ROUTLEDGE LIBRARY EDITIONS:
LANGUAGE AND LITERATURE OF THE
MIDDLE EAST

Volume 8

IRANIAN FOLK NARRATIVE

IRANIAN FOLK NARRATIVE

A Survey of Scholarship

JULIET RADHAYRAPETIAN

Routledge
Taylor & Francis Group

LONDON AND NEW YORK

First published in 1990 by Garland Publishing, Inc.

This edition first published in 2017
by Routledge
2 Park Square, Milton Park, Abingdon, Oxon OX14 4RN

and by Routledge
711 Third Avenue, New York, NY 10017

Routledge is an imprint of the Taylor & Francis Group, an informa business

© 1990 Juliet Radhayrapetian

British Library Cataloguing in Publication Data
A catalogue record for this book is available from the British Library

ISBN: 978-1-138-68297-9 (Set)
ISBN: 978-1-315-45973-8 (Set) (ebk)
ISBN: 978-1-138-69905-2 (Volume 8) (hbk)
ISBN: 978-1-138-69906-9 (Volume 8) (pbk)
ISBN: 978-1-315-51541-0 (Volume 8) (ebk)

Publisher's Note
The publisher has gone to great lengths to ensure the quality of this reprint but points out that some imperfections in the original copies may be apparent.

Disclaimer
The publisher has made every effort to trace copyright holders and would welcome correspondence from those they have been unable to trace.

IRANIAN FOLK NARRATIVE
A Survey of Scholarship

Juliet Radhayrapetian

GARLAND PUBLISHING, INC. • NEW YORK & LONDON
1990

Library of Congress Cataloging-in-Publication Data

Radhayrapetian, Juliet.
   Iranian folk narrative: a survey of scholarship / Juliet
Radhayrapetian.
      p.   cm. — (Garland reference library of the humanities; vol.
1285) (Garland folklore library; vol. 1)
   Thesis (doctoral)—UCLA, 1987.
   Includes bibliographical references.
   ISBN 0–8240–7145–X (alk. paper)
   1. Tales—Iran—History and criticism. I. Title. II. Series.
III. Series: Garland folklore library; 1.
   GR290.R33   1990
   398.2'0955—dc20   89–27418
                                                                CIP

For my mother, Hisham,

Giselle, Lillie, and my

teachers past and present

Contents

Editor's Preface

The Garland Folklore Library series consists primarily of meritorious Master's theses and deserving doctoral dissertations in the field of folklore which for one reason or another were not published upon their initial completion. In theory, all theses and dissertations are supposed to be contributions to the collective knowledge of a given discipline, but in practice it seems the vast majority are simply filed and forgotten. Sometimes the dissertation is too technical; sometimes it is too long for it to be welcomed for publication by cost-conscious university presses. Sometimes the dissertation is eminently publishable, but its author by the time the dissertation is finished is so heartily sick of the subject that he or she wants to put it aside forever.

In any case, there are a number of outstanding dissertations in folklore which warrant a wider readership and which belong in the library of any educational institution or individual with a serious interest in folklore. A few of these are in fact already well known to professional folklorists who may have bothered to send for them through inter-library loan or in more recent times purchased copies from University Microfilms International in Ann Arbor, Michigan. However, it should be noted that not all dissertations are available through UMI. The appearance of selected folklore dissertations and theses, both old and new, in the Garland Folklore Library series will make it much easier for libraries and individuals to obtain these significant studies.

Among the most important hitherto unpublished folklore dissertations are such works as motif and/or tale type indices, historic-geographic (comparative) in-depth studies of single folktales or ballads, and surveys of specialized folklore scholarship, e.g., of a particular country or group. There are in addition valuable field collections of folklore data to be found in dissertations. Clearly, there is no dearth of dissertations in folklore which could and should be published. Folklore field data, for example, never ceases to be of value—even years after its collection. It is the intention of the Garland Folklore Library series to make a number of folklore theses and dissertations available to the growing worldwide community of folklorists.

In the study of Indo-European folk narrative which began in the early nineteenth century, one critical geographical-cultural area which is less well known than some others is Iran. Whether or not the origin of Indo-European folktales is really India as was fervently advocated and argued in the nineteenth and early twentieth centuries, there can be no question that folktale traditions in ancient and modern Iran are essential for investigations of the links between Asian and European folktale cognates. Unfortunately, much of the necessary textual material has not yet been translated from Farsi and the same holds true for the scholarship devoted to such narrative data.

It is for this reason that folk narrative specialists interested in the Indo-European tale generally will warmly welcome Dr. Juliet Radhayrapetian's admirable survey of narrative scholarship in Iran. In this dissertation, Dr. Radhayrapetian gives a detailed account of early descriptions of traditional storytelling in Iran as found in travelers' reports followed by critical overviews of the development of interest in folkloristics in Iran as found among Western as well as native scholars. While the names of Arthur Christensen and L.P. Elwell-Sutton may be known to folklorists for their pioneering efforts in the study of folktales in Iran, the names of the Iranian folklorists will be new to most folklorists. The dedicated struggle of these individuals to establish folkloristics as a legitimate academic enterprise in Iran has striking parallels in many parts of the world—in times past and present.

Juliet Radhayrapetian was admirably qualified to undertake the project she chose for her dissertation. Born in Tehran in 1950, she took her B.A. in English (1971) and her M.A. in Linguistics (1973) from Tehran University. It was at that time that she learned the Old Persian and Middle Iranian languages. Her training in folklore proper came from UCLA where she earned her M.A. in folklore and mythology in 1977 and her doctorate in 1987 with the completion of the present study. Her thorough discussion of the relevant literature will make many of the results of Iranian folk narrative scholarship available in English for the first time. Her inclusion of samples of actual folk narratives from both the early travelers' reports and modern scholars (in her appendices) will give the reader a tiny taste of actual legends and folktales which will very likely succeed in whetting the reader's appetite for more. Folklorists have good reason to be grateful to Juliet Radhayrapetian for making what was essentially terra incognita intelligible to a non-Farsi reading folklore public.

Alan Dundes

Acknowledgments

This dissertation would not have been possible without the encouragement and support of several individuals. I owe my greatest debt of gratitude to Professor Mehrdad Bahar, who reinforced my special interest in folklore and mythology and encouraged me to pursue my studies in this field. During my graduate studies at Tehran University, he was the outstanding teacher and a supportive friend. Without his unfailing efforts I would not have been able to receive the scholarship which provided me with the financial support to continue my education in this country. Special thanks are due to Professor Amin Banani, the chairman of my doctoral committee, who had confidence in my potential and provided valuable support for the approval of my doctoral proposal. He has offered constant encouragement and support. I am deeply grateful for the time and invaluable insight contributed by the members of my committee who carefully read the dissertation and provided me with useful suggestions for revisions. In particular I would like to thank Professor Robert A. Georges, who exemplifies the highest ideal of a teacher and a scholar. I am grateful, too, for the consistently generous gifts of time he has given to the reading and criticism of my dissertation.

Without the support of friends and family this dissertation could never have been completed. I wish to thank all my friends for their understanding and encouragement. I am specially thankful to my husband, Hisham Kasim, who gave me the most emotional support during the writing of this dissertation. Without his love, sacrifices, and constant encouragement this project would never have been accomplished. My mother has been the most influential teacher. I am grateful to her for teaching me to value learning and education and providing me with constant support. I am also thankful to my eighteen-month-old daughter, who has provided me with love and happiness, though she had to sacrifice many hours of well-deserved care and attention.

Iranian Folk Narrative

CHAPTER I

Introduction

While no field of study that can be identified as folkloristics *per se* existed in Iran until recently, numerous individuals—ranging from travellers to philologists—generated a data base that is of primary importance to contemporary Iranian and other folklore scholars. There is hardly a mention of these early contributors as such in the scant body of Iranian folklore scholarship. In fact, the bibliography for Iranian folkloristics does not exceed a few articles and/or introductions to Iranian folk narrative collections.[1]

For centuries Iran hosted numerous travellers and visitors of diverse nationalities and backgrounds. Many of these travellers left behind documents in which they recorded their observations during their residence in Iran. These embody a vast range of firsthand information about the land and its people at different periods of time. Though the data recorded by travellers have been employed widely by researchers in such disciplines as history, archaeology, anthropology, and philology, these source documents have not received their due recognition and utilization in Iranian folkloristics. A few scholars have occasionally used these data as historical reference in their discussions of selected narratives.[2] There also exist general remarks praising travellers for their detailed description of Persian life and customs.[3] Yet no real attempt has been made to study the kinds, and to assess the importance, of the data contributed by travellers and philologists. Philologists who recorded narrative texts in the attempt to document and describe Persian dialects have received more recognition for their contribution to Iranian folklore than have travellers, probably because they presented and identified selected record *as* narrative texts, a practice that travellers have not generally followed.[4] However, the contributions of neither philologists nor travellers have been adequately explored as a fundamental part of the data base for folk narrative research which has evolved over the years.

The subjects of this dissertation are the nature and history of Iranian folk narrative scholarship, of which contributions of philologists and travellers are conceived to constitute an important part. It is necessary, therefore, to begin by posing and answering three questions: (1) what is meant by *folk narrative*; (2) what is *Iranian* folk narrative; and (3) what kinds of data are relevant to the study of Iranian folk narrative?

For the purpose of this dissertation, the term *folk narrative* refers to those narratives in prose form which are identified in the Persian language as *Hikāyat, Dāstān, ·Afsānah, Naql, Qissah, Rivāyat, Sarguzasht, Hadith,* and *Usturah*.[5] With the exception of the last two, these are by no means mutually exclusive terms, nor are they direct equivalents of terms commonly used in Euro-American folkloristics or folk narrative research.[6] Most of the Persian categorical terms are used by both scholars and members of the general populace, and different terms are used to identify what are called in English *fairy tales, legends, myths, romances,* and *fables.* Yet despite the interchangeability and lack of equivalency, there are certain characteristics which folk narratives share. They all are transmitted principally by word of mouth from person to person, and they are known or hypothesized to have enjoyed a long and widespread popularity among the Iranian people. Though familiarity with the Persian language and Iranian traditions is common among people living in countries other than Iran such as Afghanistan, Uzbekistan, and Tajikistan, this dissertation focuses only on data recorded and research conducted in Iran by Iranian and foreign scholars or on data recorded in Iran, but studied outside that country by scholars.

Actual collections and studies of Iranian folk narratives, as well as information about Iranian oral tales and taletelling recorded by travellers and philologists, form the data base of folk narrative scholarship in Iran. This is not meant to suggest that travellers and philologists can or should be regarded as early folklorists, even though some of them did actually conduct research and present material which deals exclusively with Iranian folklore. Rather, it is my intention to emphasize the significance of the data they provide; to characterize their role in the overall development of Iranian folkloristics; and to demonstrate that any historical survey of Iranian folkloristics would be incomplete without a consideration, characterization, and discussion of these documents.

To compile a working bibliography for this dissertation, I consulted various sources, including those by or about travellers, philologists, and both native and foreign scholars who studied phenomena that can be identified as *folklore.* As a starting point, I consulted such general works as *The Encyclopaedia of Islam;* L. P. Elwell-Sutton's *A Guide to Iranian Area Study;* Iraj Afshar's *Fihrist Nāmah-yi Kitābshināsihā-yi Irān (A Bibliography of Bibliographies on Iranian Studies);* and *Rāhnamā-yi Tahgigāt-i Irāni (A Guide to Iranian Studies).* Next I examined general bibliographies on Iran, such as Sir Arnold Wilson's *A Bibliography of Persia;* A. Kazemi's *Fihrist-i Kitābhā-yi ālmani dar bārah-yi Irān (A Bibliography of German Books on Iran);* Y. M. Nawabi's *A Bibliography of Iran; A Catalogue of Books and Articles on Iranian Subjects, Mainly in European Languages;* L. P. Elwell-Sutton's *Bibliographical Guide to Iran;* and Muhsin Saba's *English Bibliography of Iran* and *Bibliographie Française de l' Iran.* The basic list of material obtained from these and other general bibliographies on Iran was supplemented with items from such sources as Pearson's *Index Islamicus* and Iraj Afshar's *Fihrist-i Magālāt-i Fārsi (Index Iranicus).* In addition, I perused many Persian and Western periodical indexes to discover the most recent scholarship. Most of the general bibliographies on Iran and periodical indexes provided entries in the three main categories of the working bibliography. To obtain material relating to a specific category, I consulted other specialized bibliographies and sources, such as *Fihrist-yi Tusifi-yi Safarnāmah-hā-yi ālmani-yi Mujud dar Kitābkhānah-yi Milli-yi Irān* (*Annotated Bibliography of German Travel Books in the National Library of Iran*) by Sh. Babazadah; *Fihrist-i Tusifi-i Safarnāmah-ha-yi Inglisi-yi Mujud dar Kitābkhānah-yi Milli-yi Iran* (*Annotated Bibliography of English Travel Books in the National Library of Iran*); and *Fihrist-i Tusifi-i Safarnāmah-hā-i Faransawi-yi Mujud dar Kitabkhanahi-yi Milli-yi Irān* (*Annotated Bibliography of French Travel Books in the National Library of Iran*) by M. Jaktaji. M. Zamani's *Kitābshinashi-yi Farhang-yi 'Ammah va Mardomshināsi-yi Irān* (*A Bibliography of Folklore and Anthropology of Iran*) yielded numerous entries on research conducted by Iranians, together with Persian translations of foreign scholarship. This book and the two periodical indexes *Fihrist-i Maqālāt-i Mardumshināsi, Intishārāt-i Mu 'assasah-yi Mutaāli 'āt va Tahqiqāt-i Ijtimā'i* (*An index of Anthroplogical Articles: Social Sciences Research Institute Publications*), and *Fihrist-i Mundarajāt-i Majallih-hā-yi 'ilmi va 'Ulum-i Ijtimā±yi Irān* (*Contents Pages, Iranian Science and Social Sciences Journals*) were the major sources I used to obtain references to journal articles describing research conducted by the Iranian scholars. I also utilized the public catalogue of the University Research Library, UCLA, as well as catalogues published on Iran by institutions such as the University of Chicago, Harvard University, the New York Public Library, the British Museum, and the Library of Congress.[7] Bibliographies and references cited in the footnotes of folk narrative collections and studies provided additional material.

The working bibliography for the purpose of this dissertation consists of three major categories: 1) travel journals and notes; 2) research conducted by Iranian and Western philologists; 3) narrative studies and collections by Iranian and Western scholars. To maximize the variety of sources examined and to obtain a broad perspective, I include in the bibliography works by travellers of various nationalities, from different periods, and with diverse backgrounds and interests. However, for practical purposes and due to the huge quantity of material available in this category, I had to be selective and limit the list to a few examples from each period, country and/or group. In selecting sources from the second category, I concentrated on those philological studies which include narrative texts in both dialect and in standardized orthographies or translations. The sources in the third category are subdivided into two groups: (1) narrative collections and (2) research conducted by Iranian and Western scholars on Iranian folk narratives.

Most of the material included in the working bibliography is available in the UCLA University Research Library (including Special Collection), the Wayland D. Hand Library of Folklore and Mythology in the Center for the Study of Comparative Folklore and Mythology, and the William Andrews Clark Memorial Library. Other material was obtained from other institutions through the interlibrary loan service. Political circumstances and postal restrictions made it impossible for me to obtain many recent publications which are only accessible in Iran.[8] The accompanying bibliography lists only those sources actually consulted and surveyed.

In examining the different kinds of source material, I looked for specific and differing kinds of information. When perusing works by travellers and philologists, for example, I was mainly concerned with the kinds of data recorded, data-gathering methods utilized, and ways stories and storytelling were conceptualized. When considering written reports of research conducted by Western and native scholars on Iranian folk narratives, I expanded on the above list and also noted information about researchers' apparent preoccupations, methodologies, motives, objectives, the presence or absence of analysis, and means of classifying data. For narrative collections, I was mainly interested in discovering whether or not the collections were preceded by introductions or accompanied by documentation, and if so in determining what kinds of information were included concerning Iranian folkloristics, data-gathering and recording techniques, sources, and classification of narratives.

The specific objectives of this dissertation are as follows: 1) to describe the history and nature of Iranian folk narrative scholarship, with an emphasis on the nature and significance of the data contributed by travellers and philogists; 2) to characterize the objectives, preoccupations, and approaches of Iranian and Western scholars engaged in collecting, recording, and/or analyzing Iranian folk narratives; 3) to discuss and investigate the trends dominating contemporary Iranian folkloristics; 4) to explain how and why the data provided by non-folkorists—such as travellers and philologists—constitute a fundamental part of the data base upon which contemporary folklorists can and do draw.

To accomplish these objectives, I introduce chapter two with a brief historical sketch in which I discuss factors responsible for the large numbers of travellers to Iran, followed by a discussion of their objectives, motives and interests. In characterizing the data presented in works authored by travellers, I discuss the factors that influenced their conceptualizations of folk narratives and storytelling, and describe the kinds of the data they recorded, and comment on their data-gathering techniques and approaches, as well as their attitudes toward the data. I conclude the chapter by providing an evaluation of the data provided by travellers.

In chapter three, I characterize Western scholars' contributions to Iranian folk narrative scholarship. I make reference to, and draw examples from, the writings of researchers in such disciplines as Iranology, anthropology, folkloristics, and philology. The focal point of the chapter is the work of philologists, particularly their objectives, motives, and methodologies, as well as the data they present and the ways in which they utilized data recorded by travellers.

In the fourth chapter, I discuss native scholars and the evolution of folkloristics in Iran. First, I characterize factors responsible for the foundation of Iranian folkloristics. Next, I examine scholars' concepts of folklore and folk narratives and their methodologies, preoccupations, and objectives. I also review and assess predominating trends in Iranian folklore scholarship.

The dissertation concludes with a chapter in which I describe and evaluate the accomplishments of Western and Iranian scholars, and suggest new research directions for Iranian folk narrative scholarship. I present in appendices selected examples of the kinds of data recorded by travellers and philologists, and a bibliography of sources consulted for this research.

In transcribing Persian terms, I follow the romanization tables used at the Library of Congress. Dates of Persian sources are given in terms of the Persian solar calendar (*hijrī*), followed by the date converted to Christian era (for example, 1327/1948). Each Persian title is transliterated according to the style recommended by the Library of Congress, followed by an English translation (given in parentheses). In translating quotations from Persian sources, I make every effort to keep the translation as close to its original Persian as possible without disturbing meaning and to insure fluency or exactness.

NOTES

1. See for example, A. Boulvin, *Contes populaires persans du Khorassan*, 2 vols. (Paris, Travaux de l 'institut d 'études Iraniennes de l 'université de la Sorbonne nouvelle, 1975); and I. Osmanov, A. Bertels, and P. Aliev, compilers, *Persidskie Skazki* (*Persian Tales*), (Moscow, 1958). The introduction to the latter work is by D.S. Komissarov and has been translated into Persian by A. Azmudah as "Qissah-hā-yi Fārsi," in A. Azmudah, translator, *Haft Maqālah az Irān-shināsān-i Shuravi* (*Seven Articles by Russian Iranologists*) (Tehran: Markaz-i Nashr-i Sipihr, 1972), 71-79; and F. Machalski's article "Notes on the Folklore of Iran," in *Folia Orientalia*, 12 (1970), 141-154. The information presented in these and other similar sources, regarding folkloristics in Iran is generally limited to the chronological enumeration of the foreign and/or Iranian scholars and their contributions, with hardly any analysis or in-depth study.

2. Arthur Christensen, *Contes persans en langue populaire*, (Paris, 1916); and C. M. Gibbon, "Some Persian Folklore Stories Concerning the Ruins of Persepolis," *Journal of the Asiatic Society Bengal*, 5. No. 8 (1909): 279-297. The latter source is stated regardless of the negative results of search by its author. Gibbon acknowledges that his efforts were fruitless for locating in the travel books on Iran

references to the stories he recorded. Yet for the purpose of this discussion, the mere consideration of travel books as sources of reference is of importance.

3. F. Vahman, "Jam' Avari-i Afsanah-ha-yi Irani," ("Collecting Iranian Folk Narratives"), *Sukhan*, 18 (1347/1968): 171-177; and E. P. Elwell-Sutton, "Collecting Folktales in Iran," *Folklore* 93, No. 1 (1982): 96-104. This kind of statement usually appears in introductions to collections or Persian translations of travel books, regional folklore collections, and historical studies of different aspects of Iranian culture.

4. To record texts in dialect, some philologists asked their informants to narrate stories. If informants could not remember any at the time, the philologists themselves would narrate tales and ask the informants to repeat them in their own dialect. Arthur Christensen has made a note of this method in his *Persische Märchen* (Düsseldorf-Koln: Eugen Diederichs Verlag, 1958), p. 283.

5. See, for example, M. J. Mahjub, "Mutali 'ah dar Dastan-ha-yi 'Ammiyanah-i Farsi," ("A Study of Iranian Folk Narratives"), *Majallah-i Danishkadah Adabiat*, 10:1 (1340/1961): 68,-112. On page 72 he enumerates seven of these terms and comes to the conclusion that one cannot come up with a final judgment about the exact meaning of these terms.

6. Classification and definition of categories of folk narrative are ongoing subjects of discussion and debate among American and European folklorists. Yet for the practical purposes, a general understanding regarding the underlying characteristics of each category exists among scholars. After that, the clarification and/or modification of the defining characteristics and criteria become the scholar's choice.

7. University of Chicago, *Catalogue of the Middle Eastern Collection, First Supplement* (Boston, Massachusetts, 1977); *Harvard University Catalogue of Arabic, Persian, and Ottoman Turkish Books,* (Cambridge, 1968); Labib Zuwiyya-Yamak, ed., *Harvard College Library Catalogue of Persian Books,* (Cambridge, Massachusetts, 1964); New York (City) Public Library, *List of Works in the New York Public Library Relating to Persia,* (New York, 1915); Edward Edwards, *A Catalogue of the Persian Printed Books in the British Museum,* (London, 1922); United States Library of Congress, Reference Department, Iran; *A Selected and Annotated Bibliography, Compiled by Hafiz Farman,* (Washington, 1951).

8. To minimize the limitations caused by this situation, I continually consulted the University Research Library's catalogue supplement and ORION computer records for acquisitions of new materials by the library (holdings of both of which are constantly

updated). In addition, the Near Eastern bibliographer at the University Research Library was most helpful in informing me about newly-acquired Persian books and periodicals, as well as helping me to locate sources.

CHAPTER II
Early Contributors

Although there are travel books on Iran that date back to at least the time of Alexander the Great,[1] a sizeable number of travellers' reports did not begin to appear until the Middle Ages. In the East, the expansion of Islam and the establishment of the Arab Empire encouraged and facilitated travel throughout the vast Muhammadan world. This was the "period during which the traveller could pass from the confines of China to the Pillars of Hercules, from the banks of the Indus to the Cicilian (sic) Gates, from the Oxus to the Shores of the Atlantic, without stepping outside the boundaries of the territory ruled over by the Caliph in Damascus or Baghdad."[2] Factors responsible for the ever-increasing interest in travel among the Muhammadans were, in one way or another, related to religion, politics, and commerce. Every Muslim, within the limits of health and financial possibilities, was obliged to make the pilgrimage to Mecca (*Hajj*) at least once in his lifetime. Thus, a constant stream of pilgrims every year headed towards Mecca from different parts of the world. On the other hand, learning and pursuit of knowledge was highly stressed in the religion and the teachings of Muhammad as can be inferred from the famous saying attributed to him, "Seek knowledge even if it be in China."[3]

As the Empire of Islam expanded and new countries were added to the territory, it became an administrative necessity for the central government to have accurate and firsthand knowledge about the newly acquired countries, mainly the boundaries, routes, population, and revenues. While some of this information was available at the central government, travellers and merchants played the important role of providing the firsthand observations.[4] This need for information led to "the collection of itineraries and other actual geographical knowledge (which in turn) brought into existence the different books on "the roads and countries (*al-masalik wal mamalik*).[5] The works of such authors as Ibn-Khurdadbih, Al-Istakhri, and Ibn Hawqal belong to this category.[6] Regional geographies, such as that of Ibn Balkhi's *Farsnamah*,[7] which is a description of the province of Fars in Iran, was another category emerging as a result of travellers' accounts. The same "Brotherhood of Islam" which facilitated travelling of the pilgrims provided new markets for commerce, and as a result there were more travelling and travel books. (Whether travelling was stimulated by mere curiosity and love of travel (Ibn Battuta, Abu Dulaf), or to perform pilgrimage (Nasir Khosraw), or for trade (al-Muqaddasi) or administrative and political purposes (Iban Fadlan, Hafiz Abru), the records left behind by Arab and Iranian travellers and geographers of the Middle Ages embody more than just geographical and/or topographical information. These "travellers had many-sided interests and possessed a keen sense of observation and took pains to obtain information of various kind. . . ."[8] As a result, these documents also provided insight into the beliefs, manners, and customs of the peoples visited by travellers. Legends, etiological tales, local legends, and other kinds of folk narratives are cited side by side with descriptions of towns and roads. One special characteristic of these sources in comparison to the itineraries of the European travellers of the later centuries is the geographical and/or historical emphasis of their authors, which keeps these sources from automatically falling under the category of "travel books." Consequently, with very few exceptions, these treatises are primarily treated as descriptive geographical sources.

The Eastern traveller was said to have left home and gone on the road for religious, political, and/or commercial reasons or just to quench his thirst for adventure. The Western traveller was not an exception either. The horror which was created in Europe by the Mongol conquest and the Mongols' attacks on Eastern Europe in the middle of the thirteenth century led the Pope and the kings of France and England to send missionaries and emissaries to the court of the Great Khan in the hope of putting an end to their aggression in Europe, converting them to Christianity and establishing trade routes between the East and the West. Thus, in 1245 Pope Innocent IV sent a delegation headed by a Franciscan friar (John Pian de Carpini) to the Great Khan. A few years later another friar-traveller (William of Rubruck) was sent out as the representative of Louis IX, King of France.[9] Yet these friars were not the first Europeans to visit Persia in the Middle Ages. Rather, the credit goes to the Jewish merchant Rabbi Benjamin of Tudela, whose period of travels extended from A.D. 1160 to 1173.[10] Within a very short period of time he was followed by Rabbi Petachia of Ratisbon who, like his predecessor, was a highly-motivated merchant who visited and acquainted himself with the condition of his Jewish brothers living in other parts of the world. His objective was to write down what he saw and heard in order to inform his people, the house of Israel.[11] After the two friars (Pian de Carpini and William of Rubruck), the Latin mission which had started in the late thirteenth century continued to head toward the East until mid-fourteenth century.[12] But, "although the best travel books belonging to this period were written by missionaries, the real impetus to travel was given by trade, and the most frequent journeys to Persia, India and Cathay were made by merchants."[13] The greatest of them all was Marco Polo, whose two visits to Iran occurred between the years 1271 and 1294.

As the Renaissance began, religion lost its role as a main motive for travel, and politics and commerce became the major factors. Thus, individual traders or government-organized delegations and emissaries headed toward Persia in the hope of establishing trade and/or political relationships.[14] European countries tried to ally with Persia against their powerful and common enemy, the Ottomon, while at the same time competing with each other to obtain exclusive import and/or export rights. Trade companies were established by different European countries one after another: the English East India Company in 1599, the Dutch East India Company in 1602, and the French East India Company in 1664. Mention should also be made of the Portuguese who, from the late fifteenth to the first half of the seventeenth centuries, maintained a strong lead in commerce in Iran and established a firm foothold in the Persian Gulf. They stood as a powerful rival to other European countries, mainly England, until 1622, when they lost the battle to the Iranians and the English and had to give up their settlements at Hormoz on the Persian Gulf. The grandeur and political power of the Safavid dynasty attracted numerous travellers on diplomatic and commercial missions to Iran. Thus, travel literature written in many European languages was remarkably enriched in the seventeenth century. However, these favorable conditions did not last long, for "the disordered condition of Iran during the decline and fall of Safavid rule made the country unattractive both to travellers and traders."[15]

By the middle of the eighteenth century a new kind of traveller appeared in Iran. This breed of traveller, who was motivated by pursuit of knowledge and art, was later on followed by the "tourist." Many travellers of the latter group headed toward the East, influenced by the romantic stories. Braaksma best describes them as "travellers (who) had fallen under the spell of the so-called Oriental literature of the Arabian Nights, and later of the Ruba'ayyat, and were constantly set on finding a romantic and glamourous Persia."[16] The scholarly interest in Iran, which was kindled in the latter part of the eighteenth century, was primarily of a literary nature. Studying the Persian language and literature and subsequently translating Persian texts into European languages was primarily practical. It was meant to facilitate the task of those envoys who travelled to the country on political and/or commercial missions.[17] Through the translation of books such as the *Arabian Nights* the notion of the romantic East was created in the minds of-the Westerners, of whom Braaksma talks, as noted above. On the other hand, through the accounts of the travellers who visited and reported on the historical sites of the country, Westerners became aware of relics and headed toward Iran to visit and/or study them. Thus, archaeology became another subject of interest and an important factor in attracting travellers.[18] In short, in the nineteenth and twentieth centuries travellers with diverse scholarly backgrounds and interests visited the country; and there emerged a new type of traveller, whom L. P. Elwell-Sutton calls "the serious student of Persia."[19] Many of these travellers—such as Sir John Malcolm, Lord Curzon, Sir Percy Sykes, and Sir Arnold Wilson—went to the country on political missions. The travellers' widening scope of interest had direct effects on the nature and content of the travel literature of the nineteenth and twentieth centuries. Travel books became more interesting and informative, and a greater emphasis was put on describing people and their ways of life rather than the topography of towns and villages.

Certain factors influenced conceptualizations of the data travellers provided. The length of residence in the country was one important factor. It goes without saying that a lengthier residence in the country gave a traveller greater opportunities to acquaint himself with the land and its people. Thus, a visitor such as a political envoy who brought messages to the king did not stay in the country any longer than his mission required, and travellers passing through the country on their way to other parts of the world could not gain or provide an extensive amount of firsthand information. The data gathered by this type of traveller was highly dependent on the extent of his interest and curiosity as well as the knowledge and interest of his guide or interpreter. The itineraries left behind by this type of traveller are usually topographical, with general remarks about roads, towns or areas visited, accounts of revenue and products, and descriptions of the court of the king (in the case of political envoys). These travelogues are occasionally interspersed with etiological accounts, legends, superstitions, customs, and manners. Most of the travel books of the Middle Ages— especially those of the Arab travellers and European missionaries or envoys—fall into this category, though such works were also plentiful in later centuries, too. Examples include itineraries left behind by the Arab traveller of the tenth century, Ibn Fadlan; the two Italian envoys, Josafa Barbaro and Ambrogio Contarini, sent by the Venetian government in the fifteenth century; and the sixteenth-century traveller Ludvico di Varthema.[20]

The personal interest and background of the travellers, together with the purpose(s) for travel, had a significant influence on the nature of the data they provided. Often the background or interest of a traveller differed from the purpose of travel, or the travel itself was of a multipurpose nature. Rabbi Benjamin of Tudela provides the best example; "his primary object was to visit the synagogues of the principal cities through which he passed, and to describe the number and condition of the Jews whom he found in them."[21] As a merchant he was interested in acquiring commercial information. On the other hand, the friars who were sent to Iran in the Middle Ages, besides having missionary purposes, were bearers of political messages or emissaries sent to establish trade relationships. This combination and diversity of purposes and interests widened the scope of the data conceptualized and/or gathered by travellers.

Visitors who came to the country with religious missions or backgrounds focused more on the spiritual beliefs of the people, searching for similarities and/or differences between Christianity and Islam. They were more interested in gathering information about the religious minorities of the country, mainly information about their condition of life, numbers, centers of concentration and religious activity, and authorities. Consequently, in the itineraries of this type of traveller, interest in people and their customs, beliefs, and manners overshadowed the interest in geographical and/or topographical data. Legends relating to religious personalities and/or places appeared more frequently in their records. The best example of this category is the work of the Arab traveller and theologian Ibn Battuta, who undertook his travels because of his theological interest and love of travel. He set out on a pilgrimage to Mecca, then continued his journey to other parts of the world for twenty years. His work, which was intended primarily to present a descriptive account of Muhammadan society in the second quarter of the fourteenth century, reveals his interest in people, especially religious leaders, rather than in places.[22] In the same manner, the traveller who was in Iran for trade purposes was more concerned with centers of trade, safety and the conditions of roads, climate, products, weights, measures, and taxes of each region. Yet this type of traveller, due to the nature of his profession, travelled more and was in close contact with differing classes of people. As a result, he had a better chance to observe those aspects of life which a diplomat or a tourist would be likely to miss or overlook. To prove this point, it suffices to mention names of such great travellers and merchants as Tavernier, Chardin, Hanway, Marco Polo and the accounts left behind by those of a less fame, such as Francisco Balducci Pegolotti of the fourteenth century; Nicolo Conti, the Italian merchant of the fifteenth century; and Athanasius Nikitin, the Russian horse-trader of the fifteenth century. On the other hand, the diplomatic envoys were more interested in the administrative aspects of the country, its government, politics, economy, the king, and the customs and manners of the court. Their work contains more oral history and narratives or legends about the kings. The Spanish Don Roy Gonzalez di Clavijo, who was sent by Henry III of Castile in 1403, gives a vivid description of Timur and his court; Catarino Zeno, an envoy from Venice to the court of Uzun Hassan, besides providing political and historical information of the time describes the king and his court; Englebert Kaempfer, the German traveller, gives a precise and detailed description of the administrative organization of Iran in the seventeenth century.[23]

Knowledge of the Persian language was another influential factor in conceptualization of the data. This is true despite the fact that some travellers who did not have a command of the language and who were at the mercy of their interpreters nevertheless recorded data of considerable importance. Sir John Chardin puts great emphasis on the knowledge of the language for, he believes:

> to make a true relation of a country, it is necessary that they who describe it should know the Language; else they must commit a thousand errors not passable among persons of Judgement, . . . therefore it is my Opinion, that whoever publishes his Travels and Observations of a Country which he

has not learnt the Speech shall never make any perfect and accomplish'd.[24]

A comprehensive—that is to say, a textual as well as contextual—recording of a storytelling or performing of narrative(s) depends on one's comprehending the narrator's language and the nature of his interaction with the audience. Travellers who witnessed storytellings and who were unable to provide information other than to mention the event or describe the narrator's physical appearance are not rare. Ella Sykes refers to a storytelling she witnessed in the following way:

> . . . we had to pass round the city on our way to them, and found a crowd assembled at the big gate of the town, listening to a professional storyteller, who was reciting poems to his audience, with violent gesticulations.[25]

Arthur Arnold, who visited Iran in the summer of 1675, gives the following description of a wandering professional storyteller:

> A dervish clad in white, his face encircled with long black hair, screams eulogies of Haussein, supposed to be peculiarly acceptable when the Mohurrem is drawing near.[26]

Yet at times there were travellers who, despite their unfamiliarity with the Persian language, went further in their description, providing a more detailed, though not complete, picture. One such example is Victoria Sackville-West, whose literary background and interest were responsible for the style of the following passage:

> In the Meidan a dervish was sitting on the ground telling a story to the crowd; they sat round him in a circle with lips parted and eyes popping nearly out of their heads as the holy man worked himself up into a state of frenzy over the exploits of his hero (for Persian stories are usually heroic, and Firdusi's epic of the kings their favorite recital). With his long beard, high hat, and orange nails, and fierce little eyes flashing out of his hairy face, he seemed spinning his tale for the last five hundred years and was only now working up the climax. It was evening; the Meidan

> was sparsely populated. . . . Fanatism, barter, dusk and the story-
> teller, all gathered together, in this Eastern city. . . . There was
> the dervish, still churning up the turmoil of his story; a horseman
> had drawn rein, and sat in the saddle, listening. . . . Someone had
> lit a brazier which produced strange effects of shadow amongst
> the crowd, and threw a fitful light on th the face of the dervish.
> The gutteral language spurted as though in ecstasy from his lips.
> He jerked his hands in wild gesticulation.[27]

The first two examples do not give any information about the audience; Sackville-West's description only depicts the fascination of the crowd. While Arnold informs the reader that it was Houssein, the grandson of Muhammad, that the *Dervish* was *screaming* (not reciting or narrating) about, Sykes and Sackville-West are vague about the nature of the storyteller's narrative, though the latter assumes that the narrative was of a heroic nature because "Persian stories are usually heroic." Sykes remains silent about the storyteller, Arnold describes his physical appearance, and Sackville-West provides, in addition, some information about his style. Recordings of this nature—as short and incomplete as they are—have value because, in one way or another, they provide information about narratives, narrators (professional or nonprofessional), and/or audiences.

Travellers' attitudes and approaches to the data and their documentation or study of the people and traditions and customs greatly influenced their conceptualization and presentation of the data. Almost all the travellers who had a chance to familiarize themselves with the customs and manners of Persians, and who chose to comment on their characteristics and ways of life, invariably testify to these people's love of stories and storytelling. Ella Sykes states:

> Persians of all ranks are like children in their love of stories.
> From the Shah downwards they listen with delight to the public
> story-tellers, most of whom belong to the order of dervishes,
> and make the round of the country, always drawing small crowds
> in every town.[28]

A majority of these comments are complimentary and in admiration of the Persians, who have a "stock of opposite quotations from the poets and a rich fund of anecdotes,"[29] and who are "Gifted with a delightful sense of humour, a ready wit, and for centuries accustomed to amuse themselves around the campfires, in their gardens or in the course of long journeys by caravan by telling stories, reciting poetry and capping verses, . . . have prodigious memories, are brilliant raconteurs and have an untold wealth of humorous stories and anecdotes."[30] Yet there are other remarks which reveal the unappreciative attitude of the travellers. So the wealth of stories and legends and amazing memory are denigrated and attributed to the lying tendencies of the people by a traveller like Ferrier, who states, "As to the Persians they are never at a loss to account for the origin of ruins or towns, for with their inventive faculties they make up any history they like and fabulous indeed are their traditions."[31] Other travelers go even further than merely scorning Persians for their love of stories and extend their unfriendly attitude toward the people themselves, calling them semi-savages, idolators, barbarous, superstitious, etc. Fortunately, for purposes of this study, both groups, those who favored and those who disdained Persians and their traditions, have presented examples as proof of their statements. The end result is a collection of remarkable data. Both groups of travellers draw and hold the attention of their readers by presenting interesting information about a nation which, for historical, geographical, political, economic, and/or romantic reasons, has been of great interest to the West, while also noting differences in ways of life, religion, government, customs, and traditions that existed between the people they visited and those familiar to their readers. This *otherness*, together with the way it was conceptualized and handled, became the significant factors in shaping travellers' and consequently their readers' attitudes toward the people. Those travellers who held Western ways to be superior and perfect were quick to criticize, pity, and/or ridicule Persians for being different. Others who were less ethnocentric expressed their feelings of having been charmed and amused by the people and their simple way of life. Travellers were so much involved in their constant conscious or unconscious comparisons that when faced with similarities, they did not hesitate to express their astonishment or try to justify them, as a remark by Sir Henry Layard reveals:

> A similar legend, in different versions, will be familiar to my readers. Whence Saleh and the Lures obtained it I know not. I often heard versions of well-known classical stories among these wild people.[32]

Travellers' attitudes toward the narratives they recorded can be inferred from the comments that accompany the data. The nature and presence or absence of these comments are significant factors in categorizing the data presented. A majority of travellers describe what they saw and heard without further comments about the narratives and/or the informants. Such narratives usually begin with general remarks, such as "the legend is that," "the legend runs/has it . . . ," "popular legend avers that . . . ," "the Persians have a story that . . . ," "according to Persians . . . ," or "they have a story that. . . ." Thus, unless explicitly stated, it is difficult to determine whether or not the narrative was transmitted orally to the traveller. In such cases verifying the sources of the narratives as oral ones requires a thorough study of the travel book as well as the traveller's background. Travellers have not always been vague about their sources, however, for there are also narratives which are introduced with statements such as "as they said . . . ," "we were informed . . . ," or "the people told us . . . ," and in many cases the informants are mentioned by name.

A second category of travellers are the ones who chose to provide more than just brief descriptions or text, and who include additional comments, some of which are true manifestations of their authors' attitudes toward the data and/or the people. Those without much appreciation for the narratives they heard label them "idle nonsensical stories," "strange," "ridiculous," "trash," and "absurd." Others reveal their interest by introducing the narratives with terms such as "pleasant," "good," or "ingenious." Some travellers chose to share their disbelief in what they heard by comments such as "Rumour relates, but apparently without any very certain foundation, that. . . . "[33] or "Tradition says . . . I suspect that tradition is in this case somewhat of a romancer—not an uncommon thing."[34] On the other hand, there were travellers whose attitudes toward the data were not so critical, as the following examples illustrate: "A good story is told of him (Nasir Ud-Din Shah) the truth of which I have no reason to question,"[35] or "all these things (concerning the three Magi) were told Messer Marco Polo by the people of the town. And they are all truth."[36] The travellers who were not much concerned with the true or false nature of narratives—which constitutes a considerable majority—either chose to withhold any comments in this regard, or simply to comment briefly on the matter. For example, Edward G. Browne states, "whether this story is true or false I cannot say, neither did I pay much attention to its recital."[37] In another instance he writes, "Where this shrine is I do not know, neither did I make any attempt to test the truth of the legend."[38] Several travelers, still preoccupied with determining the true or false nature of the data, took one step forward in studying the narratives and either refuted or rationalized some of the data (Friar Jovani di Marignolli, Adam Olearius, Ferrier, Ibn Hawqal), or perused the writings of their predecessors in search of historical evidence (Chardin). Other comments accompanying narratives are either descriptive, providing information about the main theme of narrative, or in the case of more recent travellers, discussion of the origin(s) of narratives with reference to the folkloristic theories of the time. One such example is presented by S. G. Benjamin:

> Another story of the evening is one which is widely current in Persia. It may have some mystical relation to the so-called solar myths about which Professor Max Muller, Wolf and others have expended such floods of hypothetical ink.[39]

Sir John Malcolm, in his *Sketches of Persia*, allotted several pages to a discussion of the origins of fairy tales, revealing his commitment to the Indian origin thesis.[40]

The third category of travellers consists of those who were particularly concerned with the quality and the quantity of the data they recorded. In order to make their accounts brief and avoid tiring the reader, some travellers discarded those materials which they did not consider important and/or interesting (Istakhri), while others decided against presenting too many narratives lest their credibility be questioned by the reader (Friar Odoric of Pordenon). Another group of the travellers selected among multiple examples and focused upon one or two narratives which they judged to be the most interesting (Sir John Malcolm) or peculiarly oriental (S. Benjamin). There were also a few extreme cases in which narratives were deleted because of the seemingly serious nature of the work (G. A. Oliver) or due to high printing costs (H. L. Rabino).

Few travellers have stated their motives and methods for gathering and recording data. Leading motives ranged from pure curiosity and personal interest—as in the case of Jonas Hanway, who admits, "When I was in PERSIA my curiosity led me to collect several anecdotes, particularly concerning NADIR"[41]—to a more scholarly approach as illustrated by a quotation from the work of Edward G. Browne, "Anxious to become further acquainted with the folklore of the country, I succeeded in engaging the muleteer in conversation."[42] Sir John Malcolm is one individual who combined utilitarian and scholarly motives in recording and translating narratives:

> I made translations, not only of history and poetry, but of fables and tales, being satisfied that this occupation, while it improved me in the knowledge of the language, gave me a better idea of the manners and mode of thinking of this people than I could derive from any other source.[43]

There were also travellers whose immediate interests in soliciting narratives were not stimulated by their inquisitive mind or scholarly purposes, but rather by their boredom and/or fascination in listening to storytellers. C. B. Stewart, for instance, states, "While I was at Khaf, there was a renowned story-teller, for whom I used to send in the many dull evenings I spent there alone, to amuse me."[44] Similar remarks are made by C. J. Wills, who had a professional storyteller "beguile the tedium of the long evenings."[45] Nevertheless, the principal motive for gathering and recording narrative data, though not always explicitly stated by travellers, was to entertain their readers by describing marvelous, incredible, or strange stories which provided information about the people they had visited.

Since a majority of travellers did not describe their data-gathering methods explicitly, one can only hypothesize what they might have been from comments accompanying the narratives. Earlier travellers, especially the Arab and Persians in the Middle Ages who were concerned with their credibility in the eyes of their readers, were specific in informing the reader about their sources and/or methodology. Examples are found in the works of Ibn Hawqal, Al Muqaddasi, Istakhri, and Mas'udi. They usually obtained their information from the works of their predecessors, hearsay (sources of which were sailors, merchants and other travellers), and what they themselves heard and observed. Yet their description of their methodology was usually limited to general remarks about all the material gathered and recorded, not just for narratives. Occasionally there were remarks made by travellers which provide information about their methodology for gathering and recording stories and storytellings. Al Muqaddasi, for instance, reports that when he "entered Al-Sus (Susa)" he "sought out the mosque, looking for a sheikh from whom" he "might hear some of the traditions."[46] Direct inquiry was another method of obtaining information and was employed by Abu Dulaf and Marco Polo.[47] Though travellers' primary motive for employing this method was to obtain information or explanations regarding etymologies and/or out of the ordinary phenomena or places, the outcome of their inquiry usually included legends, etiological tales and local legends. Most travel books were written or dictated some time after the return of the traveller to his or her homeland on the basis of memory and notes they had taken in the country.[48] Thus, the more detailed the notes, and the fresher and more vivid the memory, the more elaborate the accounts.

One important element in studying the data recorded by travellers, in the scope of this dissertation, is to determine whether or not the data were transmitted to the traveller orally and during firsthand interaction, and to figure out if the data were elicited by the traveller or volunteered by the narrators. Whenever the traveller starts a narrative with the statements, "I was told by . . . that," "the people told me/us . . . ," "I heard . . . ," or " as they said . . . ," and similar remarks, then it can be posited with some degree of certainty that the data were obtained in firsthand situations. That the narratives were volunteered or elicited can only be inferred on the basis of comments provided by travellers. The following passage, in which Sir John Malcolm expresses his frustration from constantly hearing stories about Shah Abbas the Great, reveals that the data were volunteered, in this case despite the nonresponsiveness of the traveller:

> I was really quite tired with hearing of this most gallant, most sage, most witty, and most munificent monarch, at his seat of glory, and when sixty miles to the northward of that city, we were entering the delightful little town of Nethenz . . . , I said to myself, "Well, we are now, thank God, clear of Abbas and grand palaces. . . . Hajee Hoosein, who was riding near me, said, as if he had read my thoughts, "This is a charming place. . . . When Abbas the Great—" I pulled up my horse, and looked at him with a countenance that indicated anything but anxiety for his story; but not observing, or not choosing to observe, he continued. . . . [49]

Edward G. Browne writes about a similar experience:

> Haji Safar began to tell me a long rambling story about the creation of *Buzmajja* whereby he sought to account for its harmlessness. He related his story, in the dreamy, visionary manner which occasionally came over him, and in the soft lisping accent of the south. I was not paying much attention to his narrative the upshot of which appeared to be. . . . "[50]

The remarks frequently made by travellers about the Persians' ready wit and love of story and storytelling suggests that a good number of the narratives might/must have been volunteered in the course of conversation. Yet gathering data was not always an easy task to accomplish, especially when people were doubtful about the intentions of the traveller. One of the travellers who had difficulty gathering the data and was not always successful in his interactions with his informants was Sir Henry Layard, who was in Iran pursuing his archaeological interests. He voiced his complaint:

> I was among barbarous people, who entertained the greatest suspicions of my motives for visiting their country, it was often dangerous to be seen putting pen or pencil to paper.[51]

Ferrier describes people's attitude toward those who questioned the credibility of a legend. After relating the legend, he states, "This is a good specimen of a Persian tale, and absurd as it is, it finds believers amongst them, even the educated. To seem to doubt its truth might bring one into trouble "[52]

As noted earlier, travellers' comments do not usually provide much information about informants. Those who travelled to the country before the invention of motor cars, whether on horseback or in caravans, had the chance to have their interpreters, guides, muleteers, fellow travellers, or the local people as their primary sources of firsthand information. Thus, many stories were communicated to them by members of these groups. Some travellers made references to this mode of obtaining the data; the following are but a few examples. Ibn Hawqal informs us, "One of the nobilities of Sistan, on the road to Egypt in the year 360 A.H. told me. . . . "[53] Armenius Vambery, who also had his fellow travellers as informants, says, "Such and similar stories I was regaled with by my fellow-travellers in connection with the Salt desert of Persia."[54] Edward G. Browne states, "A little further on, . . . we came to the ruins of a little village. . . . Concerning this, one of the muleteers told me a strange story."[55] As can be inferred from these and other examples, and unless stated by the traveller to the contrary, a majority of the data seem to have been volunteered by informants. In the case of those travellers who had lengthier residences in the country, more inquisitive minds and/or interest in the people and their stories, and a knowledge of the Persian language, the list of volunteering informants expanded to include the travellers' friends, hosts/hostesses, and/or professional storytellers. Information about the informants, when available, most often includes their names, style, repertoire, and/or profession. Edward G. Browne, fascinated by the skills of his host and informant, states:

> We had a most delightful evening, the Khan, being one of the most admirable conversationalists I ever met. Some of his stories I will here set down, though it is impossible for me to convey an idea of the vividness of description, wealth of illustration, and inimitable mimicry, which, in his mouth, gave them so great a charm."[56]

To explain the style of a professional storyteller Sir John Malcolm writes:

> Mullah Adeeneh, the story-teller to his majesty . . . told me, that he considered it as much as his head was worth, to tell a tale twice without variations to the king of kings. "Besides my own inventions," said he, "I have a great book, containing anecdotes on all subjects, and an infinite quantity of amusing matter, which I select at pleasure, and adapt my story to the circumstances of the moment, and to the characters of those who form my audience."[57]

C. J. Wills comments about the informant, mentioned above (p. 13), who entertained him on several occasions:

> Dervishes are often professional story-tellers, the costume being merely donned for effect; or as in the case of a highly gifted story-teller of my acquaintance, one Aqa Nusserulla of Shiraz, a man who earned a good living by his erudite and interesting tales, the cap only was worn, and that merely when engaged in his public recitals; he also carried the big iron axe, with which he gesticulated in a manner really graceful and artistic. I often, as I grew more acquainted with Persian, had this man in to beguile the tedium of the long evenings and he would sit by the hour under the orange-trees, rattling off an endless story freely interspersed with poetical recitations, which were always apposite and well given—in fact, they were intoned. He never allowed the interest of his tales to flag, and never left off save at a point so interesting as to assure a request for his attendance the succeeding evening, adopting the principle of the lady of the "Arabian Nights." I frequently, on passing through the Maidan, or public square, of Shiraz saw Aqa Nasserulla surrounded by a

gaping crowd of peasants, porters, and muleteers squatting in a circle, he striding up and down and waving his axe as he told his story of love or fairy land; then he recognized my presence by merely the slightest drop of his eyelid, for his harvest of coppers would have been blighted had he betrayed to his gaping listeners his intimacy with a "Feringhi" [Foreigner]. . . . The tales told in the bazaar to the villagers were mostly bristling with indecency; but the dervish never transgressed in this respect on getting a hint from me that that sort of thing was unpleasing, and his stories were always of great interest, intensely pathetic at times, and at others very comic. His power of imitation was great; the voices of his old men and women were unmistakable, while the sex of the lovers were equally distinct, and his laugh was infectious and sympathetic.[58]

Besides the general description of storytelling, usually the professional form of it, several travellers also reported their firsthand experiences. These general descriptions, which usually appear in the sections in which the traveller lists different forms of the Persian entertainments, or when the subject of description is the tea or coffee-houses or *Dervishes*, present information about the style and physical appearance of the professional storyteller, the nature of the narratives, the atmosphere and/or the audience and their reaction. Travellers have reported two main kinds of entertainment involving storytellings; those which are enjoyed at home, and the ones which are performed in public places. While the storytellings of the first kind may or may not include professionals, the second category is performed only by them. Lady Sheil's description of a Persian visit bears considerable resemblance to several other accounts of similar occasions recorded by other travellers:

A Persian visit is a formidable ceremony involving a prodigious consumption of time. Pipes, coffee; pipes, tea; and pipes twice again is the usual routine. They are vivacious intelligent people; and I am told the men are often agreeable in conversation relating anecdotes, and quoting passages from poetry and history with readiness and animation.[59]

Depending on the skill of the narrator, the complexity or formality of the visit, or presence of a professional storyteller, the description becomes more detailed and informative. An example is James Morrier's report of the dinner ceremony held in honor of the English envoy. After a detailed description of the evening and other entertainments performed, he continues:

> After this concert . . . appeared from behind a curtain a dirty-looking negro, dressed as a *fakeer* or beggar, with an artificial hump, and with his face painted white. This character related facetious stories, threw himself into droll attitude, and sang humorous songs.[60]

As one can infer from Morrier's statement and the reports of many other travellers, inviting or hiring a professional storyteller—when the visiting ceremony was of a more elaborate kind—was an essential part of the entertainment provided by the host. Kings, princes, and high ranking government officials had storytellers at their employment. Edward Waring comments on this:

> After the dancers, came another description of people . . . They are called Lootees, a kind of buffoon; and as I learnt, have free access to the prince and governor, whom they amuse by a variety of indecent anecdotes and stories, which they relate, or invent, of the inhabitants of Sheeraz. Both the prince and the governor keep a set of these wretches. . . .[61]

Professional storytellers were also much in demand during the month of fasting (Ramazan), as Wills explains: "The long nights of Ramazan are enlivened by numerous festivities; dinner-giving takes place throughout the month. . . . The story-tellers are now in great request, and drive a roaring trade going from house to house."[62] Yet based on the remarks of travellers, Persians' fascination with narratives and their eagerness for hearing storytellers perform was not limited to occasional elaborate ceremonies, or just to one month of the year.

The professional storytellers either performed at people's homes by invitation, or chose public places such as markets and street corners as their stage of performance. Tea or coffee-houses were also centers which provided professional storytellings for their customers. Descriptions of the wandering storytellers are usually given by travellers in their discussions of *Dervishes*. These descriptions provide information about their religious background, appearance, and style. Basset gives the following general description.

> The dervishes are religious tramps . . . men of this class frequent the public places, where they recite passages from the poets to the people gathered in the Bazaars, and Maidans.[63]

Tavernier's report provides more detailed information:

> These *Dervi's* come every afternoon about three or four a Clock into the *Bazar* of *Ispahan*, every two, an old one and a young one, choosing his quarter. They go from Shop to Shop, instructing the People upon some Point or other of the Law: the young *Dervi's* answering the old ones at certain times. Their habit is only two Sheep-skins or Goat-skins, the one hanging before, the other behind, with a great leathern Girdle, four five fingers broad, garnish'd with several great Plates of Latten. They throw another Sheep-skin cross their shoulders, which they tye before, under their Chins. Upon their heads they only wear a little Lamb-skin in form of a Bonnet, letting the feet hang down to their Necks, over their Cheeks. They carry a great Club in their hands . . . Between their Girdles and their wasts they stuff a company of pitiful Flowers, or else a sort of Herbs, which after Exhortation, both the young, and the old *Dervi's* bestow upon the merchants and Tradesmen, from whom at the same time they receive Alms.[64]

Adam Olearius's remarks about *Dervishes* provide information about the function of storytellers. At the time of his visit to the country, political relations between Iran and its Turkish neighbor were anything but friendly. The *Dervishes* through their narratives and by fanning the religious animosity of their Shi'ite audience against the Sunnite Turks provoked nationalistic emotions:

> There is yet another sort of Ecclesiasticks in *Persia*, who are thought to be descended from *Aly*, instead where of the *Turks* have the *Dervis*. . . . These are called *Abdallas's*, and are a kind of Monks or Friars. They are very meanly clad, with a kind of

sleeve-less Coat, of several pieces, quilted like Mattresses. Some
of them wear only a hairy skin, having at the waste . . . a Serpent
of brass, given them by their Doctors, when they make their
profession, as a mark of their Learning. . . . These *Abdallas*
trudge up and down the Markets and other public places, to
assemble the people, and Preach to them the Miracles of their
Saints, and to curse *Abubeker, Omar, Osman* and *Hanife,* as also
the Saints of the Usbeques Tartars, of whom they relate
ridiculous and obscene stories, to make them abominable and
despicable. This Contributes somewhat to the establishment of
their Religion, and heightens in the Children the hatred they
have against the Turks, for those are the Chief Auditors of these
Market-Lectures; and thence it comes, that these *Abdallas* are
never seen near the Frontiers of *Turkey.* There are some of
them, who take whatever their Auditors give them . . . for after
they have spent about half an hour in talking and telling of
stories . . . they have some small money given them,
whereupon they dismiss the assembly, to go and Preach in
some other place. They have in their hand a Hatchet or Scepter
of wood, wherewith they make their Gestures, and handle
them. . . . [65]

Travellers other than Olearius directly or indirectly refer
to other functions of narratives and storytelling among Persians.
Samuel Benjamin attributes the popularity of the anecdotes
about the ruling class and the freedom people enjoy in relating
them to the function these narratives have in releasing people's
aggression.[66] Sir John Malcolm discusses the didactic function
of narratives and represents them as a medium through which
people communicate with their superiors, or criticize them
without the fear of punishment. He also discusses the effect of
narratives, especially the maxims of Sa'dee, the famous poet of
the thirteenth century, "in restraining the arbitrary and unjust
exercise of power."[67] Ulens de Schooten lets her informant
explain the function of narratives as preservers of tradition and
history:

This is what Malek Mansur told me. To survive, nomads have
been always obliged to fight. They lead a wandering life and do
not accumulate documents and archives. But in the evenings,
around fires that are burning low, the elders will relate striking

events, deeds of valour in which the tribes pride themselves.
Thus the epic tale is told from father to son, down through the
ages.[68]

John Baptist Tavernier's description of the coffee-houses and
the storytellings performed in those places reveals yet another
function of narratives; that of entertaining the audience by
storytelling and in this manner swaying their attention from
more serious problems, especially those involving the
government and the ruling class. As a result, those frequenting
these public places were left with no chance to discuss politics
or to criticize the government:

> Upon the North-Front of the *Meydan*, are made under the
> *Portico's* separation for Chambers, that look upon the *Piazza*,
> where people go to smoke Tobacco and drink Coffee. The Seats
> of those Rooms are plac'd as in so many Amphitheaters and in
> the midst of every one stands a large Vessel full of running
> Water, wherewith their Pipes be cleans'd when they are overfoul.
> All the *Persians* that have any spare time fail not every day to
> resort to those places between seven and eight in the morning,
> where the Owner of the Room presently brings them every one
> their Pipe and their Dish of Coffee. But the Great *Sha-Abas*, who
> was a man of grant understanding, finding those places were only
> so many Meeting-houses, where men assembl'd to talk and
> prattle of State-affairs, a thing which no way pleas'd him; to break
> the neck of those petty Cabals, he order'd that a *Moulla* should
> be sure to be betimes at every place before the rest of the
> People came thither, and that he should entertain those
> Tobacco-whiffers, and Coffee-quaffers, sometimes with a point of
> the Law, sometimes with History, sometimes with Poetry. This
> custom is still observ'd: so that after this entertainment has
> lasted two or three hours, the *Mulla* rising up crys to every one
> in the Coffee-Room, *Come my Masters, in good time let's all
> now retire every man to his business.* Straight every one retires
> upon the *Mullah's* words. . . .[69]

Chardin's report on the coffee-houses, on the other hand, sheds
more light on the atmosphere and the narrators:

> These houses, which are spacious and large Rooms, and rais'd in
> different Figures, are generally in the finest Parts of the Cities,

because there is the Rendezvous, and place of Diversion for the Inhabitants. There are many, where there are Basons of Water in the Middle, especially in the great Towns. These great Rooms have Estradas, or Galleries, quite round about, three foot high, and three foot deep, more or less according to the bigness of the Place, made of Wood or Stone to sit upon after the Eastern Manner; they open them at Day-break, and it is then and in the Evening, that they have the most Company; they serve you very exactly there with Coffee, very quick, and with abundance of Respect; there they converse; for there is the Place for News, and where the Politicians criticize upon the Government, with all the Freedom in the World, and without being disturb'd: The Government not troubling it self with what the World says: Here they play at those innocent Games I have been speaking of, which are like Draughts, or Chests; and besides *Dervishes*, or Poets, take their Turns to Perform. The discourse of the *Mollas*, or *Dervishes*, are upon Moral Subjects, and like our Sermons; but it is not look'd upon to be scandalous not to be attentive to them; no Body is oblig'd to quit his Game or Conversation for that. A *Molla* stands up in the Middle, or at one End of the *Cahue Kahne*, or Coffee-House, and begins to preach with a loud voice; or else a *Dervish* comes in all at once, and harangues the whole Company, concerning the Vanity, Riches, and Honours of the World: It often happens, that two or three are talking all at a Time, one at one End and one at another, and sometimes one shall be a Preacher, and the other a Repeater of Romances: In short, with Regard to that, there is the greatest Liberty taken in the World; the serious Man dare not say a Merry Thing; each makes his own Harangue, and listens to what he likes. The Discourses generally end in saying: There is enough said, go in the Name of God about your Business; then those who have held these Discourses, ask somewhat of the Auditory, which they do very Modestly, and without any importunity; for if they should do other wise, the Master of the Coffee-Room would not suffer them to come in again, so that those given them who will.[70]

A greater body of the stories narrated in these coffee-houses are those of Firdowsi's epic poem *Shah Namah*, and those who specialized in it were known by the name of *Shah Namah Kahn*, or *Naggal*, that is to say, the reciter of *Shah Namah*. Yet the performances of this type of narrative were not limited to coffee-houses; they, like other professional storytellers, would go to people's houses on request, or perform at other public places. Waring provides some information about this type of narrator:.

> Another amusement, among those who can afford it, is listening to a Shah Namu Khoon, a person who repeats and acts various passages of Ferdousee's epic poem called the Shah Namu. This is an amusement of a very superior kind, and one which a stranger is sure to delight in. They act the different description of the poet with the great spirit, particularly the account of the battle between Roostam, the hero of the poem, and Sohrab.[71]

Some wandering storytellers or *Dervishes* carry large pieces of canvas upon which the major characters and scenes of a story, be it religious or a love story, are painted in sequence. As the storytelling evolves, the narrator draws the attention of the crowd to the relevant scene or hero/heroine on the canvas hung on the wall or unrolls it gradually. When the narrating is over and the storyteller has received offering from the crowd, he rolls up the canvas and heads toward another marketplace or wherever he can find an interested audience. These storytellers are known as *Pardahdar*, in reference to the canvas they carry. A short description is given by Basset:

> Near the gate of the village a dervish discoursed to a crowd of boys and girls concerning the prophets. The likenesses of these revered persons painted upon a large canvas were suspended on the wall of the village to the delight of the little folks.[72]

Another group of storytellers, though not considered as narrators by profession, are *Rawza-Khans* or reciters of sermons.[73] In travellers' accounts they are presented by their common titles: *Mulla* or *Sayyid*. These are clergymen who preach sermons at mosques or at religious ceremonies at people's houses. Their sermons usually consist of praising God, the Phrophet, and the twelve Imams (descendants of Muhammad); discussing and commenting on religious, moral, and/or social issues while drawing frequently on accounts attributed to the Prophet and Imams (*Hadis*). Narrating the misfortunes and martyrdom of Hussain—Muhammad's grandson and the third Imam of the Shi'ites—and the members of his family and his followers at Karbila is the high point of each sermon. To insure maximum results in arousing feelings of sorrow and sympathy among members of the audience, the sufferings of the martyrs are narrated in a pathetic chanting tone. Often in the accounts of travellers the distinction between the *Rawza-Khans* and *Dervishes* is not made clearly, and they have been mistaken for one another. Very few travellers make any remarks about them, probably due to the religious nature of the ceremony itself and the exclusion of non-Muslims. Al-Mugaddasi makes a very short statement: "In Jurjan the public preaching is done by the jurists, and the storytellers."[74] James Basset reports:

> The term *rosakhan* denotes the readers of pathetic poems and eulogies. The call for readers at *takeahs*, and places of morning for Imams, has given rise to an order of persons who devote themselves to this occupation.[75]

Ferrier provides a lengthy account of the performance of a *Sayyid*, who was his fellow traveller in the caravan of pilgrims and who preached a sermon at one of the caravan's stops:

> In the evening, after he had eaten his dinner, he preached a sermon, the subject of which was taken from the life of one of the Imaums, and marvelous were the details. The Persian language is well adapted to flights of poetry, sallies of buffoonery, is emphatic and exaggerative, all of which is highly exciting to Persian ears. A tale indifferently well told, though most improbable in fact, will interest a Persian audience intensely; and if in a sermon the Syud thoroughly understands his business, and arranges his subjects skillfully developing it by degrees, and in a way to rouse little by little the emotions of his hearers, which he will easily do by dexterously throwing in the marvellous and the sentimental, he reaches the climax; his voice falters, he is overcome with feigned emotion, and a deluge of tears is seen to flow down the cheeks of his audience. His own are always at his commands; if he is telling a tale, he is sure to shed them at the proper moment; for example, when his hero sprains his ankle, or wants to smoke and there is no Kalioon; but if he is dying of thirst, or falls into the hands of his enemy oh!

Then the groans and lamentations are past belief; the men cry like calves, the women like does, and the children bawl loud enough to make a deaf man hear; and the unfortunate victim who like myself, is condemned to listen to all this trash, has no recourse but to stop his ears, or resign himself to be kept awake by these scenes of desolating grief. The tale or the sermon finished, the Syud proposes a cheer for the Prophet, and after that, one for Ali, the same for Hussein, for Hassan, for Abbas, for the sainted Imaums (and there is a long list), and, lastly, one for himself the Syud. These exhibitions sometimes last two hours.[76]

Besides general description of storytelling and narrators, some travellers document their firsthand experiences, providing detailed information about the style of the narrator and the reaction of the audience. This type of documentation is usually found in the travel accounts of more recent travellers. This can be attributed to lengthier residence; the eagerness and more possibilities for learning the Persian language; the shift of interest from places to people; and last but not least, travellers' awareness of and interest in folklore and folkloristics of their time. Sir Henry Layard, who had a knowledge of the Persian language and travelled among the Bakhtiari tribes, describes his experience in the following manner:

I frequently witnessed whilst in Mehmet TakiKhan's camp the effect which poetry had upon men who knew no pity and who were ready to take human life upon the smallest provocations or for the lowest greed . . . they would stand until late in the night in a circle round Mehmet Taki Khan, as he sat on his carpet before a blazing fire which cast a lurid light upon their ferocious countenances—rather those of demons than of human beings— to listen with the utmost eagerness to Shafi'a Khan, who, seated by the side of the chief would recite,with a loud voice and in a kind of chant, episodes from "Shah Namah" describing the deeds of Rustam, the mythical Persian hero, or the loves of Khosrau and Shirin. Or sometimes one of those poets or minstrels who wandered from encampment to encampment among the tribes would sing with quavering voice the odes of Hafiz or Saadi or improvise verses in honour of the great chieftain, relating how he had overcome his enemies in battle and in single combat, and had risen to be the head of the Bakhitiari by his valour, his wisdom, his justice, and his charity to the poor. The excitement of these ruthless warriors knew no bounds. When the wonderful exploits of Rustam was described . . . their savage countenances became even more savage. They would shout and yell, draw their swords, and challenge imaginary foes. When the death of some favourite hero was the poet's theme, they would weep, beat their breasts, and utter a doleful wail, heaping curses upon the head of him who had caused it. But when they listened to the moving tale of loves of Khosrau and his mistress, they would heave the deepest sighs—the tears running down their cheeks—and follow the verses with a running accompaniment of "Wai!Wai!"[77]

Sir Arnold Wilson has recorded a more detailed account of the storytellings he witnessed, in which he describes and praises the skill of the narrators and depicts the audience reaction.[78] This lengthy description appears in appendix I of this dissertation.

A thorough study of the narratives recorded by travellers reveals that they made no serious attempts to categorize the data. The most common terms used by them in presenting the data are story, legend, tradition, fable, and tale. These terms, however, are used arbitrarily merely to present the data and not to categorize them. There are numerous instances in which narratives are presented without classifying terms. Yet the data, judged by the criteria used by Euro-American scholars to identify categories of folk narratives, include examples of legends, local legends, etiological tales, fables, oral history, anecdotes, memorats, and folktales. A selection of narratives recorded by travellers is presented in appendix II. A review of the data leads to the conclusion that legends, local and etiological, are the predominant category. Some narratives are recorded by different travellers with few or no variation. However, at times these variations are rather significant and result in providing different versions of a narrative. The following three examples illustrate the fact. Fedot Afanasiyev Kotov, the seventeenth-century Russian merchant, reports about a mosque as follows.:

At Netenz there is no city; the town stands among hills and is small and the bazaar streets are bad. . . . There are many

vegetables of all kinds and above the town a very high mountain
rose up, called Shekho, on the top of which was a stone mosque.
They say that there was a Shah in Netenz who used to disport
himself in the fields and his falcon flew onto that mountain and
was killed. The Shah therefore ordered a masque to be built
over the falcon to his memory.[79]

Adam Olearius, another traveller of the same century, attributes
the legend to Shah Abbas:

> As you come into the City (of Natanz), you leave on the right
> hand two very high and picked Mountains, one whereof hath on
> the top of it a great Tower, built by *Schach-Abas*, in the memory
> of the advantage, which one of his Falcons had in that place over
> an Eagle, which he set upon overcame, and kill'd, after a very
> sharp engagement.[80]

Sir John Malcolm reports yet another version, which was
narrated to him by his informant on the road to Natanz, in the
course of conversation in the defense of Shah Abbas. The
informant justifies the king's violent temper:

> "He had violent bursts of passion, but these were not frequent,
> and then he used to be very sorry for what he did when in one
> of his paroxysms. . . . There," said he, as we entered Nethenz,
> "There is an instance of the truth of what I say; you see that
> little dome on the summit of the hill which overhangs the town.
> It is called Goombez-e-Baz,or the dome of the Hawk. It
> happened one day that this monarch, fatigued with hunting, had
> sat down on the top of that hill with a favourite hawk on his
> hand; he called for some water and a cup was brought from a
> neighbouring spring; the hawk dashed the cup from the king's
> hand as he was about to drink; another was sent for, but the bird
> managed to spill it likewise; a third, and a fourth shared the same
> fate. The monarch, in a rage, killed the hawk. Before he had time
> to take another cup, one of his attendants noticed that the water
> was discoloured. This gave rise to suspicions; and the spring was
> found to have been poisoned with the venom of a snake or
> some plant. Shah Abbas, inconsolable at his rashness in
> destroying the bird which had saved his life, built this dome to
> its memory, and is said to have often visited it."[81]

Besides different versions of a narrative having been reported by various travellers, there are also instances where the same legend is attributed to different characters or localities.

As stated earlier, in recording their observations, travellers were primarily interested in describing differences, for as Braaksma puts it, "The travel-book derives its principal attraction from the novelty of the things that are the object of its description. . . ."[82] Yet travellers did not always stop at recording the "differences," and this is particularly true in the case of later ones. Once they became familiar with novelties, they began to pay attention to the similarities that existed between East and West. In Cocchiara's words, these "similarities in turn, clearly gave rise to the principles of humanity and brotherhood."[83] Concluding his discussion on the importance and influence of records of the European travellers to the East in motivating and enhancing folkloristics, Cocchiara states:

> In both cases [investigation of differences and similarities], however—in the feeling that the voices of others were no longer curiosities but contingent and actual voices—was the powerful presence of the *filorientalismo*. The *filorientalismo* reconciled, in the conscience of the time, those motivating forces that later gave a new organization to the study of peoples, in the sense that at last this study would come to include usage, beliefs, superstitions—everything that is, if not the whole tradition of the people, certainly an indelible part of it.[84]

The role of travel books in the enhancement of folkoristics in Iran in general and folk narratives in particular is not less significant. In these travel books are recorded valuable information about the customs, traditions, and in a better term the folklore of Persians throughout centuries, which cannot be obtained from any other source. These are records of firsthand observations, and "often a faithful mirror of the state of civilization at almost every period of its development."[85] The bulk of the travel books available on every period not only facilitates the task of the researcher for obtaining the most credible results through comparing and contrasting the information they embody, but it also provides a wide range of material for the study of different aspects of Iranian folklore.

Through their description of the manners and traditions they observed, travellers drew the attention of scholars of different fields to the country and its people. Thus, the significance of travel books on Iran is not just limited to preserving the data that scholars can draw on, or facilitating historical surveys.

NOTES

1. Sir Arnold Talbot Wilson, "Some Early Travellers in Persia and the Persian Gulf," *Journal of the Central Asia Society* 12 (1925): 68-70; for further information and references see Chapter I, "Griechen und Römer," in Alfons Gabriel, *Die Erforschung Persiens; die Entwicklung der abendländischen Kenntnis der Geographie Persiens* (Wien: A. Holzhausens Nfg., 1952), pp. 5-19.

2. T. W. Arnold "Arab Travellers and Merchants, A.D. 1000-1500," in *Travel and Travellers of the Middle Ages*, ed. Arthur Percival Newton, p. 89 (New York: Alfred A. Knopf, 1926).

3. S. M. Ali, tr. *Arab Geography; Being the Translation of Section II of M. Reinaud's Introduction Générale à la Géographie des Orientaux (Géographie d'Abulfěda, tome i)* (Aligarh: Institute of Islamic Studies, Muslim University, 1960), p. 9.

4. J. H. Kramers, "Djugrafiya," in *The Encyclopaedia of Islam A Dictionary of the Geography, Ethnography and Biography of the Muhammadan Peoples, Supplement*, ed. M. Th. Houtsma, A. J. Wensink, H. A. R. Gibb, W. Heffening and Levi Provencal (Leiden: E. J. Brill, 1938), p. 64.

5. *Ibid.*

6. Abu'l-Kasim Obaidallah ibn Abdallah Ibn Khordadbeh, *Kitab al-Masalik wa'l-Mamalik*, edited by M. J. De Goeje, Bibliotheca Geographorum Aribocorum VI (Leiden: E. J. Brill, 1889); Abu Ishaq Ibrahim Istakhri, *Masalik va Mamalik; Tarjumah-yi Farsi-yi al-Masalik va'l-Mamalik az Qarn-i V/VI Hijri Ta'lif-i Abu Ishag Ibrahim Istakhri (Masalik va Mamalik by Abu Ishaq Ibrahim Istakhri;* Persian Translation of *Masalik va'l Mamalik from V/VI Century A.H.)*, edited by Iraj Afshar, (Tehran: B.T.N.K., 1347/1969); Ibn Hauqal, *The Oriental Geography of Ebn Haugal an Arabian Traveller of the Tenth Century*, tr. Sir William Ouseley (London, 1880); Ibn Hawqal, *Surat al-Arz*, tr. Ja'far Sho'ar (Tehran: Instisharat-i Bonyad-i Farhang-i Iran, 1345/1966).

7. Ibn Al-Balkhi, *Fārsnāmah; Qadimtarin Tārikh va Jughrāfiya-yi Fārs bā Mugaddamah va Havāshi bih Kushish-i 'Ali Naqi Bihruzi Fārsnāmah; The Oldest History and Geography of Fars, with an*

Introduction and Notes by 'Ali Naqi Bihruzi) (Shiraz: Ittihadiya-i Matbu'ati-yi Fars, 1343/1964); cf. Ibnu'l Balkhi, *The Farsnama of Ibnu'l Balkhi*, edited by G. le Strange and R. A. Nicholson (London: Luzac and Company, 1962).

8. Nafis Ahmand, *Muslim Contribution to Geography* (Lahor: Sh. Muhammad Ashraf, 1972), p. 13.

9. Manuel Komroff, ed., *Contemporaries of Marco Polo, Consisting of the Travel Records to the Eastern Parts of the World of William of Rubruck 1253-1255; The Journey of John Pian de Carpini 1245-1247; The Journal of Friar Odoric 1318-1330 and The Oriental Travels of Rabbi Benjamin of Tudela 1160-1173* (New York: Liveright Publishing Corp., 1973); see also Willem van Ruysbroek, *The Journey of William Rubruck to the Eastern Parts of the World, 1253-55, as Narrated by Himself with Two Accounts of the Earlier Journey of John of Pian de Carpine Translated from the Latin and Edited, with an Introductory Notice, by William Woodville Rockhill* (London: Hakluyt Society, 1900). Though the information given by the two friars in their records about Iran is limited, the importance of the accounts lies in the fact that these were the only reports of their kind in the first half of the thirteenth century. While both friars recorded traditions and customs of the people they visited—particularly those of the Tartars—Carpini's account is far more detailed and contains more information on those subjects.

10. Benjamin of Tudela, *The Itinerary of Rabbi Benjamin of Tudela*, translated and edited by A. Asher, 2 Vols. (New York: "Hakesheth" publishing Co., 1840).

11. Ben Jacob Pethahiah, *Travels of Rabbi Petachia, of Ratisbon, Who in the Latter End of the Twelfth Century Visited Poland, Russia, Little Tartary, the Crimea, Armenia, Assyria, Syria, the Holy Land and Greece*, translated, by A. Benisch (London: Longman and Co., 1861), pp. iv, vi.

12. Sir Henry Yule compiled a collection of travel accounts of these friars in his *Cathay and the Way Thither*, 2 Vols. (London: Hakluyt Society, 1866). See also Jordanus de Severac, Friar. *Mirabilia Descripta, The Wonders of the East by Friar Jordanus*, translated by Sir Henry Yule (London: Hakluyt Society, 1863).

13. Eileen Power, "The Opening of the Land Routes to Cathay," in *Travel and Travellers of the Middle Ages*, edited by A. P. Newton, p. 136, (New York: Alfred A. Knopf, 1926).

14. The following sources provide further information in this regard: George N. Curzon, *Persia and the Persian Question*, 2 Vols. (London: Longmans, Green, and Co., 1892), I, 18-20: Wilson, pp. 74-76, 81; Q. Hommayun, *Asnād-i Musavvar-i Urupāyān az Iran az Avāyil-i Qurun-i Vostā ta Avākhir-i Qarn-i Hijdahum (European Illustrated*

Documents of Iran from the Beginning of the Middle Ages to the Eighteenth Century), 2 Vols. (Tehran: University Publications, 1348/1969), I, 38-99.

15. Arthur J. Arberry, *British Contributions to Persian Studies* (Edinburgh: Longmans, Green, and Co., 1942), p. 11. Further information on the political situation of the period can also be found in Arnold T. Wilson, *Persian Gulf; An Historical Sketch from the Earliest Time to the Beginning of the 20th Century* (Oxford: The Clarendon Press), Chapter XII, pp. 171-191.

16. M. H. Braaksma, *Travel and Literature; An Attempt at a Literary Appreciation of English Travel-Books about Persia, from the Middle Ages to the Present Day* (Gronigen: J. B. Walters, 1938), p. 77.

17. Sir Williams Jones, the co-founder of the Asiatic Society of Bengal in 1784, in the preface to his *A Grammar of the Persian Language*, 6th ed. (London: W. Blumer & Co., 1804), p. X, lists some of the factors responsible for the interest of the members of the East India Company in studying the Persian language:

> . . . the servants of the company received letters which they could not read, and were ambitious of gaining titles of which they could not comprehend the meaning; it was found highly dangerous to employ the natives as interpreters, upon whose fidelity they could not depend; and it was at least discovered, that they must apply themselves to the study of the Persian language . . . These factors were also applicable to the envoys of other nationalities.

18. M. J. Dresden has enumerated the travellers who visited Persepolis from the fourteenth to the nineteenth century, and sets the beginning of the nineteenth century as the date for the appearance of interest in the archaeological exploration of Iran. "Survey of the History of Iranian Studies," *Handbuch der Orientalistik*, vol. 4, part 2, no. 1 (Leiden, 1968), 169-170.

19. L. P. Elwell-Sutton, *A Guide to Iranian Area Study* (Ann Arbor: J. W. Edwards, 1952), 36.

20. Ibn Fazlan *Safar Namah-yi Ibn Fazlan (The Itinerary of Ibn Fazlan)*, tr. A. Tabatabai (Tehran: Intisharat-i Bunyad-i Farhang-i Iran, 1345/1966); Josafa Barbaro, *Travels into Tana and Persia, by Josafa Barbaro and Ambrogio Contarini* (London: Hakluyt Society, 1873); Ludvico di Varthema, *The Itinerary of Ludvico di Varthema of Bologna from 1502 to 1508, as Translated from the Original Italian Edition of 1510, by John Winter Jones, F.S.A. in 1863 for the Hakauyt Society with a Discourse on Varthema and his Travels in Southern Asia by Sir Richard Carnac Temple, BT* (London: The Argonaut Press, 1928).

21. Arnold T. Wilson, "Early Spanish and Portuguese Travellers in Persia," *The Asiatic Review* 22 (1926), 641.

22. Ibn Battuta, *Travels in Asia and Africa*, 1325-1354, tr. and selected by H. A. R. Gibb (London: Routledge and Kegan Paul Ltd., 1929), p. 12.

23. Ruy Gonzalez Clavijo, *Embassy to Tamerlane, 1403–1406*, tr. Guy Le Strange, ed. E. Denison Ross (London: George Routledge and Son, Ltd., 1928); Charles Gray, tr. and ed. *A Narrative of Italian Travels in Persia in the Fifteenth and Sixteenth Centuries* (London: Hakluyt Society, 1873); Englebert Kaempfer, *Dar Darbar-i Shahanshah-i Iran (At the Court of the King of Kings of Iran)*, tr. by K. Jahandari (Tehran: Anjuman-i Asar-i Milli, 1350/1971).

24. Sir John Chardin, "II. The Coronation of Solyman the Third," *The Travels of Sir John Chardin into Persia and the East Indies. The First Volume Containing the Author's Voyage from Paris to Isphahan to which is Added the Coronation of His Present King of Persia, Solyman the Third* (London: Moses Pitt, 1686), p. 124.

25. Ella C. Sykes, *Through Persia on a Side-Saddle* (Philadelphia: J. B. Lippincott Company, 1898), p. 112.

26. Arthur Arnold, *Through Persia by Caravan* 2 vols. (London: Tinsley Brothers, 1877), I, 210.

27. Victoria Sackville-West, *Passenger to Tehran* (London: Leonard and Virginia Woolf, 1926), pp. 121-122.

28. Ella C. Sykes, "Persian Folklore," *Folklore* 12 (1901), 261. Travellers such as Gertrude Bell, Sir John Malcolm, Jonas Hanway, Adam Olearius, J. B. Fraser, C. E. Stewart and Sir Arnold Wilson are among those who have commented or alluded to the Persians' love of stories and storytelling.

29. Edward Denison Ross, *The Persians* (Oxford: The Clarendon Press, 1931), p. 27.

30. Olive Suratgar, I *Sing in the Wilderness: An Intimate Account of Persia and the Persians* (London: E. Stanford, 1951), pp. 211-212.

31. J. P. Ferrier, *Caravan Journeys and Wanderings in Persia, Afganistan, Turkistan and Beluchestan: with Historical Notices of the Countries Lying Between Russia and India*, tr. by William Jesse, ed. H. D. Seymore (Karachi: Oxford University Press, 1976), p. 69.

32. Sir Henry Layard, *Early Adventures in Persia, Susiana, and Babylonia*, 2. vols. (London: John Murray, 1887), II, 227.

33. Curzon, I. 149.

34. Ferrier, p. 102.

35. Samuel Greene Wheeler Benjamin, *Persia and the Persians by S. G. W. Benjamin* (Boston: Ticknor and Company, 1887), p. 193.

36. Marco Polo, *The Travels of Marco Polo, Translated into English from the Text of L. F. Benedetto by Professor Aldo Ricci, with an Introduction and Index by Sir E. Denison Ross* (New York: The Viking Press, 1931), p. 36.

37. Edward Granville Browne, *A Year Amongst the Persians* (Cambridge: Cambridge University Press, 1927), p. 64.

38. *Ibid.*, p. 97.

39. S. G. Benjamin p. 215.

40. Sir John Malcolm, *Sketches of Persia, from the Journals of a Traveller in the East,* 2 vols. (London: John Murray, 1827), I, 129, 132-133; II, 91.

41. Jonas Hanway, *An Historical Account of British Trade over the Caspian Sea, with a Journal of Travels from London through Russia into Persia and Back through Russia, Germany and Holland,* 2 vols. (London: T. Osborne, 175-4), I, xvi. He provides examples of this category, along with other legends.

42. E. G. Browne, p. 180.

43. Malcolm, I, 128.

44. C. E. Stewart, *Through Persia in Disguise, with Reminiscences of the Indian Mutiny . . . by Colonel Charles E. Stewart ed. from his Diaries by Basil Stewart* (London: G. Routledge and Sons Ltd., 1911), p. 313.

45. C. J. Wills, *In the Land of the Lion and Sun, or Modern Persia: Being Experiences of Life in Persia during a Residence of Fifteen Years in Various Parts of that Country from 1866 to 1881* (London: Macmillan and Co., 1883), p. 44.

46. Anthony Collins Basil, *Al-Muqaddasi: The Man and His Work, with Selected Passages Translated from Arabic* (Ann Arbor: Dept. of Geography, University of Michigan, 1974), p. 236. A detailed description of his general methodology appears on pages 142-143, where among other sources he refers to "having been present at the assemblies of storytellers and public preachers."

47. Mis'ar Ibn al-Muhalil Abu Dulaf, *Safarnamah-yi Abu Dulaf dar Iran dar Sal-i 341 Hijri (Travel Accounts of Abu Dulaf in Iran in 341 A.H.),* ed. by V. Minorsky, tr. by A. Tabatabai (Tehran, 1342/1963), pp. 74-75, 84-85; Marco Polo, p. 34.

48. Travellers' reliance on their memory for recording their observations made the elimination of some of the data inevitable.

49. Malcolm, I, 259.

50. Browne, p. 252.

51. Layard, I, 2.

52. Ferrier p. 103.

53. Ibn Hawqal. *Surat al-Arz*, pp. 153-154.

54. Armenius Vambéry, *The Life and Adventures of Armenius Vambery Written by Himself* (New York: F. A. Stokes Company, 1914), p. 86.

55. Browne, p. 211.

56. *Ibid.*, p. 190.

57. Malcolm, II, 61.

58. Wills, pp. 44-45.

59. Lady Mary Leonora (Waulf) Sheil, *Glimpses of Life and Manners in Persia* (New York: Arno Press, 1973), p. 89. A selection of other travellers' descriptions of Persians' entertainment is included in Appendix I.

60. James Morrier, *A Journey through Persia, Armenia and Asia Minor, to Constantinople, in the Year 1806 and 1809* (Philadelphia: M. Carey and Wells and Lilly, 1816), p. 121.

61. Edward Scott Waring, *A Tour to Sheeraz by the Route of Kazroon and Feerozabad* (London: W. Blumer and Co., 1807), p. 55.

62. Wills, p. 285. Cf. C. J. Wills, *Persia as It Is; Being Sketches of Modern Persian Life and Character* (London: S. Low, Marston, Searle and Rivington, 1886), p. 198.

63. James Basset, *Persia, the Land of the Imams, A Narrative of Travel and Residence 1871-1885* (London: Blackie and Son, 1887), pp. 308-309.

64. John Baptist Tavernier, *The Six Travels of John Baptist Tavernier, through Turkey and Persia to the Indies, during the Space of Forty Years* (London: Moses Pitt, 1685), pp. 155-156.

65. Adam Olearius, *The Voyages and Travels of the Ambassadors from the Duke of Holstein, to the Great Duke of Muscovy, and the King of Persia, Begun in 1633 and Finish'd in 1639* (London: Thomas Daring and John Starkey, 1662), p. 378.

66. Benjamin, pp. 170-173.

67. Malcolm, I, 130-132.

68. Marie-Thérèse Ullens de Schooten, *Lords of the Mountains, Southern Persia and the Kashkai Tribe* (London: Chatto and Windus, 1956), p. 52.

69. Tavernier, p. 154.

70. Sir John Chardin, *Sir John Chardin's Travels in Persia, with an Introduction by Brigadier-General Sir Percy Sykes* (London: The Argonaut Press, 1927), pp. 241-242. Chardin's remarks about people's freedom in discussing politics at the coffee-houses seem to contradict Tavernier's statements in that regard. But it should be noted that Tavernier's reference is to the time of Shah Abbas the Great (1587-1629), and not to the time of his own visits. The visits of Tavernier to

Iran occurred between the years 1629 and 1675; the three travels of Chardin to Iran were made between the years 1665 and 1677.

71. Waring, pp. 55-56.

72. Basset, p. 204

73. The term *Rawza* is originally derived from the title of a book about Muhammad and his family with an emphasis on the martyrdom of Hussain, by Mulla Hussain Va'iz Kashifi, *Rawzatu-Shuhada' (Mausoleum/Garden of Martyrs)*. He was a moralist and a well-known preacher (*Va'iz*) of the fifteenth century.

74. Al-Muqaddasi, p. 228.

75. Basset, p. 309.

76. Ferrier p. 57. His unfriendly attitude can be inferred from the text.

77. Layard, I, 487-489.

78. Sir Arnold Wilson, *S. W. Persia, Letters and Diary of a Young Political Officer 1907-1914* (London: Oxford University Press, 1942).

79. Fedor Afanasiyev Kotov, "Of a Journey to the Kingdom of Persia & C.," in *Russian Travellers to India and Persia: 1624-1798, Kotov, Yefremov Danibegov,* tr. and ed. by P. M. Kemp (Delhi: S. L. Kaeley, M.A., 1959), p. 16.

80. Olearius, pp. 264-265.

81. Malcolm, I, 260-261.

82. Braaksma, p. 115.

83. Giuseppe Cocchiara, *The History of Folklore in Europe*, tr. by John N. McDaniel (Philadelphia: Institute for the Study of Human Issues, 1981), p. 42.

84. *Ibid.*, p. 43.

85. Braaksma, p. 7.

CHAPTER III

Western Scholars' Contribution to Iranian Folkloristics

The considerable number of the travel books of the sixteenth and seventeenth centuries, with their detailed, vivid descriptions and drawings, played a significant role in stimulating Western scholars' interest in Iran. The wide range of information documented in these sources introduced the European reader to the art, literature, languages, customs—in short, the culture of this Eastern country. Thus, the first examples of the European travellers who came to the East exclusively in pursuit of knowledge and not for political, commercial, and/or religious reasons, appeared in the eighteenth century.[1] The observation and description period led to the serious and systematic study of the Orient. This, in turn, provided the impetus for the inception of "Orientalism," from which, later on, Iranian studies branched out.

The scholarly interest and achievements in the field of Iranian studies and their development into a discipline have been greatly influenced and/or directed by the discovery and translation of the *Avesta*; the emergence and development of linguistics as a field of study; the Romantic Movement in Europe; and the colonization of the East by Europeans. Of the various fields of Iranian studies, only a few have been directly or indirectly responsible for the enhancement of folkloristics in Iran. Therefore, in surveying the development of Iranology and assessing Western scholars' contributions, only the pertinent fields are discussed in this chapter.

The study of Oriental languages in its primary stages originated in Europe for theological purposes, for better comprehension of the Bible. "The discovery and translation of the *Avesta* by Anquetil du Perron (1731–1805) marked a new era in philology as well as in the study of religion,"[2] writes A. V. William Jackson. It gave a new dimension to the Western scholarly interest in Iran and became a milestone in history of Orientalism and Iranian studies. This epoch-making translation was the product of its translator's long residence and extensive research in India. Determined to obtain firsthand information about Zoroastrianism, Anquetil du Perron left for India in 1754 and did not return to Europe until 1761. Ten years later, in 1771, he published a French translation of the *Avesta* on the basis of the manuscripts that he had managed to gather during his travels and residence in India. Prior to the appearance of this translation only a small number of books on the old religion of Iran and some translations and Persian grammar books existed in Europe.[3] The comparison and, as a result, the discovery of similarities between the *Avesta* and Sanskrit generated systematic research and study of the *Avesta* in the nineteenth century. Rasmus Rask, one of the founders of comparative linguistics, travelled to India and Iran between the years 1819 and 1822, and brought back a collection of Avestan and Pahlavi manuscripts.[4] Eugene Burnouf (1801–1852), the originator of the systematic study of the *Avesta*, used Sanskrit to translate the *Avesta* and to resolve the ambiguities that existed in certain passages. The translations and the significant contributions of these two scholars generated the serious and extensive study of the Avestan and Pahlavi sources in the following centuries.

The results of a scientific expedition organized by the Danish government and sent to the East under the leadership of Carsten Niebuhr in 1761 provided new sources for the study of pre-Islamic Iran. In the course of his travels, Niebuhr copied a number of inscriptions, among which were those at Persepolis. Earlier travellers such as Josafa Barbaro (1472), Garcia de Silva

Figueroa (1618), Pietro della Valle (1622), Cornelius le Brun (1704), and Sir John Chardin (1711) had either commented on the existence of these inscriptions or had provided copies of some samples. In 1802 the foundation for the systematic study of the Old Persian inscriptions was laid by the achievements of the German scholar Fridrich Grotefend (1775–1853) in deciphering the cuneiform inscriptions of the Achaemenian kings. His work was continued by scholars such as Silvestre de Sacy (1758–1838), who interpreted Sassanian inscriptions; Rasmus Rask; Eugene Burouf; Jules Oppert; Sir Henry Rawlinson (1810–1895); and Antoine Meillet (1866–1936). Translation of the *Avesta* and the deciphering of the inscriptions provided the material for an extensive study of the languages, history, culture, and religions of pre-Islamic Iran. The enthusiasm for the study of Avestan and other old Iranian languages was intensified by the findings of the philologists of the time. In a lecture delivered to the Asiatic Society in Calcutta in 1786, the English Orientalist Sir William Jones (1746–1794) pointed out the genealogical relationship of Sanskrit, Greek, and Latin. He also suggested that these three languages might have sprung from a common source no longer in existence. The findings of Franz Bopp (1791–1867), the German philologist and founder of comparative grammar, drew European philologists' serious attention to the study of Avestan. Through the grammatical comparison of Greek, Sanskrit, Latin, Persian, and the Germanic languages, he proposed the common origin of these languages. Scholars such as Jacob Grimm (1785–1863), Rasmus Rask, and Theodor Benfey were among other contributors to comparative philology. The preoccupation of these and other philologists with the comparative study of Indo-European languages, and the importance shared by *Avestan* and Sanskrit as the most archaic languages of the group, guaranteed serious study of Iranian languages in the following centuries.

As time and scholarship advanced, the philological and religious studies of Iran became more independent from Oriental and/or Indo-European studies. An extensive amount of research was conducted by Russian and European scholars in the nineteenth and the twentieth centuries. With the gradual accumulation of data and the discovery of new material and languages, specialization and generation of new fields of study were inevitable. Once scholars had managed to read and interpret manuscripts and to decipher inscriptions, they attempted to describe the grammatical rules of these languages. The next step was to concentrate on the content of these documents from the past and to study Zoroastrianism and other pre-Islamic religions of Iran.

The Avestan, Middle Iranian, and Manichaean sources which were primarily studied by scholars as philological and religious data also provided material for the study of Persian mythology. In addition to myths, these sources also contain a number of legends. A survey of scholarship in the field of Iranian mythology points to the strong influence of linguistic methodologies. This is mainly due to the linguistic background and preoccupation of the scholars involved, as well as the nature of the texts, which require knowledge of pre-Islamic languages of Iran. The comparative method of scholarship is the dominant trend in the majority of the earlier, and in a good number of the later, stages of the study of Persian mythology, the sources of comparison being India and/or other Indo-European countries. While the influence of the comparative linguistic method is evident in the researches of the scholars who studied Persian mythology in an Indo-European context, the selection of India as the primary source of comparison might be attributed to additional factors. As in the case of the old languages of the two countries—that is to say, Avestan and Sanskrit—great similarities exist between their mythologies. The state of Indian studies, due to the colonial interests of the West in that country and the Romantic Movement in the European continent, was far more advanced than that of Iranian studies. The quantity of the available Vedic and Sanskrit sources, as well as the historical, geographical, linguistic, and religious closeness and ties of the two countries, were other contributing factors for the selection of India as a major source of reference and comparison. As stated by Georg Morgenstierne, "Most Iranologists have come to this field of research via Indological or Semitic studies."[5]

Another impetus for the development of Iranian studies came in the second half of the eighteenth century, when, in

1754, the British Empire established her domination over India. The fact that the scholarly interest in, and the study of, the East were enhanced and at times initiated by political and/or economic goals of Western governments verifies the statement that "Orientalism was largely stimulated by, and in a sense nurtured in the bosom of, colonialism."[6]

Soon after their settlement, the English servants of the East India Company recognized the necessity of learning the Persian language, which was at the time the official language of the court of India. Before long, the delegation members of other European countries who were in the area on political or commercial missions shared the experience. A serious study of the Persian language was undertaken; manuscripts were collected; grammar books were written; bilingual dictionaries became available; and translations of Persian literary and historical sources began to appear. Meanwhile, the information presented in the missionary reports, together with the fact that the old religion of Iran and Zoroaster's teachings had numerous devout followers in India, spawned religious studies. Eventually the study of the Persian language and culture, which had in this manner originated by and for practical rather than scholarly purposes, was carried on and developed by researchers. The establishment of government-organized societies and institutions for the study of Oriental languages, which had started in the late seventeenth century, continued throughout the eighteenth and the following centuries in various countries in Europe, the Soviet Union, and the United States.[7]

In the last quarter of the nineteenth century, the research conducted by a group of philologists known as the neogrammarians on the systematic sound changes of language promoted scholarship in the fields of phonetics and dialectology in Europe and directed the attention of philologists from the study of the archaic forms and stages of language to the contemporary ones. According to the findings of the neogrammarians, all changes in the sound system of a language followed the same pattern in the currently spoken languages and dialects as they did throughout the development of the language since prehistoric times. The introduction of structural linguistics in Europe by Ferdinand de Saussure in the early nineteenth century, and the distinction he made between diachronic and synchronic linguistics further stimulated the concentration of scholars on modern languages and eventually dialects. Synchronic linguistics is the study of a language at a given point in time, without considering the past or future developments of the language. In diachronic linguistics however, the emphasis is on the study of the historical development of a language for purposes of determining the systematic structural changes that have taken place in successive stages and resulted in the development of the present form of it from the old one. Once research in the field of dialectology commenced, factors other than mere linguistic purposes intensified the enthusiasm and efforts of scholars and amateurs to record and/or study dialects. The common belief was that dialects had to be recorded before they were forgotten, contaminated, or replaced by the standard language, the assumption being that dialects would inevitably become extinct.[8] Besides, dialects were considered valuable sources of information about the cultural background of their speakers.

While the preoccupation of the historical linguistics promoted the study of Old and Middle Iranian, and practical necessities motivated and generated scholarly research of standard modern Persian, more than one factor contributed to the study of modern Persian dialects. Curiosity and the interest of travellers in the people they visited, advancement of philological scholarship in Europe, and the discovery of the Turfan manuscripts were most influential in the development of Persian dialectology. Long before the establishment of linguistics and dialectology as serious fields of scholarship, travellers to Persia made reference to, or provided information about, the peculiarities of the language spoken by the inhabitants of certain towns or areas they visited; and they pointed out the similarities and differences that existed between standard Persian and the forms spoken by the inhabitants. At times the information included comments or narratives regarding the nature of the dialect. One such example is the following, reported by several travellers. The narrative concerns the Simnani dialect, which during the present century has been recorded and studied by Western and Iranian scholars. In his study of this dialect, Arthur Christensen characterizes the following legend and attributes it to Fath Ali Shah, a king of the Qajar Dynasty. The following version was reported by James Bassett in 1887:

> Although the people speak modern Persian, yet among themselves they use the Simnonee. There is a story descriptive of this jargon which is often told by people of this region. It is that one of the kings of Persia appointed a learned man to investigate and report upon the various dialects and languages of Persia. The savant traversed the kingdom in the prosecution of his mission. On his return to the court he was given an audience by the king. The courtiers and great men were assembled. He discoursed in a learned manner of the many tongues he had heard. At length he came to speak of the people of Simnon. He now remained silent a moment, and, taking an empty gourd, he put into it a few small stones; then holding the gourd up and shaking it, he cried out, "Here you have the language of Simnon."[9]

During the nineteenth and the twentieth centuries, a good number of dialect specimens were recorded by European and Russian political envoys who were aware of, and interested in, philological studies. Many of them had to reside and serve in remote parts or towns of the country. Led by their curiosity and personal interest, and stimulated by the flourishing scholarship in the fields of philology, ethnography, and folklore studies, these diplomat-scholars contributed to Persian dialectology and eventually folklore studies through their recording and/or analyses of various modern Persian dialects. Alexander Chodzko (1804–1891), the Polish diplomat, resided in the country for eleven years (1830–1841). He learned the Persian language and conducted research on standard Persian as well as the dialects of the northern parts of Iran. He is among the pioneering folklore students in Iran. His major contributions include *Specimens of the Popular Poetry of Persia, as Found in the Adventures and Improvisations .of Kurroglou* (London, 1842); *Grammaire de la langue persane* (Paris, 1852); and *Théatre Persan Choix de Téazlés* (Paris, 1878).[10] General Sir Albert HoutumSchindler (1846–1916) held several important posts in the Persian service, including that of telegraph adviser to the Persian government. Travelling through different parts of the country to survey the possibilities of a telegraph project gave him the chance to record and study different dialects.[11] Lt. Col. Douglas Craven Phillott (1860–1930), the British consul in Iran, is the author of numerous articles on different aspects of Iranian folklore. Yet his contribution is not limited to his recordings of tales, proverbs, falconry, folk speech, beliefs, and other traditions.[12] He also published works on the grammar of standard modern Persian.[13] Another scholar in this category is Colonel David Lockhart Robertson Lorimer (1876–1962), the English consul in Iran. His residence in the southern parts of the country provided him with the opportunity to collect and study specimens of Kirmani and Bakhtiari dialects. In 1916, with the collaboration of his wife, he published a collection of Persian folk narratives originally recorded in these two dialects.[14] The scholarly contributions of Basil Nikitin (1885–1960), the Russian consul to Iran, were mostly on, but not limited to, the study of the Kurds—their language, folk narratives, and social and political background.[15] The documenting and studying of the dialects by these and other politician-scholars not only provided other researchers with firsthand material but also enriched and enhanced study in the fields of Persian philology and folklore.

In assessing the contributions of the political envoys, mention should also be made of the family members who accompanied the delegates during their travels. These family members—mainly sisters or wives—enjoyed the advantage of having more leisure time; and frequently they had a better opportunity to study those aspects of Persian life that could not have been studied by the envoys themselves, such as women's habits and customs. Reference was made earlier to Mrs. Lorimer, who "obtained the texts of the Kirmani portion of the Persian Tales . . . and a number of nursery rhymes."[16] A larger number of the observations made by the family members were recorded in the form of travel books. Some examples include Mrs. Jean Dieulafoy, who went to Iran in 1884 with her husband, Marcel Dieulafoy, and accompanied him during his archaeological surveys of the country; and Victoria Sackville-West, who in 1925 and 1927 travelled to Iran to visit her husband, Harold Nicholson, the Counsellor at the British Legation in Iran.[17] The contributions of Miss Ella C. Sykes, sister of Sir Percy Sykes, besides the account of her travel and residence, also include her work on Persian narratives and folklore.[18]

In the first decade of the twentieth century, the unexpected discovery of manuscript texts of Middle Iranian languages—Parthian, Khotanese Saka, Sogdian—in Chinese Turkistan (particularly in Turfan) provided scholars with an abundance of new material. Archaeological excavations and discoveries also made new inscriptions and data available. While the newly-discovered manuscripts and inscriptions shed light on some obscure problems of the Old and Middle Iranian languages and provided fundamental sources for the study of Iranian religions (specifically Manichaeism), they also produced new problems and ambiguities. To search for solutions, scholars had either to turn to Indian sources or to the Persian language itself.[19] The similarities that existed between Middle and modern Persian, and the discovery of the fact that some terms though extinct in modern Persian existed in certain dialects, became influential factors in stimulating the recording and studying of modern Persian dialects. Georg Morgenstierne (1892–1978), a specialist in Indo-Iranian studies and dialectology, refers to the significance of dialects in facilitating the task of philologists: "It was the old Persian inscriptions which provided the key to the ancient cultures of the Near East, and in the mountains of Iran archaic dialects are still spoken which throw a backward light on the development of the Indo-European languages."[20] Another statement of the same nature was made much earlier by Clement Huart in his preface to de Morgan's *Mission Scientifique en Perse* (1904). In his short survey of the history of studies on Kurdish language he explains:

> Certaine formes archaique conservées en kurde, disparues en persan moderne et qui se rattachaient directement au Zeñd, étaient faites pour piquer la curiosité des linguistes, qui souhaitaient de plus abondantes lumières sur ce sujet obscure; mais la difficulté de se les procurer ne diminuait guère. Cependant, petit à petit, les voyageurs et les résidents europeens mettaient au jour le resultat de leur observation.[21]

Russian scholars have conducted extensive research in the various fields of Iranian philology and folklore and have played a significant role in the development and enhancement of scholarship in these disciplines. That the Russian scholars have had an equal, if not larger, share than that of their European colleagues in contributing to the study of Iranian philology and folklore is testified by the amount of their scholarship. In Russia, as in other countries, "interest in the study of Iranian languages was brought about by practical need, i.e., the development of diplomatic, trade and cultural relations. . . ."[22] The importance of studying standard modern Persian for practical purposes having been recognized, systematic studies of the language got underway gradually; and Persian became an academic subject of instruction and study in the Soviet Union. Later on, these studies were followed by systematic recording and analysis of other Persian languages and dialects. Recording of examples from the Persian language had appeared in Russia as early as the fifteenth century in the travel accounts, such as that of Afanasievich Nikitin.[23] However, the systematic recording and collection of Persian dialect specimens started in the early eighteenth century in Russia. Trained "Commissionaries and emissaries of the Russian imperial court were sent out to explore the empire. Their records provided valuable data for the awakening of interest in Europe, including Russia, in the languages of the world and their interrelationship."[24] These kinds of exploratory trips continued to be arranged and financed by government centers and academies in the nineteenth and twentieth centuries. To fulfill the practical need for the knowledge of the standard Persian language, a number of dictionaries, grammar books, and textbooks were written. At the same time, specimens of different dialects were gathered and published, the first example being Alexander Chodzko's *Specimens of the Popular Poetry of Persia, as Found in the Adventures and Improvisations of Kurroglou* (1842). The book contains specimens of folk poetry belonging "to the inhabitants of Northern Persia, and those of the Coasts of the Caspian Sea."[25] The pioneering work of Chodzko on recording dialect specimens was followed by fieldwork and research conducted by I. N. Bérézin, a professor at Kazan University. In 1842, he travelled to Iran and was engaged in collecting data until 1845. His trip was sponsored by Kazan University. The outcome of his trip and research appeared in 1853 in his work on the dialects of Northern Iran.[26] In the same year his book on Persian grammar was published. A few years later (1860–1861), Boris Andreevich Dorn and G. V. Melgounof were sent to Iran by the Russian Academy of Sciences to study the current dialects of the northern parts of Iran.

Along with studying the current Persian languages and dialects, the Russian scholars investigated Middle and Old Iranian languages beginning in the middle of the nineteenth century. Among those who contributed to these studies, mention should be made of such scholars as K. G. Salemann, V. Zhukovski, V. F. Miller and his son B. V. Miller, E. E. Bertels, A. A. Freiman, F. Rosenberg, R. Galunov, N. Marr and I. M. Oranski.

Because of his pioneering scholarship and significant contributions to Iranian dialectology and folklore, Valentin Zhukovski (1858–1918) is considered one of the most important scholars in these two fields of study. In 1883, he was sent to Iran by St. Petersburg University to conduct research. He resided in the country for three years, during which time he learned Persian and collected a good number of dialect specimens. The Persian grammar written by him and Carl Salemann (1849–1916), another prominent scholar in the field of Iranian studies, was first published in 1889.[27] After almost a hundred years, the book is considered to be "accurate, (and) still useable for the classical language";[28] and its excellence is attributed largely to Zhukovski, "who had years of field experience in Iran."[29] The first volume of his *Materials for the Study of the Persian Dialects*, in Russian, appeared in 1888.[30] Commenting on the philological significance of this work, I. M. Oranski states:

> Of utmost importance for the study of dialects of Iran was the posthumous edition of the 2nd and 3rd parts of the well-known work by V. A. Zhukovsky "Material for the study of Persian dialects" (Petrograd, 1922)—a work that made a tremendous impact on the development of this branch of knowledge.[31]

Though the nature of this and some of the other works of

Zhukovski is principally philological, his contribution to the study of Iranian folklore is as significant. This is primarily due to his extensive recordings of Iranian folklore examples, specifically folksongs and narratives, and his attracting the attention and interest of other scholars to the existence and importance of these genres.

Zhukovski was a professor of Persian at St. Petersburg University, a post that he held for over thirty years. This gave him the opportunity to add to the list of his contributions by training researchers such as Alexander Alexandrievich Romaskevich (1885–1942) and Vladimir Alexeievich Ivanov (1886–1970). Both these scholars, besides contributing to the other fields of Iranian studies, conducted a considerable amount of fieldwork and research on different genres of Iranian folklore. A. A. Romaskevich, following the instruction and in the footsteps of his teacher, devoted attention to recording and studying folk narratives. He travelled to Iran in 1927 and gathered dialect specimens in the form of folk narratives and songs. His collection of Persian folk narratives was published in 1934.[32] V. A. Ivanov contributed to Iranian dialectology, folklore, and ethnology with over twenty scholarly articles.[33] Besides folk narratives and songs he recorded and studied some genres of folk speech.[34]

The influential and extensive contributions of the Russian scholars to the field of Iranian studies—particularly dialectology and folklore—were a continuous endeavor throughout the nineteenth and the twentieth centuries. While European scholars have contributed more to the study of the Old and Middle Iranian languages, Russian scholars have emphasized modern languages. Special interest of European scholars in the old languages of Iran can be attributed to the development and progress of comparative linguistics in Europe. While the same linguistic trends played a role in the research conducted by the Russian scholars, the reason for their greater contribution and scholarship on the Iranian folklore and modern languages can be explained by the geographic, linguistic, cultural, and historical closeness of Iran and the immediate Soviet neighboring areas. Other than the obvious practical advantages of learning the Iranian languages for the establishment of diplomatic and trade relationships with Iran and other countries of the Near East and Central Asia, the fact that Iranian languages and dialects are spoken in some of the Soviet areas bordering Iran on the north was an influential incentive for the study of the language by government-sponsored organizations, such as universities and academies.

The political changes in Russia in the early twentieth century leading to the adoption of the Marxist ideology had a significant impact on folklore research in that country and the rest of the world. This was to a great extent due to the fact that this ideology in general gave significance to a class of people whose general descriptions in many ways matched the specifications of the "folk" as characterized by the European folklorists of the time. Consequently, studying the "folk" and their "lore" gained a political edge, in addition to being initiated by scholarly interests. One example of this ideological influence in relation to Iranian folkloristics is the fairly short sociological analysis of Persian folk narratives by D. S. Komisarov. In describing the general characteristics of some Persian narratives, he refers to instances in which the hard-working heroes who come from humble backgrounds manage to scandalize the ruthless and unjust ruling class and confront their cruelty and unfair behavior. The sovereignty of evil does not last long; the eventual victory belongs to justice and the deserving good-hearted and wise heroes.[35] It should be noted here that the number of analytical studies of Iranian folklore or folk narratives does not exceed such short remarks and a few individual studies, such as Basil Nikitin's "Un sujet de fable, variantes kurde et persane."[36] In his extensive study of Iranian folk literature, which dates back to 1956, Jiři Cejpek points out the insufficient amount of analytical research on Persian folklore and/or folk narratives. The statement is still valid:

> Until quite recently problems to do with folk-literature have very often been passed over in silence, or at best some isolated details may have been glanced at. . . . Synthesis is always difficult when there has been almost no analytical research and when comparative studies are still in a preliminary stage.[37]

The primary motivations and objectives of philologists

for studying the modern Persian languages and dialects, as indicated by themselves, were to enhance the study of Iranian philology in general and to provide adequate data for the study of those languages and dialects to enable researchers eventually to find answers to unresolved questions. In the preface to his "Le dialect de Samnan," Arthur Christensen states:.

> L'étude des dialectes est, pour la philologie iranienne, d'une importance particulière. Dans la langue persane, beaucoup de vocables iraniens ont disparu et ont été remplacés par des mots arabes, et notre connaissance des langués anciennes de l'Iran est, malgré tout ce que les recherches archéologiques des dernieres annèes nous ont apporté de nouveau de l'Asie Centrale, très fragmentaire. Les dialects vivants doivent etre mis à contribution pour combler les lacunes, dans le mesure du possible.[38]

A few years earlier E. B. Soane had made a similar statement in regard with the study of Kurdish language:

> The Kurdish dialect of Persian has so far received very little attention from Oriental students, . . . for while actually nothing more than a Persian dialect it has not submitted to the erosion which time brings about in every language. . . . Nor has it been subject to that admixture of Arabic words . . . it has preserved intact many words now obsolete in the mother language.[39]

A common factor stated by almost all philologists for studying and/or providing specimens of certain dialects is lack of adequate research and data. One such example is the comment made by V. Ivanov in his study "Two Dialects Spoken in the Central Persian desert."

> . . . it seems that so little is known about the spoken languages of Persia and so rarely does this arid and unhospitable track of desert attract the attention of travellers who have linguistical interest, that I think I am right in offering my notes . . . hoping they may be of use to students.[40]

Another motivation was the fact that philologists saw the dialects in danger of rapid changes and eventual disappearance due to modernization, literacy, and migration of their speakers to towns. At times dialectology was employed to provide data for fields other than philology. In the case of Vladimir Minorsky, it was a tool to overcome certain ambiguities in his religious studies as he states: "From the earliest days of my Oriental studies the Gurani dialect appealed to my imagination as a key to the mysteries of Ahl-i Haqq religion."[41] Practical purposes were not absent either, for D. L. Lorimer hoped that his work on the Bakhtiari dialect would be "useful to British officers who were concerned with affairs in the South-West of Persia during the war."[42]

Dialectology was also employed to provide insight into the lifestyle and the culture of the people under study, as V. Ivanov in one of his studies explains:

> The purpose of this monograph is to give a fairly representative collection of specimens of local rustic songs which may, to some extent give an idea not only of the language used by the peasants, but also of the life and general conditions in that arid and isolated corner of Persia.[43]

Ivanov's statement has inherent in it his view of folklore as being collective in nature and being a reflection of culture. These two concepts, though modified, elaborated, and expanded with the advancement of time and scholarship, have had an important impact on the research conducted by folklorists and anthropologists of the nineteenth and the twentieth centuries. When the term "folklore" was coined, the ideas of "collectivity" and "communality" were implicit in it, as it is the "lore" of the "folk"; and there is no idea of individuality in it. Commitment to the notion of the "collectivity" of folklore made scholars put more emphasis on similarities and ignore differences. This preoccupation with the consistencies of human behavior in time and space also resulted in scholars' generalizations about the "folk" and their "lore." But in time and with the expansion of the data base, researchers began to pay attention to differences; and due credit was given to individuals and their creativity. Scholars' belief in the interrelationship between folklore and culture has been another influential factor in folklore scholarship. Anthropologists as well as folklorists raised questions about the reasons, extent, and forms of this interrelationship and presented various explanations for the tallying and/or non-tallying of folklore with culture. Franz Boas (1858-1942) considered folktales as mirrors of culture and stated that whatever had value and meaning for the members of a society is reflected in their folklore. A similar idea was expressed by Chodzko in his analysis of Persian folksongs:

> Feeble, disheartened, poor, and enervated, the Persia of this day struggles for a precarious existence, in fear of two mighty neighbours—Russia on the north and England on the South. Popular poetry, being an exact expression of the moral state of a nation, cannot lie. Consequently, we find nothing evidencing a manly spirit in any of the songs of the modern Persia.[44]

In another example, Ivanov expresses his disappointment and surprise in not being able to find evidence of the tallying of folklore with the Kurdish people's way of life. In reference to Kurdish folksongs he states:

> On the whole these tristichs appear to belong to an "impressionistic" school. . . . They are "static" in their motive, defining some emotional movement from physical experience, with the utmost economy of words. They never contain a "story," however short, but always deal with a single individual fact. It is singular that a people with such a long fighting past, like the Kurds of Khurasan, take little interest in epic poetry. My long and persistent search for poems of this kinds was unavailing. I found but a few "cycles" of tristichs dealing with events...the subject was usually death of a hero. [45]

An almost identical remark is made by Jan W. Weryho:

> What is surprising is the lack of modern heroic poems among a people as warlike as Sìstanìs. Blood-feuds between tribal chiefs are still a characteristic feature of Sìstanì society and a constant topic of conversation. Yet no poems are being composed to describe them. . . . But perhaps the short quatrain, particularly the only form of verse in Sìstanì nowadays, is not a suitable means for heroic poetry. Perhaps formerly there existed in

Sĭstān long epic ballads, similar to those of Baluchis, but that we shall never know.[46]

Few researchers have included analytical remarks, textual or contextual, to accompany their recording of dialect specimens. The contextual analysis is mainly based on the researchers' notion of folklore as a reflection of society or culture. This kind of analysis is usually limited to determining the presence, absence, and/or the extent of the interrelationship between culture and folklore. Where the researchers choose to do a textual analysis, comparative and/or motif annotations are the prevailing ones. One such example is Ivanov's textual analysis of a narrative in the Birjandi dialect:

> The Persian tale is rarely simple; usually it consists, as in the present case, of a number of motives. . . . The motives of bewitching, especially by a woman, turning the rival into a cow . . . etc., all these are well known from the Arabian Nights and other similar collections. The main portion of the tale, the story of the reward for the virtuous maiden and punishment for the wicked one, is apparently a genuine folk-tale. It resembles so closely the folk-tales of many European nations. A Russian folk-tale treats the same subject almost word for word. . . . The motive of the naked maiden hiding herself in the foliage of a tree when surprised by a prince at her bathing is one of the most popular, and almost inevitable in all Persian tales of some length. . . . The marriage of the virtuous maiden to the prince resembles the motive of Cinderella. . . .[47]

Most of the philologists provide information regarding their methodology and the circumstances of their fieldwork. The information usually includes the date and/or the period during which, and the area in which, the fieldwork was conducted, the process of selecting and/or training informants, the methods of soliciting and recording data, fieldwork difficulties, and informants. The following is a typical example:

> In 1918–1920 during my residence in that part of Persia, I collected about 400 specimens of Kurdish poetry and tales which gave a more definite idea of the language which the Kurds of Khorasan speak.[48]

Philologists' primary purpose for recording prose texts and folksongs was to analyze the syntax of the dialect under study. To record the specimens, the informants were either asked to provide narratives of their own choice, or philologists would tell stories which they chose from well-known collections of folk narratives and ask the informants to reproduce them in their dialect. In comparative studies of two or more dialects, philologists often used the same narrative to facilitate the task of discovering similarities and differences in the vocabulary and grammar of those dialects. This is one reason why certain narratives commonly appear in the specimen recordings of different philologists.

Though not all philologists explicitly describe details of their methodology, the number who do is not few. In his "Notes on the Gabri Dialect of Modern Persia," D. L. Lorimer states:

> My first step was to work out the grammatical forms of the dialect . . . with the help of a man who himself talked the Yezdi sub-dialect. . . . Having in this way acquired some knowledge of the ordinary forms and structure of the language, I set him as themes the subjects of marriage, birth, and "burial" customs. . . . I then procured the services of two or three Kermani Gabrs, of whom I eventually selected one . . . as the most intelligent and articulate. He was a school master of the old type. . . . I made him tell me stories which I took down from dictation. . . .[49]

A reference to the direct method of eliciting data, which presumably was employed by most philologists, appears in another study by D. L. Lorimer. His introductory notes to a Badakhshani text read as follows:

> This text was the result of an attempt to explain the parable of the Parodigal Son to my informant and get him to give a version of it in Badakhshani. He had, however, strong views as to what would naturally occur in such a family crisis.
>
> This second version of the same parable represents an attempt to get my informant to render it sentence by sentence. . . .[50]

Arthur Christensen is another scholar who describes his data-gathering method:

> D'abord j'ai traduire à mon Mīrzā l'anecdote persane des deux femmes qui se querellaient à propos d'un enfant (le "jugement de Salomon"), anecdote dont il existe déjà des traductions dans plusieurs dialect iraniens, et une autre historiette. . . . Ensuite, mop mirzā a préparé pour moi trois petites pièces. . . .[51]

Another description of this methodology is presented by Christensen in his "Contribution a la dialectologie iranienne." After referring the reader to the introductory notes in the work mentioned above, he continues:

> . . . puis je fis traduire à Zabīh-ollāh l'anecdote du jugement de Salomon et trois petites anecdotes tirées de mes, "Contes persans en langue populaire" J'ai demandé à Zabīh-ollāh, s'il savait des contes qu'il pût me raconter en guilākī, et le lendmain il avait un text tout préparé . . . . Ensuite il me dicta le text guilākī phrase par phrase . . . .[52]

As can be inferred from these and other similar statements made by scholars regarding their methodology, the recorded specimens were mostly dictated by the informants or were written down during their leisure time following the scholars' directions. With the invention of recording machines, however, the task of philologists became much easier. In gathering data, philologists' emphasis was on the text itself; and since the specimens were not recorded in a natural setting, there was no chance to study the social context. Bearing this fact in mind, travellers' records with a variety of valuable information regarding narrating, audience, narrators, and narrating situations provide more significant data from a folkloristic point of view.

Though the data recorded by philologists include narratives of such genres as fairy tales, local/historical/ etiological legends, and animal tales, the majority of the texts consist of short folk narratives known in Persian as *Hikāyat*. No real attempt has been made by philologists to classify these data. Scholars usually refer to these narratives as anecdotes, short narratives, specimens, and texts. Of the sources studied for the purpose of this dissertation only two specify the genre of the narratives.[53]

Collecting the data was not always an easy task for researchers. At times their scholarly intentions were misunderstood by the people under study and resulted in minimal or no cooperation at all. Åge Meyer Benedictsen is one scholar who airs his complaint in this regard:

> Mon travail dans le pays d'Awromān, s'est effectué dans des conditions tres défavorable. Le "sultan," qui ne comprenait pas mon intérêt linguistique, me regardait avec une méfiance croissante. On interrompait toujours de nouveau mon travail . . . on désirait me voir partir au plus tôt. "Qu'est-ce que tu veux savoir?" me demandait le "sultan"; un boeuf s'appelle comme ça, un fusil comme ça, un cheval comme ça; il ne faut pas longtemps pour noter cela, et puis, inšallāh, tu reviendras à ta partie." Le soupçon du chef rendait les gens tantôt timides, tantôt grossiers, et me força de partir plus tot que je ne l'eusse désiré. Dans un certain village on me refusa le feu et l'eau pour me faire partir.[54]

Jan W. Weryho provides another example:

> Upon my arrival in Sistan I first found it very difficult to establish any contact with the natives. Shi'a bigots regard an Unbeliever as "najes" (unclean), any contact with whom produces pollution. Also association with a foreigner might mean trouble with the Police.[55]

To these problems should also be added the communication difficulties. Most philologists had little or no knowledge of the dialect under study; and if the informant was not fluent in standard Persian, they could hardly understand each other.

Finding the right informant was another problem for philologists to overcome. While some preferred educated informants, others felt that for linguistic purposes illiterate informants were ideal. In any case, locating a suitable informant was not easily achieved. In one instance V. Ivanov states:

> The informer selected for the work should be trained, instructed,

tested, etc. Often he is so unintelligent that he must be dismissed. Circumstances permit such training rarely, and therefore to obtain a complete story in prose is rather a rare success.[56]

The emphasis is always on the intelligence of the informant—the presence or absence of it. In reference to the Awromani dialect and the informants involved, De Morgan complains:

> . . . malheureusemant l'ignorance de ces gens est telle, et leur intelligence est si bornée, que j'ai eu la plus grande peine à recueillir les elements de leur langage.[57]

D. L. Lorimer's statement regarding his informants goes as follows:

> I have . . . collected large quantities of popular poetry and prose tales. This I have written down from the mouths of several Bakhtiari of the upper, or at least of the more intelligent classes. . . .[58]

Yet he later admits that his "informants did not make up for their deficiency in number by any special brilliance of intellect." On the other hand, when satisfied with their informants' performance, philologists unanimously used the word "intelligent." It does seem that by noting the intelligence of their informants, philologists were intent on convincing their readers of the validity of their data. Such emphasis is also embedded in philologists' perceptions and presuppositions about their informants, who were mostly "peasants" or illiterate people who lived in rural areas, as Ivanov states:

> . . . it is almost hopeless to try to get explanations from the unsophisticated peasant or shepherd, which the average Kurd generally is.[59]

Some philologists, besides having the problem of locating the right informant, also had difficulty recording data. When informants were given a choice of telling the tales they knew, on many occasions the results were less than satisfactory, either

because of the informant's short memory or the philologists'
difficulty in recording the specimen. V. Ivanov comments about
his experience:

> Kurdish fairy tales are interesting from the folklore point of
> view. . . . Unfortunately, I found these tales beyond my power to
> write down from dictation. The primitive Khorasani Kurds find it
> impossible to tell them slowly and distinctly. Every demand for
> repetition leads to a complete change of sentence, and
> sometimes even to a complete change of the subject itself. The
> literate disdain all knowledge of such "old women's nonsense,"
> and it was with great difficulty that I succeeded in obtaining a
> few stories in prose. . . .[60]

To avoid such problems, some philologists preferred to narrate
short, well-known narratives and ask their informants to
reproduce them in their own dialects. Thus, narratives were
mostly dictated and/or written down by the informants rather
than being told at their normal pace and in their usual
circumstance. Therefore, the opportunity for the philologists to
observe and comment about the narrating style of their
informants was non-existent. There are, however, occasional
statements regarding an informant's good memory or his or
her extensive repertoire. Other information regarding the
informants usually includes their age, profession, and name.

While philologists provided a bulk of firsthand recorded
folk narratives, the grammar books and manuals of standard
Persian brought about the impetus for translation of
manuscripts of Persian folk narrative collections. To provide
European students of the Persian language with easy and
interesting reading material, the authors of Persian grammar
books included some short narratives in their works. These were
usually taken from well-known narrative collections; and because
of their simple plots and language, these texts provided suitable
reading material for the learners of the language. Of the earlier
examples of these grammar books, mention should be made of
Francis Gladwin's *Persian Moonshee*,[61] which, in the section on
"Persian Stories in an Easy Style," includes seventy-six short
narratives (*Hikāyat*) with English translations; *Elementa Persica*
by Georg Rosen, with a collection of eighty-nine short

narratives;[62] and *A Grammar of the Persian Language* by Duncan Forbes, with a selection of seventy-four short narratives.[63] Even in more recent works, folk narratives are still considered as suitable reading material.[64]

The narratives recorded in the reading sections of Persian grammar books and manuals generated interest in the original sources. Eventually, translations of narrative collections began to appear. Every effort was made by the enthusiastic translators to locate manuscripts of narrative collections and present them in European languages for their readers. On the other hand, the translation of *The Arabian Nights* at the beginning of the nineteenth century, with all the glitter and splendor described in the stories, captured the interest and fascination of European readers and made them eager for more.

Translations of the Persian narratives fall under two categories: exact translation of narrative collections and/or manuscripts, and modified or adapted versions. The section on "The Persian Tales" in Henry Weber's *Tales of the East* is a translation of the Persian collection *Bahār-i Dānish* (*The Garden of Knowledge*), composed in 1650;[65] *Gulzara, Princess of Persia*, is a translation of a manuscript found in Bengal;[66] Auguste Bricteaux's *Contes persans* is a translation of a manuscript in the Berlin Royal Library;[67] and Reuben Levy's sources for his *The Three Dervishes and Other Persian Tales and Legends* are

> from various manuscripts in the Bodleian Library. The majority are taken from collections of short tales of varied authorship, collected by different hands and brought to England by such travellers and officials as Sir William Ouseley and his brother . . . [68]

Narrative translations of the second group, often taken from various sources, were modified to appeal to the taste of the European readers. Ethel Mary Wilmot-Buxton's *Stories of Persian Heroes Retold from the Shāh Nāmeh of Firdawsi*,[69] and *Persian Wonder Tales Adapted from Persian* by C. F. Mackenzie,[70] are both intended for young readers, therefore the narratives are curtailed and simplified. Ella C. Sykes, as was the case with Wilmot-Buxton, had the *Shāh Nāmah* of Firdawsi as the original source for her *Story Book of the Shah*.[71] Though not limiting her readers to a specific age group, Ella Sykes also adapted the narratives and the characters to fit the interest of her readers:

> I have endeavoured to make such characters as Jamshed . . . interesting to English readers, and have given local colour to my book by depicting, from my own experiences in the country, some of the aspects of Persia, and the different manners and customs of its inhabitants, as they are at present day.
>
> In many cases I have taken only the bare outline of the story, filling it in with suitable incidents, and have tried to avoid the repetition and verbosity of the original, which would not appeal to western mind, as it does to the eastern.[72]

A similar method is followed in *Tales of the Persian Jenii Retold by Frances Jenkins Olcott*,[73] in which narratives taken from different sources are modified and molded into a continuous story. Of other collections mention should also be made of *Fairy Tales of a Parrot Adapted from the Persian*,[74] based on the Persian collection *Tooti Nāmah*, and W. A. Clouston's *Some Persian Tales from Various Sources*,[75] which is a collection of what Clouston calls "tales of common life" taken from different Persian and Indian sources.

It was not until the development of dialectology that firsthand recorded collections of narratives began to appear. Contributions and philological studies of scholars such as Oskar Mann, Arthur Christensen, V. Ivanov, Georg Morgenstierne, and D. L. Lorimer, to name a few, contained valuable data in the form of dialect specimens. Narratives collected at firsthand appeared as early as the beginning of the twentieth century. Among the pioneering works were D. C. Phillott's "Some Current Persian Tales, Collected in the South of Persia from Professional Story-tellers" (1906);[76] *Contes persans en langue populaire* (1918) by Arthur Christensen; and *Persian Tales, Written down for the First Time in the Original Kermani and Bakhtiari and Translated by D. L. R. Lorimer and E. S. Lorimer* (1919). A short collection of tales by Henri Massé appeared in 1925.[77] The stories are transcribed in colloquial Persian and were recorded from the same informant who provided

Christensen with the data for his *Contes persans en langue populaire.*

As time went on, Russian and European scholars became more involved in recording narratives and increased the number of narrative collections. During his residence in Iran, L. P. Elwell-Sutton recorded a number of tales from an informant which appeared in his *Mashdi Galeen Khanom, The Wonderful Sea-horse and Other Persian Tales* in 1950.[78] Though Anne Sinclair Mehdevi obtained the narratives recorded in her *Persian Folk and Fairy Tales* firsthand, she was not very faithful to the texts narrated by her informants.[79] As she states in the introduction, she either retold, split, or combined the narratives she had recorded. The significance of Arthur Christensen's *Persische Märchen* lies not only in the narratives themselves, but also in the lengthy and informative introduction in which he reviews the study of Iranian folk narratives.[80] An English translation of the narratives only appeared in 1971 under the title *Persian Folktales.*[81]

Though some folkloristic studies such as Ella Sykes' "Persian Folklore" and R. A. Nicholson's "Some Notes on Arabian and Persian Folklore" appeared early in the present century, most research on Iranian folklore has been conducted since mid-century.[82] Studies of Iranian mythology, which had commenced in the late nineteenth century, flourished in the early decades of the twentieth century, with a great number of books and articles on Iranian mythology either in an Indo-European or Indo-Iranian context or as a separate subject matter.[83]

The most extensive study of Persian folk narratives is Jiři Cejpek's "Iranian Folk Literature" in Jan Rypka's *History of Persian and Tajik Literature.* In addition to detailed descriptions of various forms of Iranian folk narratives and a discussion of the interrelationship between folklore and literature, Jiři Cejpek's study also covers relevant and important subjects such as narrating, the role of audience, classification of narratives, and textual and contextual analysis. He dwells on the significance of social analysis of narratives, stating:

It would be a mistake to regard and treat tales merely as a

form of fiction. When studying them one has to find out about
the way they were composed as well as about the social milieu in
which they came into being.[84]

In every segment he makes references to the works of the
European and Russian scholars, the contributions of the latter,
however, being predominant. Since only few Russian scholars'
contributions to the fields of Iranian folklore and/or folk
narrative research have been translated into European
languages, Cejpek's extensive coverage and bibliography of
their works is of great significance.

Studies of Persian folk narratives are not usually as lengthy
as that of Jiři Cejpek's. Rather, they are in the form of essays
appearing in scholarly periodicals, such as J. P. Asmussen's
"Remarks on Some Iranian Folk-tales Treating of Magic Objects,
Especially AT 564."[85] Another study on the same subject, though
from a different perspective, was authored by L. P. Elwell-Sutton.
In "Magic and the Supernatural in Persian Folk-Literature,"
Elwell-Sutton discusses the influence of Iranians' religious
background and belief in the supernatural on their folk
narratives.[86] Elwell-Sutton's contribution to the study of Iranian
folk narratives includes several other essays. In "The Role of the
Darvish in the Persian Folk-tales," after presenting examples of
the portrayal of the *Dervish* in narratives and examining the
characteristics attributed to him, he concludes:

> . . . in the *darviš* of the Persian folk-tale we have a
> remarkable blend of two quite distinct traditions—the Islamic
> Sufi element from the west, with its background of Hellenism
> and Mesopotamian ideology, and an eastern element derived
> either from the direct influence of Hindu folk-literature, or
> possibly a survival from the original springs of Indo-Iranian
> culture.[87]

In the short introductory remarks to "The Unfortunate Heroine
in Persian Folk-Literature," Elwell-Sutton makes the statement
that since the unfortunate heroine, despite the male-dominated
culture, overcomes evil and disaster and in the end is rewarded
with a handsome prince or other happy ending, "the folk-tale
has kept alive an older tradition of feminine independence."[88]

He also regards the unexpected good luck of the heroine and her triumph over disasters as an ironical social statement. Unfortunately, no further discussion or elaboration follows these statements. Another scholarly study by Elwell-Sutton is his essay "The Influence of Folk-tale and Legend on Modern Persian Literature," in which he discusses the influence of folk narratives on the works of the contemporary Persian writers.[89] In his short study of two popular characters in Persian folk narratives, Elwell-Sutton emphasizes the significance of the "examination of the regional and national differences and idiosyncrasies" as they appear in folk narratives. He believes that "the particular form that an internationally known motif or story-type takes, . . . in any given region, is a valuable aid to the understanding of the mode of thought, cultural traditions, superstitions, and way of life of the people of that area."[90] His most recent work is "Collecting Folktales in Iran," a short review of the work done by Western and Iranian researchers on collecting folk narratives. In Sean Sweeny's short article of the same title, however, the emphasis is on encouraging Iranians to collect folklore, and on the methodology to be used.[91] In a lecture delivered at Tehran University, Adrienne Boulvin reviewed the development of folkloristics in Western countries and Iran and encouraged systematic collection and recording of folk narratives. She pointed out that narrative collections would on a national level provide the Iranian researchers with the necessary data, and in an international scope they would facilitate comparative folklore studies and the research regarding the migration theory of narratives. She emphasized that for folk narratives to be effectively employed in any kind of research, they have to be systematically classified and analyzed.[92]

The emphasis in the research conducted by Western scholars has been on collecting and recording different genres of folklore before they disappear or are forgotten. Yet some analysis has also been done. Persian folk narrative studies are mostly either descriptive or textual analysis with literary overtones. The close interaction and relationship which exist between Persian literature—classic or modern—and folklore provide sufficient data for comparative and textual studies of what is also known as the polite and popular literature.[93] In the absence of the literary overtone, and when textual study is involved, researchers either reconstruct the origins of the narratives, attempt to locate and compare numerous versions, or discuss the form, content, and/or structure of certain group of narratives.

At times scholars have chosen to limit their data base to a certain narrative, such as Arthur Christensen's "La princesse sur la feuille de myrte et la princesse sur la pois," an essay in which the author traces the narrative to several classical Persian sources and gives references to its European versions.[94] Another example is B. Nikitin's "Un sujet de fable, variantes kurde et persane," which is based on the comparison of the Persian and Kurdish versions of a fable, together with some remarks regarding the social context of the fable.[95] There also exist studies with a wider scope, where either a certain category of narratives is chosen for study, or a specific topic is examined in the general area of Persian folk narratives, examples of which include B. Nikitin's "Quelques fables kurdes d'animaux" and Arthur Christensen's two essays "Les sots dans la tradition populaire des Persans," and "Juhi in the Persian Literature."[96]

Western scholars' contributions have been fundamental to the generation and enhancement of folklore studies in Iran. They have accomplished this not only by their research, but also by cultivating an awareness and interest among Iranians in folklore studies as a serious field of scholarship. Western scholars have consistently pointed out the insufficient data base and limited research on Iranian folklore, the significance of its study—contrary to the Iranians' belief—and they have directly or indirectly encouraged the Iranians to get involved. Of the researchers who have contributed to the study of Iranian folklore, philologists have played the most important role. The bulk of narratives recorded by them as dialect specimens, their interest and research in the field of Iranian folklore, and their drawing the attention of Western and Iranian scholars to folk narratives and their significance are of great value to Iranian folklore scholarship.

NOTES

1. V.V. Barthold, *La découverte de l'Asie; Historie de l'orientalisme en Europe et en Russie traduit du Russe et annoté par B. Nikitine* (Paris: Payot, 1947), p. 140.

2. A.V. William Jackson, "Our Interest in Persia and the Study of Her History, Language, and Literature," *International Congress of Arts and Sciences* 3 (1906): 361.

3. M.J. Dresden, "Survey of the History of Iranian Studies," p. 171. See also, Shuja'al-Din Shafa, *Jahān-i Irānshināsi* (The World of Iranology) (Tehran, 1969), pp. 42–44.

4. For further information regarding Rasmus Rask's contributions, see Georg Morgenstierne, "Iranian Research in the North," *Le Nord* 2–3 (1941):135–137.

5. *Ibid.*, p. 137.

6. Hamid Enayat, "The Politics of Iranology," *Iranian Studies* (Winter 1973): 3.

7. For some examples, see Shafa, pp. 44–47.

8. The same kind of thought prevailed during the early stages of folklore scholarship and resulted in a rush to collect folklore before it was forgotten.

9. Bassett, pp. 195–196. The same story is presented by Rev. James Bassett in his article "Grammatical Notes on the Simnuni Dialect of the Persian Language," *Journal of the Royal Asiatic Society* (1884): 120–139.

10. Of these and other contributions of Chodzko, his *Specimens of the Popular Poetry of Persia, as Found in the Adventures and Improvisations of Kurroglou* has been of greater significance to Iranian folklore study.

11. Edward G. Browne has provided information regarding the life and contributions of Houtum-Schindler in his article "The Persian Manuscripts of the Late Sir Albert Houtum-Schindler, K.C.I.E.," Journal of the Royal Asiatic Society (1917): 657–694.

12. See, for example, D. C. Phillott, "Some Persian Riddles Collected from Dervishes in the South of Persia," *Journal of the Royal Asiatic Society*, 2, no. 4 (April 1906): 86–93; "A Note on Sign-, Gesture-, Code-, and Secret-language, etc., amongst the Persians," *Journal of the Royal Asiatic. Society*, 3, no. 9 (1907): 619–622; "A Persian Nonsense Rhyme," *Journal of the Royal Asiatic Society*, 2, no. 7, (1906): 332–333; "Some Street Cries Collected in Persia," *Journal of the Royal Asiatic Society*, 2, no. 7 (1906): 283–285; and "Some Lullabies and Topical

Songs Collected in Persia," Journal of the Royal Asiatic Society, 2, no. 3 (1906): 32–53; "Two Persian Equivalents for Peter Piper," *Journal of the Royal Asiatic Society*, 2, no. 10 (1906): 529; "Note on the Huma or Lammergeyer," *Journal of the Royal Asiatic Society*, 2, no. 10 (1906): 532–533; and "Bibliomancy, Divination, Superstitions amongst the Persians," *Journal of the Royal Asiatic Society*, 2, no. 8 (1906): 339–342.

13. *Higher Persian Grammar* (Calcutta, 1919). For a complete list of his contributions, see M. Hedayat Hosain, "Douglas Craven Phillott (1860–1930)," *Journal of the Asiatic Society Bengal* 27 (1931): clxxx–clxxxiii.

14. D. L. R. Lorimer, *Persian Tales, Written Down for the First Time in the Original Kermani and Bakhtiari and Translated by D. L. R. Lorimer and E. S. Lorimer* (London: Macmillan and Co., 1919).

15. His major work on the Kurdish people is Les Kurdes; *étude sociologique et historique* (Paris, 1975). Of his other contributions reference can be made to "Superstitions des Chaldéens du plateau d'Ourmiah," Reveu d'Ethnographie et des Traditions Populaires, Année 4, n° 14 (1923):149–181; "La vie domestique kurde," *Revue d'Ethnographie et des Traditions Populaires*, Année 3, n° 12 (1922):334–344; and "La poési lyrique kurde," L'Ethnographie 45 (1947–1959): 39–53.

16. D. L. R. Lorimer, "Is There a Gabri Dialect of Modern Persian?" *Journal of the Royal Asiatic Society* (1928): 293–294.

17. Jane Dieulafoy, *La Perse, la Chaldée et la Susiane* (Paris, 1887). Besides Passenger to Tehran, a reference to which was made in Chapter II, the other work by Victoria Sackville-West is her *Twelve Days; An Account of a Journey Across the Bakhtiary Mountains in South Western Persia* (London, 1928).

18. To these should also be added her short article on "Persian Family Life," *Journal of the Central Asian Society* 1 (1914): 3–11, which is a general review of Persian life with an emphasis on the unfortunate *position of Persian women, and "A Talk about Persia and Its Women," National Geographic Magazine* 21 (1910): 847–866.

19. For further information on the discovery of these manuscripts and their significance see H. W. Bailey, "A Half-Century of Irano-Indian Studies," *Journal of the Royal Asiatic Society* (1972): 99–110. On page 108, he states, "Every trace of Iranian language which can be found in manuscript or inscription or spoken dialect is urgently needed to win through to a full interpretation of these ancient poems."

20. Morgenstierne, p. 134.

21. J. de Morgan, *Mission scientifique en Perse*, tome V (Etudes linguistiques), (Paris, Imprimerie Nationale, 1904), p. vii.

22. I. M. Oranski, "Old Iranian Philology and Iranian Linguistics," in *Fifty Years of Soviet Oriental Studies* (1917–1967), USSR Academy of Sciences Institute of the Peoples of Asia (Moscow: Nauka Publishing House, 1967), p. 3.

23. Fedor Kotov Athanasius Nikitin, "The Travels of Athanasius Nikitin of Twer," in Richard Henry Major, *India in the Fifteenth Century* (London: Hakluyt Society, 1857).

24. Gernot L. Windfuhr, *Persian Grammar: History and State of Its Study* (The Hague: Mouton Publishers, 1979), p. 15.

25. Chodzko, p. vii. He continues about his method of collection: I collected them at different periods, during a sojourn of eleven years in those countries, from oral communications with the people—generally, the lower classes, who did not know how to read or write. Their source, therefore, is undoubtedly genuine. . . .

26. E. Bérézine *Recherches sur les dialectes persans* (Casan, 1853).

27. Carl Salemann und Valentin Shukovski, *Persische Grammatik* (Leipzig: Otto Harrassowitz, 1947)

28. Gilbert Lazard, "Persian and Tajik," in *Current Trends in Linguistics,* edited by Thomas A. Sebeok, p. 65 (The Hague, 1970).

29. Windfuhr, p. 27.

30. English translation of some of the narratives recorded by Zhukovski in his *Materials for the Study of the Persian Dialects* as dialect specimens were presented by V. Ivanov in his article "The Gabri Dialect Spoken by the Zoroastrians of Persia," Rivista degli Studi Orientali 17 (1937): 1–39.

31. Oranski, p. 23.

32. A. A. Romaskevich, *Persidski Narodnye Skazki* (Moscow, 1934). I personally have not reviewed this work.

33. For further information on the life and contributions of Vladimir Ivanov see the following articles: A. A. A. Fyzee, "Wladimir Ivanow (1886–1970)," *Journal of the Asiatic Society of Bombay,* 45–46 (1970–1971): 92–97; Farhad Daftari, "Bibliography of the Publications of the Late W. Ivanow," *Islamic Culture* 45 (1971): 55–67.

34. Examples include Vladimir Ivanov, "Some Persian Darvish Songs," *Journal of the Asiatic Society of Bengal,* New Series, 23 (1927): 237–242; "Jargon of Persian Mendicate Darvishes," *Journal of the Asiatic Society of Bengal,* New Series, 23 (1927): 243–245; "Pidar-Sukhta," *Journal of the Royal Asiatic Society* (1927): 96–97.

35. D. S. Komisarov, pp. 75–76.

36. B Nikitin, "Un sujet de fable, variantes kurde et persane," *Revue d'Ethnographie et des Traditions Populaires,* Année 3, n° 10

(1922): 129–140.

37. Jiři Cejpek, "Iranian Folk-Literature," in Jan Rypka, *History of Persian and Tajik Literature*, edited by Karl Jahn, p. 705. (Netherlands: D. Reidel, Dordrecht, 1968).

38. Arthur Christensen, "Le dialect de Sămnăn, essai d'une grammaire Sămnănīe avec un vocabulaire et quelques textes suivi d'une notice sur les patois de Săngsar et de Lăsgird," *Det Kgl. Danske Vidensk. Selskab. Skrifter, Historisk og Filosofisk*, Afd. II, no. 4 (1915), p. 227.

39. E. B. Soane, "A Southern Kurdish Folksong in Kermanshahi Dialect," *Journal of the Royal Asiatic Society* (1909): 35.

40. V. Ivanov. "Two Dialects Spoken in the Central Persian Desert," *Journal of the Royal Asiatic Society* (1926): 405–406.

41. V. Minorski, "The Gūrān," *Bulletin of the School of Oriental and African Studies*, 11, pt. 1 (1943): 76.

42. D. L. R. Lorimer, *The Phonology of the Bakhtiari, Badakhshani, and Madaglashti Dialects of Modern Persian with Vocabularies* (London: Royal Asiatic Society Prize Publication Fund, Vol. VI, 1922), p. xi.

43. V. Ivanov, "Persian as Spoken in Birjand," *Journal of The Asiatic Society of Bengal* 24 (1928): 235.

44. Alexander Chodzko, *Specimens*, pp. 401–402.

45. V. Ivanow, "Notes on Khorasani Kurdish," *Journal of the Asiatic Society of Bengal* 23 (1927): 171.

46. Jan W. Weryho, "Sīstanī-Persian Folklore," *Indo-Iranian Journal* 4 (1962): 282.

47. V. Ivanov, "Persian as Spoken in Birjand," p. 261.

48. V. Ivanov, "Notes on Khorasani Kurdish," p. 167.

49. D. L. R. Lorimer, "Notes on the Gabri Dialect of Modern Persian," *Journal of the Royal Asiatic Society* 12 (1916): 424–425.

50. D. L. R. Lorimer, *The Phonology of the Bakhtiari*, p. 167. This is a rare example of recording a narrator's personal view of a narrative.

51. Arthur Christensen, "Le dialect de Samnan," p. 229. He later on gives a detailed account of his interactions with his informant.

52. Arthur Christensen, *Contributions à la dialectologie iranienne, dialecte Guilăki de Recht, dialectes de Fărizănd, de Yaran et de Natanz, avec une supplément contenant quelques textes dans le Persan vulgaire de Teheran* (Kobenhavn, Det Kgl. Danske Videnskabernes Selskab. Historisk-filologiske Meddelelser), 17, 2 (1930), pp. 12–13.

53. Georg Morgenstierne, "Persian Texts from Afganistan," Acta Orientalia 6 (1928): 309–328. Only two texts are presented as legends; the rest are identified by numbers. Oskar Mann, *Kurdisch-Persische Forschungen; Die Mundarten von Khunsâr, Mahallât, Natănz, Nâyin,*

Sämnän, Sîvänd und Sô-kohrûd, Band 1, Abteilung 3 (Berlin und Leipzig, 1926). The text section is presented under the titles Anekdoten, Schwanke, Fablen, Märchen und Erzählungen, without any further subdivision.

54. Arthur Christensen, "Les dialectes d'Awroman et de Pawa, textes recueillis par Åge Meyer Benedictsen," *Det Kgl. Danske Videnskabernes Selskab. Historisk-filologiske Meddelelser*, 6: 2 (1921), 4.

55. Weryho, p. 277. Despite the initial difficulties Weryho later on managed to be accepted by the natives and to enjoy their company and cooperation. Folklorists, as well, encounter suspicion and interference from government officials. One such example is provided by L. P. Elwell-Sutton in "Collecting Folktales in Iran," p. 103:

> Officialdom is often suspicious of what appears to the bureaucratic mind to be a frivolous occupation concealing some more sinister purpose. I have been refused permission to travel to outlying villages, even though I carried a letter signed by the Prime Minister. In Mashhad a man who had promised to record some tales was found on arrival at his house (evidently after a visit from the police) to be too unwell to assist-and he had a very nasty-looking boil to prove it.

56. V. Ivanov, "Persian as Spoken in Birjand," p. 239.

57. De Morgan, p. 3.

58. D. L. R. Lorimer, *The Phonology of the Bakhtiari, Badakhshani, and Madaglashti Dialects of Modern Persia*, p. 9.

59. V. Ivanov, "Notes on Khorasani Kurdish," p. 170.

60. *Ibid.*, p. 172.

61. Francis Gladwin, *Persian Moonshee* (London: Wilson and Co., 1801).

62. Georg Rosen, *Elementa Persica: Persische Erzählungen mit Kurzer Grammatik und Glossar* (Leipzig, 1915).

63. Duncan Forbes, *A Grammar of the Persian Language* (London: Wm. H. Allen and Co., 1861).

64. See, for example, Charles Henri D. Fouchecour, *Elements pour un manuel de persan* (Publications Orientalistes de France, 1976), which includes five firsthand-recorded narratives.

65. Henry Weber, *Tales of the East*, 3 Vols. (Edinburgh: James Ballantyne and Company, 1812).

66. *Gulzara, Princess of Persia, or the Virgin Queen; Collected from the Original Persian* (1816).

67. Auguste Bricteux, *Contes persans* (Liege, 1910).

68. Reuben Levy, *The Three Dervishes, and other Persian Tales*

and Legends (Oxford: Oxford University Press, 1923), p. vii.

69. Ethel Mary Wilmot-Buxton, *Stories of Persian Heroes Retold from the Shah Nameh of Firdausi* (New York: Thomas Y. Crowell Company, 1908).

70. C. F. Mackenzie, *Persian Wonder Tales Adapted from the Persian* (Glasgow: Blackie and Son Limited, 1928).

71. Ella C. Sykes, *Story Book of the Shah, or Legends of Old Persia* (London, 1901).

72. *Ibid.*, p. vi.

73. Frances Jenkins Olcott, *Tales of the Persian Jenii Retold by Frances Jenkins Olcott* (London, 1919).

74. Stephen A. Condie, *Fairy Tales of a Parrot Adapted from the Persian* (London: Ernest Nister, 1892).

75. W. A. Clouston, *Some Persian Tales from Various Sources* (Glasgow, 1892).

76. D. C. Phillott "Some Current Persian Tales, Collected in the South of Persia from the Professional Story-tellers." *Memoires of the Asiatic Society of Bengal*, 1, no. 18 (1905–1907): 375–412.

77. Henri Massé, "Contes en persan populaire," *Journal Asiatique*, Tome 206 (1925): 71–157.

78. L. P. Elwell-Sutton, Mashdi Galeen Khanom; *The Wonderful Sea-horse and other Persian Tales* (London: Geoffrey Bles, 1950).

79. Anne Sinclair Mehdavi, *Persian Folk and Fairy Tales* (New York: Alfred A. Knopf, 1965).

80. The introduction was translated into Persian in 1956. Arthur Christensen, "Qissah-hā-yi Irāni," ("Iranian Narratives"), K. Jahandari, tr., *Sukhan*, 7, no. 2 (1335/1956): 17–25, 148–263.

81. Alfred Kurti, *Persian Folktales* (London: G. Bell and Sons, 1971).

82. Ella C. Sykes, "Persian Folklore"; R. A. Nicholson, "Some Notes on Arabian and Persian Folklore," *Folklore* 41:4 (1930): 345–358. Both articles are descriptive in nature, with emphasis on and examples of Persian folk belief.

83. For a partial bibliography, see, for example, Abd al-Hamid Abi al-Hamd, *Bibliographie française de civilisation iraniene par Abdolhamid Abolhamd et Nasser Pakdaman* 3 Vols. (Tehran, 1972–1974), Vol. 2, 69–76; and J. D. Pearson, *A Bibliography of Pre-Islamic Persia* (Mansel, 1975).

84. Jiři Cejpek, p. 649.

85. J. P. Asmussen, "Remarks on some Iranian Folk-tales Treating of Magic Objects, Especially AT 564," *Acta Orientalia* 28: 3–4 (1965): 220–243.

86. L. P. Elwell-Sutton, "Magic and the Supernatural in Persian

Folk-literature," *Ve Congres International d'arabisants et d'islamisants* Actes. 5 (1970): 189–196.

87. L P Elwell-Sutton, "The Role of Darvish in the Persian Folk-tale," *Proceedings of the 26th International Congress of Orientalists* 2 (1968): 203.

88. L. P. Elwell-Sutton, "The Unfortunate Heroine in Persian Folk-literature," *Yādnāmah-i Irāhi-yi Minorsky (Minorski's Iranian Memorial Volume)* edited by M. Minuvi, Iraj Afshar, p. 37 (Tehran: Tehran University Publications, 1969).

89. L. P. Elwell-Sutton, "The Influence of Folk-tale and Legend on Modern Persian Literature," *Iran and Islam* (Edinburgh: Edinburgh University Press, 1971), pp. 247–254.

90. L. P. Elwell-Sutton, "Scaldheads and Thinbeards in Persian Folk-Tale Literature," *Laographia dettion tes Ellenikes Laographikes Hetaireias* 22 (1965): 105.

91. Sean Sweeny, "Girdavari Āsār-yi Adabi va Āmmiānah-yi Irān," ("Collecting Iranian Folk-literature"), *Rāhnamay-i Kitāb* 4 (1339/1960): 458–460.

92. Adrienne Boulvin "Uslub-i 'Ilmi-yi Tanzim-i Mavvād-i Qissah-hā-yi 'āmmyānah," ("Systematic Methodology of Folk Narrative Classification,") *Sukhan* 21 (1971): 1159–1170.

93. See, for example, William Hanaway, "Popular Literature in Iran," *Iran: Continuity and Variety*, edited by Peter J. Chelkowski (Fourth Annual New York University Near Eastern Roundtable, 1971); William Hanaway, "Formal Elements in the Persian Popular Romances," *Review of National Literature* 2: 1 (1971): 139–160; and S. Hillelson, "The Source of a Story in the Mathnawi, and a Persian Parallel to Grimm's Fairy Tales," *Journal of the Royal Asiatic Society* (1937): 474–477.

94. Arthur Christensen, "La princesse sur la feuille de myrte et la princesse sur le pois," *Acta Orientalia* 14 (1936): 241–257.

95. B. Nikitin, "Un sujet de fable, variantes kurde et persane."

96. B. Nikitin, "Quelques fables kurdes d'animaux," Folklore XL: 2 (1929): 228–244; Arthur Christensen, "Les sots dans la tradition populaire des Persan," *Acta Orientalia* 1 (1923): 43–75; Arthur Christensen, "Juhi in the Persian Literature," *A Volume of Oriental Studies Presented to Edward G. Browne on his 60th Birthday*, edited by T. W. Arnold and Reynold A. Nicholson pp. 129–136, (Cambridge: The University Press, 1922).

CHAPTER IV

Development of Folkloristics in Iran: Native Scholars and Folk Narrative Scholarship

Though folklore studies were inspired in the West in the nineteenth century as a scholarly discipline focusing on the study of human behavior and taught through scrutinizing traditional narratives and customs principally, folklore scholarship in Iran is comparatively young and dates back only to the third decade of the present century. In the second half of the nineteenth and throughout the first few decades of the twentieth century, Iran underwent tremendous political, social, economic and cultural changes, which resulted in reforms in various aspects of life leading to the modernization of the country. Internal reforms, combined with the effects of closer contact with the Western culture and technology, opened new arenas for seekers of knowledge and those Iranians interested in the advancement of the country and its culture. Among the new fields of study was folklore scholarship. Western researchers, however, had paved the way by recording and studying Persian folklore since the nineteenth century. Their scholarship played a significant role in laying the foundations and drawing the attention of the Iranians themselves to folklore studies as a scholarly discipline.

In addition to the contributions of Western researchers, several other factors were responsible for the inception and development of folkloristics in Iran: strong nationalism that evolved before and during the constitutional movements and was later on greatly reinforced during the reign of Reza Shah; Romanticism imported to the country by Iranians educated abroad, and through translations of European literature; and the development of modern Persian literature; socialist realism introduced by Communist ideologies. The direct influence on the generation of interest in folklore studies, however, was provided by the literary renaissance of Iran in the twentieth century. The main characteristics of modern literature were a realistic approach, development of literary prose, simplification of the language and style, interest in the language and lives of common people, and addressing the masses of the nation rather than the courtiers and/or the limited number of literate individuals.

Modern Persian literature—significantly different in content and form from the classical literature—developed under totally new political, social, and economic conditions. The primary stages of change and reform appeared during the reign of the founder of the Qajar Dynasty, Aga Mohammad the Qajar, who was crowned in 1796. He managed to replace the existing feudalism with a unified and strong centralized government, creating a period of peace and expansion of administrative organizations. Men of letters and education from across the country headed to the capital to fill the new administrative positions, and in the course of time they created a new class of courtiers or civil servants. These individuals, whose earnings provided them with an average, comfortable life and leisure to cultivate letters, gradually formed the nucleus of the educated or the intellectual class.[1] It was also during this period that, as the result of the expansionist policies of great rival powers such as France, Britain, and Russia, who struggled for supremacy in Iran, the country came into close contact with Western civilization and culture. The positive outcome of the penetration of European powers into the country for the fulfillment of their economic exploitation and colonial intentions was the acquaintance of Iranians with Western technology, literature, and modes of thought. Infiltration of European ideologies into Iran and Iranians, awareness of European technological and scientific supremacy and their own inferiority and backwardness in those areas inspired movements for reforms and social justice. On the other hand, the reformist and patriotic ideas and writings of men such as Mirza Malkom Khan and Sayyid Jamalud Din Asad Abadi Afghani, successful political movements of the late nineteenth century in the East, political events in Europe—mainly the Russian Revolution of 1905 and the Russo-Japanese war of 1904–1905—and the social changes that followed, acceleration of Western power politics in Iran and their interference in Iran's internal affairs, and the oppressive nature of the Qajar Shah's despotic regime stirred up strong patriotic feelings among Iranians and intensified their oppositions to the government. Eventually, the political movements that had started in the late nineteenth century led to the Constitutional Revolution. The proclamation of the Constitution in 1906 heralded the beginning of a new era in the political and social existence of the country.

The introduction of printing in the second decade of the nineteenth century, publication of lithographed Persian literary works and translations of Western literary and scientific sources, foundation of schools (specifically *Darul-Funun* or polytechnical college in 1851), student travel grants to Europe, and the development of the press and journalism were significant reforms and influential factors responsible for the spread of education and eventually the wider diffusion of literature. As the literate class continued to grow, so did their need for knowledge and information regarding the social and cultural happenings of the country and the world. It was the writer's task to satisfy this thirst for knowledge through journalism and the translation of European literary and scientific works, as well as the publication of books dealing with issues affecting the lives of their country men. In addition to providing information and widening the scope of their readers' knowledge, journals and translations of European works also had a great impact on the modernization and simplification of Persian prose. The foundations of simplification of the language had been laid as early as the middle of the nineteenth century through the efforts of the reformist ministers of the Qajar Dynasty, Qaim Maqam Farahani (1779–1835) and Mirza Taq-i Khan Amir Kabir (d. 1852), in abolishing traditional bombastic prose and advocating a plainer style of writing in official correspondence. Other influential works in this regard were the diaries of Nasir-ud Din Shah of Qajar on the occasion of his three journeys to Europe (1873, 1878 and 1889); the publication of Hajj Zaynu'l-Abidin Maragheh-i's (1837–1910) *Siyāhat Nāma-yi Ibrāhim Beg* (*The Travel Diary of Ibrahim Beg*) in the first decade of the twentieth century; Mirza Ja'far Qarachadaghi's Persian translation of several plays written by Mirza Fath-'Ali Akhunduff; the translation of James Morrier's *The Adventures of Hajji Baba of Isfahan* by Mirza Habib Isfahani in 1905; and the newspaper articles and other writings of Mirza Malkum Khan, Hajji Mirza Abdur-Rahim Talibuf (1855–1910) and Ali Akbar Dihkhuda (1879–1956).

The appearance of journalism in the middle of the nineteenth century and its eventual rapid development were significant factors in the Iranian literary renaissance. Edward G. Browne considers journalism "the most powerful modernizing influence in Persia."[2] This influence—rooted in the nature of the press as a printed communicative source—greatly manifested itself in both the political and literary movements of the country and bore witness to the statement that "the most important effect of the Press in every country is the awakening of political and literary opinion amongst the people . . . ."[3] Besides exerting great influence on public opinion by awakening thoughts and arousing political awareness on the eve of and during the constitutional revolution, the press played a significant role in the generation of modern Persian prose.

Due to the restrictions imposed by the despotic political regime of the time, the limited number of newspapers published in Iran in the pre-revolutionary period were void of any political value. The stimuli for generating political and social consciousness and the literary renaissance were provided by a number of newspapers published by Persian intellectuals outside the country in places such as Cairo, London, Constantinople, and Calcutta and smuggled into the country. The writers and/or publishers of these newspapers had, on the one hand, the privilege of voicing freely their liberal and patriotic views in opposition to or criticism of the government and, on the other hand, the opportunity to communicate their knowledge of Western thought and literature to their Iranian readers. After the revolution there was a great increase in the number of newspapers in Iran. With the constitutional movement new themes emerged among the literati, the most important of which were "freedom" and "the common people." To achieve the goals of informing and conveying new political ideologies to a larger audience, the journalistic language had to be comprehensible by the "ordinary people," and as close to their language as possible. So the bombastic style of traditional prose was replaced in the press by a simple, straightforward language. In addition to the newspapers with political overtone there gradually appeared a number of literary periodicals, a majority of which proclaimed their distinct goals for introducing new guidelines for literature.[4] Through printing literary reviews and samples of literature from other countries, the newspapers and literary periodicals also functioned as primary sources of world literature.

Though translations of European sources in their entirety had appeared since the early days of printing, at the time they were not very well received. The foundation of *Darul-Funun* with European teachers, and an increase in the number of the readers graduated from that school, on one hand, and new technical developments in printing on the other, gave rise to a number of translations.[5] The earliest examples of translations of European sources were the textbooks prepared by the joint efforts of the European teachers of Darul-Funun and their Iranian assistants and students and published by the school's printing house.[6] Publication of these textbooks with their simple style and comprehensible language laid "the foundation of a modern Persian scholarly prose and terminology."[7] Gradually the demand for and number of scientific and literary translations increased. To maintain the comparatively simple style of these sources, the translators had to employ a less complicated language. These translations not only paved the way for the development of modern Persian literary prose by providing models for Persian writers, but they also greatly influenced the simplification of style and language, as explained by Vera Kubičkova:

> The literary language as it then existed, bound for centuries by a system of rhetorical rules, cluttered up with phrases which no longer had any real meaning, had so estranged itself from the spoken language that it was no longer suited to the translation of a western hovel and still less a stage play. Thus here translation was, . . . an important factor in the forming of a modern literary expressive medium.[8]

Commenting on the significant role of translations during the Persian literary renaissance, Jan Rypka states:

> For many people they provided an inducement to read, they helped in the clearance of antiquated rubbish and led the language into a new course. . . . Without these translations Persian belles-lettres and the prose of the 20th century as a whole is difficult to imagine.[9]

The influence of literary translations manifested itself in the writings of the new writers, who imitated the form of these sources and produced the first Iranian novels. To awaken national pride and to reinforce patriotic feelings among their readers, some writers drew on the glories of the country's past history and wrote the first historical novels.

While the form of prose literature in the constitutional period (1896–1921) was greatly influenced by European literature, inspiration for the content came directly from the political and social conditions of the period.

> The literature of the Constitutional period was . . . mainly of a topical character; it aimed at communicating a content that should be comprehensible and give pointed expression to the ideas of the patriotic struggle then being waged. As regards form, of first importance was always the clarity of the formulation of the thought and its comprehensibility for the broad masses and an inclination to use folk-literature as a medium of expression.[10]

During the constitutional period journalistic prose continued to develop; and along with poetry it served as the medium to communicate new political ideas and to arouse social consciousness. Apart from the writings of Ali Akbar Dihkhuda, which appeared in the press as satirical essays and mostly in colloquial language, and the publication of a few historical novels, there were not any notable contributions to literary prose in this period.[11]

The form and content of modern Persian literature underwent great changes and developments during the twenty-year rule of Reza Shah (1921–1941). These developments were highly influential in inspiring folkloristic research in Iran. The significance of literary prose was recognized, and some epoch making works were produced in this period. Greater emphasis on social consciousness and the instructional role of literary prose shifted the sources of inspiration for some modern writers from the historical past to contemporary life. To portray more efficiently the existing political and social problems and short-comings, and to break further away from the traditional literary conventions, the modernists drew on the lives of "common" people and employed their language. The founder and best representative of this literary trend is Muhammad Ali Jamalzadah. His trend-setting collection of six satirical short stories, entitled *Yiki Bud Yiki Nabud* (*Once Upon a Time*), was first published in Berlin in 1922. The significance of Jamalzadah's work in the history of modern Persian literature is due to the fact that in his innovative style he reintroduced the short story as a form of prose literature and "widened the scope of written Persian by injecting a large dose of colloquial idioms into it."[12] With regard to Jamalzadah's choice of the short story as a literary medium and his contribution toward popularizing it, Hassan Kamshad writes:

> The medium chosen by the majority of younger writers since the war has been the short story. . . . Not that there is anything new about this choice of medium; the short story, in the broad sense of the term, is probably the oldest form of narrative in Persia. For the modern literary movement really to start, it needed only a man like Jamalzadah to show that this popular and principally oral form of narrative—about the adventures, passions,

and ludicrous situations of ordinary people—could be produced
in the language of the people as good *written* work.[13]

Of great importance to the literary history of modern
Persian is the lengthy introduction of *Yiki Bud Yiki Nabud*,
which was the first modern Persian literary manifesto. It was
Jamalzadah's clarion call to Iranian writers for the regeneration
of prose and the creation of a "literary democracy," which in
his view could only be achieved by simplification of the prose
language and narrowing of the gap between the formal literary
language and the colloquial speech. Inspired by his interest in
common people—their daily life and language—and the spread
of knowledge among them, Jamalzadah emphasized in the
introduction the educational function of fiction and its linguistic
contribution to people's everyday language. He stated that as a
medium of instruction, available to every class of society, fiction
provides the readers with general information regarding the
realities of the modern life and familiarizes different classes of
society with each other and other nations, since it is "the best
mirror for reflecting the moral composition and specific
characteristics of nations and peoples."[14] In his view by
preserving expressions, idioms, and slang in their proper
context, prose language becomes a reservoir of colloquial
language. In other words, narrative prose can serve as "the
phonograph of the speech of the different classes and groups of
a nation."[15] By successfully presenting the short story as a
literary prose form, depicting the life of the "common" people
and employing their language, Jamalzadah "has become known
as the undisputed founder of modern Persian fiction and the
herald of literary modernism in Iran."[16]

The significance of Jamalzadah's writing from a
folkloristic point of view is his free use of colloquial language,
providing folk speech with credibility among the literary class,
and emphasizing the fundamental importance of collecting and
recording people's everyday language. In addition to employing
folk speech in his writings, Jamalzadah also drew on folk
narratives, a trend which was later followed by other writers.[17] In
his article on folk speech, which is to a certain extent a revision
of the introduction to *Yiki Bud Yiki Nabud*, Jamalzadah

repeatedly emphasizes the necessity for collecting and recording of slang, jargon, proverbs, and idioms lest they disappear and result in poverty for the Persian language.[18] To encourage and generate enthusiasm, he repeatedly states that collecting folk speech is not only a necessity but also entertaining and pleasant.[19] He appended to *Yiki Bud Yiki Nabud* a glossary of idiomatic expressions with their equivalent meaning in literary Persian. Later on he expanded this glossary into a larger collection, which was published in 1962.[20] In the first section of the book, Jamalzadah once more points out the significance of colloquial language and its study, gives references to the existing folk speech in classical literary works, and enumerates the research conducted in the country on folk speech and dialects since the publication of *Yiki Bud Yiki Nabud.*

Jamalzadah's other contribution was his article on Persian folk narratives and nursery rhymes, a pioneering effort in analytical study of folklore in Iran. The essay, marked by his preoccupation with educating readers and familiarizing them with novelties, is based on his view that "No fairy tale, story, or narrative is without a history or historical basis, and proper research will reveal that even fairy tales narrated for children by old women have historical meanings."[21] After a lengthy description of Dadaism and Surrealism, Jamalzadah draws a comparison between the two and the world of nursery rhymes. Then he presents an analysis of the nursery rhyme that the article bears the title of. In his view the nursery rhyme under discussion is a symbolic explanation of man's intellectual evolution, a description of his universal journey through different stages of existence.

Jamalzadah's innovative style was imitated by other writers, and focusing on the lives of "common people" and employing their language in writing gradually became a tradition. But it was in the writings of Iran's foremost writer, Sadiq Hidayat, that "the tradition became not only an established but a *natural* mode of literary expression."[22] Hidayat's mastery of the style is well depicted in his literary work, in which, "besides vividly picturing his countrymen, of all classes, in their own surroundings, he puts into their mouths the speech of their city, their districts, even their quarter."[23] In his writings he "unfolded a panorama of the habits, traditions, and dialects of various groups of Persian people."[24] Yet his accomplishments are not limited to his brilliant works of prose, many of which have been translated into several European languages and analyzed critically. The list of his publications includes collections of short stories, novels, plays, travelogues, translations from Pahlavi and European sources, critical essays, and collections and studies of folklore. He was the first Iranian to study folklore and outline the methods of scholarship. Several factors provided the motivation for Hidayat's keen interest in collecting and studying Iranian folklore: his profound love for his country, its culture, traditions, language, and its glorious historical past; his strong resentment of the foreign influence on Iranian culture—namely those inflicted by the Arab and Mongol invasions; his genuine interest in the people of his country specifically the underprivileged and the common man; his short-lived association with left-wing groups; and his wide range of reading and vast knowledge of literary and cultural developments in the West.[25] The most influential factor, however, was his strong nationalism.

Sadiq Hidayat was born in 1903 in Tehran, to an aristocratic family. In 1926 he went to study in Europe on a government scholarship, and he attended universities in Belgium and France. Though at the beginning he was attracted to such professions as engineering and dentistry, he finally decided to pursue his interest in literature and Iran's pre-Islamic languages and culture. After his return to Iran in 1930, he devoted himself to writing and research. During the period of his residence in India in 1936–37—a self-imposed exile and a refugee from the tyrant regime of the time—Hidayat studied the Pahlavi language in Bombay. A deeper knowledge of Pre-Islamic Iran and translations of several Pahlavi sources were the outcome of his trip. Despite his family's prominence, Hidayat held several unimportant official positions throughout his life. In 1950 he returned to France, and in the April of 1951 he committed suicide.

Hidayat did most of his writing during the reign of Riza Shah, the founder of the Pahlavi Dynasty. As Jalal Al-Ahmad, another prominent Iranian writer states, "Hidayat is the child of the Constitutional period and the writer of the dictatorship era. . . . During his lifetime, he either witnessed political upheavals or oppressive dictatorship."[26] The political oppression and social corruption, together with the ideological policies of the period, significantly influenced Hidayat and his writings.

Reza Shah came to power with the goal of establishing stability in the country by creating a centralized government and administration, modernizing the country through industrialization and social and economic reforms, and putting an end to all forms of interference in the internal affairs of the country by the great powers. The reform plans of Reza Shah are best outlined as follows:

> In summary, the ideals of the Iran of Reza Shah were: to be independent and strong in order to preserve her national entity; to promote prosperity by the scientific development of her natural resources and the cultivation of favorable international trade; to banish want, sickness, and misery so that a healthy Aryan nation, descendant of heroic ancestors, might measure up to the bold reliefs carved on the mountainsides at Behistun and Persepolis; and to hold a place of honor among the nations of the earth and contribute her best to the culture of the world. Finally there was an increasing feeling that traditional Islamic beliefs and institutions were incompatible with a realization of the country's goals and were therefore expendable.[27]

Through the fulfillment of some of these goals Reza-Shah succeeded in transforming the country into a modernized one and creating significant social and economic reform. But his tyranny and autocratic rule turned the political atmosphere of the country into a suppressive dictatorship, replacing Iranians' hopeful anticipation of the establishment of democracy with great disappointment as the increasing power turned Reza Shah into a tyrant. The inspiration for Reza Shah's progressive objectives and eventual reforms and achievements came directly from his strong patriotism. His nationalism with visions of reviving the glorious pre-Islamic period of Iran became a characteristic feature of his period. The following statement best describes Reza Shah's ideological policies and the significant role that nationalism played in shaping them:

> The ideals underlying the changes that took place in Iran from 1921 to 1941 was threefold; a complete dedication to the cult of nationalism- statism; a desire to assert this nationalism by a rapid adoption of the material advances of the West; and a breakdown of the traditional power of religion and a growing tendency toward secularism, which came as a result of the first two ideals. At the heart of these ideals, shared alike by the Iranian people and Riza Shah himself, was an intense nationalism—from it came all other motivations.[28]

Besides nationalism, another ideology of the period, reflected in the writings of Sadiq Hidayat, is religious unorthodoxy and the view of Islam as "an alien faith imposed upon Iran by an inferior civilization."[29] The influence of a subscription to this ideology is only manifest not only in Hidayat's literary work, in which he "incorporates a deep cynicism towards the traditional Islamic Institutions with the plight of the ordinary man of Iran,"[30] but also in his study of Iranian folkore. In the introduction to *Nayrangistān*, a collection of superstitions and customs whose title comes from a Pahlavi source, Hidayat points out that those superstitions which are socially looked down upon are not products of Iranian minds; rather they are the result of contact with foreign races, and these superstitions have been forced upon Iranians through foreign and religious pressure.[31] Hidayat believes that the best way to eliminate these superstitions is to record and publish them, revealing their baselessness and decreasing their significance.[32] Unless these superstitions are printed as such, foreigners would consider these absurd beliefs to be part of Iranians' national beliefs and customs.[33] Hidayat is not, however, totally against folk beliefs and customs. He reminds the reader that there are some beliefs and customs that are not only good and acceptable, but also survivals of the glorious days of Iran, making their preservation and revival an essential national duty. Thus, he encourages research on folk beliefs and customs that are purely Iranian, some of which date as far back as the migration of the Aryan race to the Iranian plateau.[34] With regard to the state of folklore studies, Hidayat states that, apart from a small collection of superstitions that appear in one source, and whatever—correctly or incorrectly—has been recorded by travellers, no attempts have been made to collect and record Iranian beliefs and customs.[35] A noteworthy factor in this statement in view of this dissertation's subject matter is Hidayat's use of travellers' notes as sources of reference for data. Throughout the book, in his descriptions of superstitions and customs, Hidayat makes reference to Persian classical sources. The first edition of *Nayrangistān*, published in 1933, was banned on publication, and the second edition did not appear until 1956. Besides chapters on customs, beliefs, and superstitions, the book has a section on folk narratives in which Hidayat explains the magical elements and creatures that appear in Iranian folk narratives. *Nayrangistān* is the first booklength attempt at recording Iranian folklore. Hidayat collected the data from family and household members, through direct interviews with informants and correspondence with friends and acquaintances, whom he asked to provide him with the folklore of their town or region.[36] Information regarding Hidayat's data gathering methodology comes to us only through the writings of others, as he himself does not comment about it in any of his writings.

Hidayat's earlier contribution to Iranian folklore was a short collection of folksongs, first published in 1931.[37] The songs are classified under the categories of nursery rhymes, songs of mothers and nurses, games, riddles, and folksongs. He considers the headings self-explanatory, and no further information is provided. It seems the only criterion he used to categorize the data as "folksongs" is the existence of rhymed verse. That probably explains the inclusion of riddles, whose question part is in verse. Lack of distinctive classifying criteria is also responsible for inconsistencies in categorization; examples can be drawn on inclusion of a love song—categorized by Hidayat himself as such in a later work—under the category of "The Songs of Mothers and Nurses," and verses from a folk narrative as "Nursery Rhymes."[38] Except for the introductory discussion of folksongs in general, the work contains only texts, with no information about fieldwork, informants, or regions in which the songs are popular. Despite these shortcomings, *Usānah* is significant as a pioneering effort in folklore studies in Iran.

In the opening statement of his introduction, Hidayat warns against the adverse effects of modernization, which, he felt, would eventually lead to the disappearance of folk narratives, songs and beliefs, which have been transmitted from earlier generations and are kept only in memories. He blames the disappearance of folklore on Iranians' negligence and their attitude toward these national entities, for they have looked down upon. Not only have researchers made no attempts to collect them, but they have also considered them to be unnecessary and ignorable.[39] To illustrate their significance, Hidayat notes that folksongs always embody a philosophy or a moral. Some of them have literary value; and despite their simple content they compare favorably with the creations of great poets. A group of folksongs, he notes, has maintained its pre-Islamic style and is exemplary of the pre-historic era of the Aryan race.[40] In his concluding statements, Hidayat points out that *Usānah* is the first section of a two-part book, the second part being an extensive collection of folk beliefs and customs, by which he evidently means *Nayrangistān*. He had plans to expand *Usānah* in the second edition, based on the data he had in his possession; and he hoped to involve readers in this effort, expressing his gratitude in advance for their co-operation. French translations of *Usānah* and *Nayrangistān* were presented by Henri Massé in his *Croyances et coutumes persanes*. In the introduction, Henri Massé praises Hidayat for publishing *Nayrangistānn* and calls him a pioneer in folklore studies in Iran.[41] He also expresses his gratitude for the assistance and cooperation he received in his research from Sadiq Hidayat.[42]

Despite Hidayat's promise, there was no second edition of *Usānah*. In 1939, however, he wrote an essay, "Tarānah-hā-i "Amiyyānah" ("Folksongs"), which is a sequel to *Usānah*. It was published in *Majallah Musiqui* (*Music Review*) 1, nos. 6–7. Hidayat's effort in this article is to present folksongs as art forms and to point out the need to collect and record folksongs. To rectify the misconceptions of his countrymen regarding folklore in general and folksongs in particular, Hidayat states that folksongs are the primary form of poetry and music. He continues, stating that this primitive form of art is very old, going back to the time when the Indo-European races started their migrations, thus accounting for the similarities that exist between the folksongs of different nations.[43] Thus, he presents diffusion as an explanation for similarities, without discounting the "identical manifestations of genius." Pointing out the main characteristics of folksongs and folklore, which he refers to as "Tudah Shināsi" ("The Study of Masses") and "Majmu'ah Sunnat-i "Avvām," ("collection of traditions of the populace"), he states that they have been transmitted for centuries from generation to generation by the word of mouth. Having established the "oral" and "traditional" characteristics of folksongs, Hidayat continues, noting that though they belong to the masses and the common people, they possess all the general characteristics of art, and totally correspond with the artistic needs of a nation. Then he explains how in the West great composers of classical music have been inspired by folksongs and traditional music. He considers folksongs and narratives, which are composed by uneducated individuals, as the representatives of the spirit and the inner voice of a nation.[44] He reiterates the view that the composer and the place and date of origin of folksongs are unknown. He emphasizes that every effort should be made to collect examples of these art forms from the peasants and the members of populace who are the final preservers of these treasures. Hidayat points out that other than very few works, such as Zhukovski's collection of folksongs and his own *Usānah,* no real effort has been made in collecting Iranian folksongs; and he insists that unless a scientific and scrupulous gathering is undertaken, the remaining folksongs will soon be forgotten and disappear forever. In the final section of the article, Hidayat incorporates some examples of "children's songs," "love songs," "lullabies," and "wedding songs," with a further discussion of folksongs. "Tarānah-hā-yi "Āmmiyānah," in comparison to *Usānah,* ismore detailed in presenting definitions and ideas; and it certainly reflects Hidayat's development as a folklorist and a researcher.

In addition to superstitions, customs, folksongs and magic, Sadiq Hidayat collected and studied proverbs and folk narratives. In his enthusiasm for the advancement of folkloristics in Iran, he readily shared his collections of folklore and research results with others engaged in folklore studies. Though Hidayat did not leave behind a separate collection or study of Iranian proverbs, there is evidence that he had gathered a large number of them. The prominent figure in the study of Iranian proverbs is Ali Akbar Dihkhuda, who compiled an extensive collection of proverbs, *Amsal va Hikam* (*Proverbs and Aphorisms*), which was published in four volumes between the years of 1929–1932. In a speech made at Hidayat's memorial ceremony in 1952, Mujtaba Minuvi made a statement revealing Hidayat's interest in proverbs:

> Mr. Ali Akbar Dihkhoda was engaged in the writing of *Amsal va Hikam* and each of his friends and acquaintances helped him as much as they could] [with] whatever they found.
>
> Sadiq Hidayat helped him more than anybody else; he had a collection of folk proverbs in a volume of two-hundred pages where he had recorded about two thousand proverbs, he readily presented this volume to Mr. Dihkhoda and I do not know whether he ever took it back.[45]

In his quest for engaging Iranians' interest and involvement in the recording and study of folklore, Sadiq Hidayat took advantage of every opportunity. During his employment at the Music Bureau and at his suggestion, announcements were made on the radio inviting the inhabitants of different regions to send in folk narratives to be broadcast under the name of the sender. Once the narratives were received, "they were narrated on the radio after Hidayat had studied, corrected and arranged them." Some of these narratives were printed in *Majallah Musig* (*Music Review*) under the sender's name, Hidayat occasionally adding some comments.[46] One example of this procedure was "Bulbul Sargashtah" ("The Wondering Nightingale"). Hidayat's commentary appears at the end of the narrative. He states that versions of the narrative exist among most Indo-European nations, and the original version is very old. After providing several references he presents the Scottish folksong version "Song of the Phoenix."[47]

Of the narratives Hidayat collected, only a few have been published. According to the available information, he donated the rest to another compiler of folk narratives.[48] In 1939 two narratives, "Aqā Musha" and "Shangul u Mangul," appeared in *Majallah Musiqi* (*Music Review*), with an introduction regarding the characteristics of Iranian folk narratives.[49] Hidayat considers Iranian folk narratives as the most valuable and liveliest examples of Persian prose, their subject matter, novelty, and variety making them eligible to be introduced to the world as competitors with the best literary works. Yet, except for the collections presented by D. L. Lorimer, Arthur Christensen, and Henri Massé, no correct texts are available. Hidayat continues, noting that folk narratives link mankind to all the creation through a magical power. It is from this point of view that they are suitable for children, who need to re-live in their imagination human history and feel life from its very beginning.[50] Hidayat compares the variety of style and subject matter of the narratives to those of modern literature and considers narratives as the original source of the short story and novel. In the conclusion of this short introduction, Hidayat points out that the Persian folk narratives were composed in a simple, delicate, and lively language by unknown narrators and have been transmitted orally from generation to generation among members of the populace. Parallel versions of Persian folk narratives exist in European languages, Hidayat states; and he adds that they should be collected from the old and illiterate and recorded word for word with no alterations. In order to be able to make a judgment about the original version of a narrative, he states, several variants of the same narrative should be recorded.[51] Of the other two narratives recorded by Hidayat, "Lachak Kuchuluy-i Qirmizi" was printed in *Majallah Musiqi* in 1940 and "Sang-i Sabur" in 1941.[52]

Of great importance to Iranian folkloristics was a series of four essays by Sadiq Hidayat on data gathering techniques. In the first article his main emphasis is to point out the significance of folklore in shaping a nation's culture and the necessity of prompt collection. After presenting an account of the coinage of the term "folklore" in the West, he refers to Saintyves' statement that to study folklore is to study the life of the masses of populace in civilized countries, because primitive societies do not have any folklore. He then clarifies that folkloristics is no longer limited just to the study of folk narratives, songs, riddles and so on, but rather that it includes all traditions learned orally. Re-emphasizing the artistic value of folklore, Hidayat considers folk art and literature as man's best masterpieces, specifically literature, fine arts, philosophy, and religion.[53] Referring to folkloristics as a newly-developed science, Hidayat points out that in Iran the gradual movement for the study of folklore started shortly after the publication of his *Nayrangistān* in 1933. He then enumerates the contributions of Western scholars and the few Iranians, taking into consideration as well studies on dialects. The second article of the series, "Tarh-i Kulli Barāy-i Kāvush-i Folklore-i Yik Mantaqah" ("General Plan for the Study of Folklore in a Region"), is a detailed itemization of those aspects of life that should be considered in a folkloristic study of an area. This fieldwork guide was later on expanded and employed by the collectors of regional folklore. Sadiq Humayuni states that he was the first to follow the guidelines in his *Farhang-i Mardum-i Sarvistān (The Folklore of Sarvistan)*[54]. This section and the rest of the essays in the series constitute a fieldwork manual, providing information on such subjects as the qualifications of a fieldworker, methodologies of soliciting and choosing informants, directing interviews, and recording data. Hidayat's model for this fieldwork guide is P. Saintyves' *Manuel de Folklore* (Paris, 1936). For proper recording of local dialects, Hidayat included the phonetic alphabet prepared by P. Natil Khanlari and Roger Lescot. With regard to gathering and recording folklore, Hidayat insists that not only the government institutes, but every educated individual should participate; and local newspapers and magazines should encourage their readers' participation as well. After all the collected documents are printed, then the folklore specialists can study, compare, and classify the country's folklore. In his final statement, Hidayat announced plans by the periodical *Sukhan* to publish a collection of folklore, and encouraged readers to send in examples from their areas to be printed in the periodical. He also promises that prizes will be awarded for thorough collections.

In the essay "Chand Nuktah dar bārah *Vis u Rāmin*" ("A Few Comments about *Vis and Ramin*"), Hidayat combines his interest in folklore and literature. This study of the classical work by Fakhrud-Din Gurgani, a poet of the eleventh century, was first published in *Payam-i Naw* in 1945. In his analysis of *Vis u Ramin*, Hidayat is mainly concerned with pointing out the folk beliefs, customs, expressions, idioms, proverbs, and Zoroastrian and Islamic beliefs and narratives recorded in the context. Providing ample examples from the text in support of his discussion, Hidayat concludes that Gurgani based the story on a Pazand translation from the original Pahlavi and on the information and beliefs current at his time. Therefore, *Vis u Ramin* is a valuable source of information on the folklore of ancient Iran, and on the poet's period.[55] To encourage further research of the kind Hidayat states that his article is only a plan for such studies.

Hidayat's direct and indirect contributions were highly influential in drawing the attention of Iranians to the study of folklore. Through his pioneering collections and studies, he directly approached Iranians with the significance of folklore as a cultural phenomenon, with artistic values, worthy of systematic investigation for the better understanding of the glories of the past and the realities of the present. He appealed to his countrymen's nationalistic feelings; presented examples of the progress and the research done in the advanced Western countries; pointed out the few, yet important, studies conducted by the Western scholars on Iranian folklore and dialectology; and repeatedly emphasized the urgent need for collecting folklore before its disappearance; and pleaded for Iranians' immediate involvement. He emphasized, "Research on Iranian folklore is not only significant from a scientific and psychological point of view; it will also shed light on some dark philosophical and historical points."[56] As can be inferred from this and many similar statements he made, Hidayat's first objective was to establish the credibility of folklore as a scientific field of study, equal to other established fields of inquiry. Once folklore studies began to evolve, Hidayat's views and definitions of folklore became the guidelines for the field. His indisputable position as the pioneer and learned authority on Iranian folklore gave his statements such authenticity that for a long period of time researchers kept on repeating them as matters of fact, without any alterations. Hidayat's indirect contribution to Iranian folkloristics was through his literary work and studies of the pre-Islamic period. By employing colloquial expressions, folk beliefs, and customs and drawing on folk narrative themes and content in his short stories and novels, Hidayat not only provided a treasury of folklore in context, but he also popularized a style which was followed by the next generation of Iranian writers.

Hidayat's efforts gradually attracted the attention of Iranians interested in the study of their culture. Some government organizations also took part in the collection and study of folklore. Soon after its foundation, the Iranian Academy set out to provide guidelines for gathering folklore, specifically folk narratives. To implement this plan, the Academy sought the cooperation of the Ministry of Public Education. Official requests were sent out to the heads of the Education Departments of each province, asking for their cooperation in providing collections of folklore through the participation of the local school teachers and students. To facilitate the process, guidelines were provided, and Rashid Yasimi was chosen as the person in charge of preparing it. In a meeting of the representatives of the Education Departments of different regions, Rashid Yasimi presented the audience with definitions and information about the significance and functions of folklore. He briefly surveyed the history and status of folkloristics in Europe; pointed out the interrelationship existing between folklore and other fields of study, such as psychology, economics, literature, technology, religion, linguistics, history, and geography; and provided a brief classification of the genres to be collected, together with methodological guidelines pertinent to each category. With regard to folk narratives, for example, he stated that the purpose of recording them is to gain information about the thoughts and beliefs of the peasants. Narratives should be recorded exactly as they are told; no attempts should be made to correct them or eliminate absurdities or obscenities; if a narrative is told in different versions, each one of the versions should be recorded, with mention made of its locality and information regarding the age, racial background, and dialect of the informant.[57] In 1938, to fulfill its task of preserving folklore by collecting and recording it, the Academy extended its call for data to the general public. Through advertising in newspapers it invited the cooperation of those who could assist the Academy by providing it with information and publications.[58]

Subsequent to the discussions in an official meeting of Ministry of Public Education in 1936 regarding the necessity of the systematic collection and survey of folklore, the Ministry commissioned an eight-member committee to put into effect the plan for the foundation of the Institute and Museum of Ethnology in 1937. The Institute, however, did not prove to be very successful in fulfilling its goal of providing folklore data from all parts of the country. It was closed down in 1941 with the abdication of Reza Shah. A vehement critic of the Institute and the Museum of Ethnology was Sadiq Hidayat, who believed that the government's effort in this regard was just "to stage a show," which "like other imitations of the Pahlavi period turned out to be a loathsome caricature."[59] He continues, noting that the term "Mardum Shināsi" was coined and a museum was established under this name. To the layman it is not clear whether it is meant to be a museum of ethnography, sociology, anthropology or a secret intelligence office. He criticizes the lack of authenticity, continuity, and sufficient information about the items gathered in the museum. He considers the plan for sending official requests to the Education Departments of provinces to obtain folk narratives from school children just a formality and states that the collected documents are void of scientific value. The call for the data was not answered by all regions and provinces. Referring to the available data, Hidayat considers a majority of the recorded documents worthless due to the lack of information about the collector and/or the narrator; but he indicates that there are some which are usable and of value for future research.[60] Though the Institute of Ethnology has been criticized for not having emerged "out of the cultural fervor of the time," and having been "imposed from above," as "mere window dressing,"[61] despite its shortcomings, it had its own merits. On one hand, it was an official center for collection and study of folklore with the possibility of future development and fruitfulness; and, on the other, it had direct and indirect impact on public opinion about folklore.

In 1958, the Department of Popular Culture was established within the Ministry of Education. To accomplish the department's main task of collecting folklore, interested graduates in different fields of humanities were recruited. After some training in fieldwork methodologies, they were sent to villages and tribes. Due to limited resources, however, country wide collections proved to be impossible; and only some scattered surveys were conducted. In 1968 the Department of Popular Culture received a budget for its expansion, and new projects for the study of folklore got underway. The final stage of development occurred in the early 1970's. The Department of Popular Culture was replaced by an extended organization equipped with more human and financial resources, under the title the National Center for Ethnology and Popular Culture Research.

The goals of the Center, as outlined by Mahmud Khaliqi, the Director of the Center in 1974, are as follows: [62]

1. To conduct organized research in ethnology, ethnography and folkore all over the country; that is to say social, economic and cultural survey of the rural, urban and tribal areas. The research would include kinship, folklore, folk literature, beliefs, customs, folk music and dance, dialects, local clothing, food, etc....

2. To point out the changes caused in the life style of Iranians due to social evolutions and economic developments, and forecast future tendencies.

3. Effective cooperation with the organizations conducting research in fields related to the general goals of the Center, particularly research organizations of universities.

4. To maintain continuous contact with the country's museums of ethnology, and guide and support them scientifically.
5. Effective cooperation with the foreign organizations, and researchers conducting research on Iran's ethnology.[63]
6. Publication of research results in the form of reports, articles, books, magazines, films, slides and so on for public use.

To conduct surveys in the designated places, four-member groups were sent to the areas with questionnaires intended to gather information about the characteristics of the rural life, folklore, and dialect. Once the survey was accomplished, and in order to familiarize the local people with their own cultural background, an exhibition was set up in one of the towns of the region. Between the years 1968 to 1974, 384 villages were surveyed, and 32 monographs were prepared.[64] The research publications of the Department of Popular Culture and the Center for Ethnological Research at the time of Khaliqi's report included the publication of ninety-six essays, written on the basis of the research conducted in the villages, tribes, and towns, in the Center's journal, *Hunar va Mardum (Art and People)*; twenty-three books, three of which are folk narrative collections;[65] thirty-three unpublished books and monographs; and five exhibits, including one which was displayed in Paris in 1971. The Center's archives also house folklore data extracted from the classical sources of literature and history; dialect studies; collections of folk narratives and proverbs; and slides, pictures, tapes and films on folklore.[66] Among the activities of the Center toward popularizing the interest in folklore was its sponsorship of the First Festival of Folklore, held in Isfahan in October of 1977. In addition to the Center, a few other government-sponsored organizations and institutions were also directly or indirectly engaged in the collection and study of folklore. The research conducted at, and the publications of, the Cultural Foundation of Iran also includes, besides folklore, source materials from the pre-Islamic period and information about Iranian mythology. The archives of the Literacy

Organization has on deposit a collection of folk narratives recorded by the members of Literacy Corps during their residence in the rural areas. The monographs published by Tehran University's Institute for Social Studies and Research, though basically ethnological in nature, contain folk narratives current among the people of the area under study.[67] Iranian National Radio and Television also played an active role in the collection of folklore and folk narratives. The Linguistics Department at Tehran University's Faculty of Literature and Human Sciences offered a course on Iranian mythology, and the curriculum at the faculty of Dramatic Arts included, from the time of the establishment of the faculty, a course on folk literature.[68]

Following the lead of Sadiq Hidayat, other individuals interested in folklore gradually started collecting folk narratives, songs, and proverbs. The earliest contributor was the journalist Hussain Kuhi Kirmani. His first attempt at gathering folklore was a collection of 120 folksongs, published in 1931. Three years later, by the direct authorization and order of the Minister of Education at the time, Kirmani was officially commissioned to gather folklore. The result was a collection of fifteen folk narratives. Since the narratives were mainly about kings and their ministers, according to the strong censorship policies of the day, the narratives were considered a direct insult to the king (Reza Shah) himself. The book was banned, and the collector arrested. The misfortune of the collector and his narratives did not last long. Kuhi Kirmani was released after proving lack of any political intentions, and the collection was published in 1935, but not before modifications were made. All the kings and ministers in the stories were replaced by chief merchants and rulers. The narrative "Pisar-i Sayyād" ("The Hunter's Son") was totally excised, and the collection was published in 1935 under the title *Chahārdah Afsānah az Afsānahā-yi Rustāi Irān (Fourteen Narratives from Iran's Rural Folk Narratives)*. The collection was translated in its entirety by Henri Massé in his *Croyances et coutumes persanes*, and Arthur Christensen included two of the narratives in his Märchen collection. In the second edition, which appeared in 1954, the narratives were presented in their original form, and the missing narrative was added to the collection, bringing the number of the texts up to fifteen.[69] In the introduction to the second edition, Kuhi Kirmani provides information about the names and occupations of some of his informants.

A teacher and storyteller, Fazlullah Subhi Muhtadi started broadcasting on the Tehran Radio in 1938 and continued his storytelling program for several years, despite the opposition of radio officials and occasional cancellations. His program was mainly geared toward children. After telling a folk narrative and pointing out the moral of the story, Subhi Muhtadi encouraged his listeners to send him versions they were familiar with. Based on the data gathered in this manner from all over the country, he published a number of folk narrative collections. First in the series was the two-volume *Afsānah-hā* (*Folk Narratives*).[70] In the preface to the first volume, Subhi Muhtadi refers to folk narratives as the "elegant and unique foundation of Persian language and literature" and laments that "unfortunately, in our country no attention has been paid to these narratives from a literary point of view." Subhi's view of folk narratives as literary entities eliminated for him the significance of each individual version of a narrative and the creativity involved in telling them. Preoccupied with the literary value of folk narratives, Subhi Muhtadi recast each narrative on the basis of the various versions on hand, in order to produce a version as close as possible to what he felt must have been the "oldest," the "most correct, and complete" version. The recast version was then recorded in the collection as *the* version of a narrative, with remarks about other versions current in different parts of the country. On occasion, Subhi Muhtadi makes references to similar narratives existing in other nations. In his studies, Subhi was very much interested in the similarities that existed among the folk narratives of different nations; and in his comparisons he always concluded that the Persian version was the original one. He was familiar with the Grimm Brothers' collections of folk narratives and included translations of a few of their narratives in his collections. On several occasions he acknowledges the assistance he received from Sadiq Hidayat.

Subhi's career as a storyteller, collector, and publisher of folk narratives was not free of obstacles and opposition.[71] In the introduction to each of his collections, addressed to his young readers, he complains about the lack of the genuine interest among the officials in charge in the country's cultural advancement, and he discusses the problems they caused him. Though his style in recasting and reproducing the folk narratives is in violation of present-day standards of recording and presenting folklore, his contribution to Iranian folkloristics is, nevertheless, significant. Through his writings and articles, Sadiq Hidayat stimulated the educated and the intellectuals to recognize folklore, and Subhi's radio broadcasts and collections of narratives played the same role among the ordinary people. Expressing his gratitude to his young listeners for their cooperation in providing the data that otherwise would have been forgotten and disappeared, Subhi pointed out the significance of these narratives as the "roots of Iran's ancient culture" and encouraged his readers to preserve the culture of their country.

Amir Quli Amini's collection of proverbs and stories of proverbs was published in 1945. A native of Isfahan, and the editor of a local daily newspaper, Amini's primary goal in gathering the data over a period of eighteen years was to record Persian proverbs—specifically, those current among Isfahanis— together with the narratives which were the sources of the proverbs and vice versa.[72] In 1935, on the recommendation of the Minister of Education, he signed a contract with the Ministry for the publication of this collection and his future collections of folk narratives. In 1937 he handed in his collections to the Ministry of Education. After seven years of bureaucratic delays, he managed to repossess the collections and arrange for the publication himself. In the introduction he comments about the painstaking data gathering process, which required extensive time, effort, and patience, mainly because he had to solicit the data from uneducated individuals. The majority of his informants were servants, peasants, shopkeepers, and cab drivers. In his characterization of folklore and its cultural significance, Sadiq Hidayat's views are easily recognizable. He considers folklore to be a mirror of a society's thoughts, customs, and beliefs, a thorough study of which would reveal not only the present characteristics of a nation, but also provide important historical background information. He also refers to folklore as the source of fine arts and sciences and as the primary tools for the creation of the best literary and art masterpieces.[73] Though he refers to folklore as being current among all members of the society, a review of his comments about his informants reveals the fact that by the "folk" he means the illiterate or—as he puts it—the members of the lower class.

Amini's other contribution on folk narratives is *Si Afsānah az Afsānah-hā-yi Mahalli Isfahān* (*Thirty Folk Narratives from Isfahan*), which was first published in 1960. In his characterization of folk narratives, he states that they are treasure-houses of our ancestors' thoughts, beliefs, and customs which have been formed in the minds of the populace and have been transmitted orally from generation to generation among the illiterate masses. These narratives also reveal people's reactions to their leaders, and as a whole the political and social conditions of each period.[74] Amini then exemplifies the didactic function of folk narratives by drawing on some of the narratives in the collection. He provides no information about informants. Claiming to be the first to have collected proverbs and folk narratives in Iran, he expresses his hope for publication of further collections.

In 1970, Abulqasim Faqiri, a teacher and the producer of the folklore program on Shiraz Radio, published a collection of twenty-seven folk narratives that he had collected from his students and co-workers.[75] In his earlier collection *Tarānah-hā-yi Mahalli-yi Shirāz* (*Folksongs of Shiraz*), Faqiri also included some folk narratives from Shiraz.

Subhi's follower in broadcasting folklore programs on Tehran Radio is Abulqasim Anjavi Shirazi, also known as Najva, who started his programs in 1961. While Subhi was mainly concerned with collecting and telling folk narratives, Anjavi Shirazi in his weekly programs dealt with all genres of folklore. Greatly concerned with the disappearance of folklore, Anjavi campaigned for an intensive systematic collection. His radio programs were geared mainly toward the "folk"—the inhabitants of small towns and rural areas—to whom he repeatedly emphasized the significance of collecting folklore and whom he encouraged to get involved in this national task. To train interested individuals, based on Sadiq Hidayat's series of essays about fieldwork techniques, Anjavi prepared a handbook, which he sent to the listeners upon request, together with some data information sheets.[76] In the preface to the first edition, he notes the adverse effects of change on folklore, stating that modernization causes its disappearance. He defines folkloristics as the study of the life of the masses, and folklore as the popular culture which has been transmitted orally from generation to generation and exists side by side the formal culture. He then explains that folk literature includes folksongs, narratives, proverbs, riddles, and jokes, and that folklore in general includes all the activities and ceremonies performed before the birth, during the lifetime, and after the death of an individual. Since these beliefs and information are the product of the pure minds of the illiterate and the populace, one should go the old, illiterate men and women to elicit them; and one should record the data word for word. Sadiq Hidayat's statement with regard to the artistic value of folklore is quoted without the mention of his name. In fact in the preface to the first edition, Hidayat is only referred to as "one of the researchers of this field." The introduction to the second edition is longer, and Anjavi makes references to the works of his predecessors, without including Subhi. In discussing the importance and function of folklore, he rephrases Hidayat regarding the unifying effect of folklore among nations. He states that folklore eliminates animosities and creates peace and friendship among different peoples.[77]

Anjavi provides further description of his nationwide data gathering plans in the lengthy introduction to *Masal va Tamsil (Proverbs and the Stories of Proverbs)*. Without acknowledging the pioneering work of Subhi Muhtadi in employing radio to collect and popularize the study of folklore, Anjavi states that the direct communication with the "folk" through radio is "the best and most reliable method of collecting folklore in Iran."[78] Enumerating the merits of this method, Anjavi points out that since radio waves are carried to every remote and otherwise inaccessible part of the country, this methodology is the only way to achieve a nationwide collection in a short period of time, before the disappearance of the older generation. He also refers to the difficulties an outsider has in trying to conduct fieldwork in a rural community, for the development of trust and rapport between the fieldworker and the inhabitants would be impossible in a short period of time. He then concludes that the best solution is to train the interested local individuals through radio programs and correspondence. In a description of the early stages of his project, Anjavi points out the opposition he received from the inhabitants of the small towns and rural areas who considered folklore responsible for their backwardness, and from the westernized and educated individuals who belittled these efforts. To overcome these obstacles and educate the public about significance of folklore, Anjavi published several articles in the press and delivered lectures at educational institutes and on cultural programs on National Iranian Television.[79] Anjavi's efforts finally brought results, and a large collection of folklore was accumulated. The outcome was the founding of a museum which housed objects sent in from throughout the country by program listeners. It also led to the publication of collections of folk narratives, customs, beliefs, superstitions, games, and plays.

Anjavi's three-volume collection of folk narratives was published between the years 1973 to 1976. Each narrative is followed by the name, age, and occupation of the informant and the date and place of its recording. The introduction to the first volume is a description of the characteristics and function of folk narratives, of the direct influence of folk narratives on classical literature and the necessity of studying the literary classical texts from a folkloristic point of view; storytelling; and a survey of some of the research done by the Iranian and the Western scholars. Anjavi views folklore collecting and publication as a defense against the westernization of the country, for folklore provides the identifying characteristics of each nation. With the disappearance of folklore, nations lose their cultural identity. He considers folklore to be the stronghold of the country against the cultural invasion of more powerful nations. Warning mothers against the influence of foreign cultures on their young children, Anjavi states that "narrating for children is not an entertainment, rather necessity and a must."[80]

Along with the extensive efforts of Anjavi Shirazi to collect folklore on a nationwide scale, there were also individuals who, either by the support of government organizations or in pursuit of their personal interests, collected and published regional folklore. The compilers of these works chose a specific geographical region—preferably their own birthplace—and gathered examples of different genres of local folklore. These collections usually include a section on the folk narratives current in the area under study.[81] Ibrahim Shakurzadah is a compiler of the folklore of Khurasan. His collection of Khurasani folk narratives was published in collaboration with Adriene Boulvin. His other contribution is a collection of Khurasani folklore. In his discussion of folklore in general, Shakurzadah considers folklore a valid document for determining the morals, psychological, social, and political characteristics of a nation in the past. He divides folk beliefs into two categories: good beliefs and bad ones. The good beliefs are produced by wise, intelligent, and good-hearted individuals, whereas the bad customs, narratives and beliefs are spread by evil-minded and unsuccessful members of the society. The emphasis, he states, should be on popularizing the former and abandoning the latter. Commenting on his fieldwork methodology, Shakurzadah points out that he travelled to the villages of Khurasan, visited coffeehouses and other places in disguise, and conducted interviews with Khurasanis, specifically the older individuals.[82]

With the gradual recognition of folkloristics by Iranians as a scientific field of study, examples of folk narratives, songs, and speech, and essays on the definition and significance of folklore as a cultural phenomenon appeared in magazines and periodicals. Of the numerous genres of folklore, the greatest amount of emphasis has been placed on the collection and study of folksongs, narratives, proverbs, and games. Articles on folk narratives are usually descriptive, but there are also many analytical studies. Abdulhussain Zarrinkub's essay "Dar barāh-yi Afsānah-hā-yi 'Ammiyānah" ("About Folk Narratives") is descriptive, focusing on the general characteristics of Iranian folk narratives. His outlines include the timelessness of the stories; the anonymity of the characters; the simplicity of style; the beginning and ending formulas; the presence of magic and magical creatures; and the obstacles that the hero/heroine almost always have to overcome. A review of these characteristics and Zarrinkub's choice of examples reminds the reader of Stith Thompson's definition of fairy tales[83] and leads one to conclude that Zarrinkub's subject of study in this article is the *Märchen*. He refutes the concept of the communal creation of folk narratives, believing that they were created by anonymous, talented individuals, some of whom were women. With regard to the role of women as narrators, he comments that in primitive societies narrators were usually the elders, specifically old men; but after the introduction of nations to civilization, narrating tasks were transferred to women.[84] He then provides examples of legendary narrators of such collections as *One Thousand and One Nights* and concludes that the imagination and talent of women are in perfect harmony with fairy tales. That is why collectors of folk narratives in primitive societies select women informants, as though women are everywhere the treasurers of ethnic narratives and proverbs.[85] Zarrinkub concludes that undoubtedly women have been the original narrators of many fairy tales; that is why women are often the main characters. In these narratives an attempt is made to portray women as the symbols of faithfulness, chastity, and piety, whereas all cruelty and unfaithfulness are attributed to men. In "Afsānah-hā-yi 'Āmmyanah" ("Folk Narratives"), Zarrinkub addresses further issues with regard to folk narratives. He emphasizes that love of narratives is not exclusive to children, but that people of all ages and from every walk of life enjoy listening to them. He enumerates examples from different historical periods. With regard to the similarities between folk narratives of different nations, he follows Euro-American researchers in the explanations he proposes. He concludes that no single theory can explain similarities, and he does not rule out polygenesis or the effects of nations' interactions as the result of wars, commerce, and travel. He also classifies folk narratives, dividing them into imaginary narratives, in which magic and the supernatural are present; narratives about the real life; historical narratives; humorous narratives; and narratives with animals as main characters.[86]

Classification of narratives has not been a priority with the Iranian folklorists, and the attempts that have been made are superficial and non-exclusive. The major obstacle is the lack of well-defined terminology. The two essays by Zarrinkub, and his choice of the term "Afsānah" to identify both fairy tales and folk narratives in general, illustrates this problem. Since the various terms in Persian are used interchangeably to refer to different categories of folk narratives, attempts to classify narratives usually result in such categories as "narratives about . . . ," and usually the main theme or identities of the characters become the defining criteria. One such example is Samad Bihrangi's classification of Azarbayjani folk narratives. He classifies these stories under three main categories: epics combined with heroic romances and actions, and battles with kings, rulers, and the feudals; pure love stories; and narratives told to children and during the long evenings of winter for entertainment.[87] Muhammad Ja'far Mahjub utilizes a variety of criteria to categorize folk romances.[88] The classification consists of eight divisions and is based on subject matter, characters, and the historical, fictional, or religious nature of the narratives. He then comments that there are folk narratives which can be classified in more than one category. In his other study of romances from printed sources, his main criterion for classification is origin. The six categories include narratives composed by Iranian narrators; narratives of Indian origin translated from Sanskrit; narratives based on Iranian national epic and religious stories of ancient Iran; religious narratives; didactic narratives; and the narratives written by Western writers following the pattern of famous Eastern narrative collections.[89]

Besides descriptive works, Iranian folklorists and researchers have also produced some analytical studies. Some researchers have chosen certain kinds of folk narratives as their subject of study. F. Vahman, for example, concentrates on numbskull tales. He believes that these narratives have their origins in people's daily life and activities and that they are representative of the reactions and actual feelings of the members of the society towards incidents and situations.

Despite their brevity and simplicity of style, a thorough study of these humorous tales reveals many social and psychological problems.[90] Vahman presents a classification of these narratives, but categories are unclear and overlapping. He considers migration to be the reason for the existence of similar stories in different nations. In the second part of his article, Vahman traces many of the numbskull stories to classical literary sources. He concludes that in the process of collecting other genres of folklore such as folk narratives, songs, customs, and beliefs, attention should be paid to these anecdotes despite their apparent insignificance.

Hassan Javadi chose fables and their didactic and satirical function as his subject of study, the main focus being fables in Iranian classical literature. The wide use of folklore in literature and the close interrelationship that exists between the two provides researchers such as Javadi with abundant examples. He considers the fables with didactic messages the product of learned societies and the early stages of urbanization. Primitive man considered himself a part of the animal world. It was only in the early stages of civilization that man distinguished himself from animals. Since then, he has employed fables to criticize social conditions or to moralize.[91]

A group of studies focuses on the characteristics of the dramatis personae of the characters in Iranian folk narratives. One such example is H. Sadiq's study of Azarbayjani folk narratives. In addition to pointing out the specific characteristics of these narratives in view of their relationship with the Avestan and Pahlavi sources, Sadiq examines the human and animal characters of Azarbayjani folk narratives in pre-Islamic and present-day social context.[92] Sirus Parham considers the flawless character of heroes in folk narratives, and specifically in heroic epics, as representatives of the hidden wishes which have dwelled for centuries in the minds of simple people. These wishes, which remain unfulfilled in real life, show up in narratives. Besides the engaging plot of these romances, the other enchanting forces come from the pleasant wishes and from the hope for the fulfillment of high goals.[93] Study of folk narratives and myths from a psychological point of view is the subject of a series of articles by Jalal Sattari, which appeared in *Hunar va Mardum* (*Art and People*) over a three-year period.[94]

Kazim Sadat Ishkivari's comments on the narratives he gathered in Ishkivar-i Bala reveal his view of folk narratives as a reflection of man's struggle with his surroundings. He states that in folk narratives, dreams are realized, the impossible becomes possible, and goodness abounds. He continues his poetic definition of narratives as "an ancient tree with roots spread all over; at one end it extends to history, at the other to "myth' and cultural symbols . . . . It is a river which starts at the land of creation, passes through the highs and lows of centuries and the valleys of events, and reaches us."[95] He attributes the existence of different versions of a narrative to different stages of life, periods of time, and surroundings. Drawing on examples from his collection of narratives, Sadat Ishkivari comments on the influence of physical surroundings, local livelihood, and natural elements on narratives. Muhsin Mihandust also bases his study of folk narratives on data he himself recorded. He considers folk narratives to be products of man's imagination and wishes. He points out that in studying folk narratives one's focus should be on unveiling moral and philosophical messages embedded in each story. He defines oral literature as narratives, songs, lullabies, proverbs, riddles, and any prose or poetry whose composer is unknown; and he considers oral literature to be the forerunner of, and model for, written literature. Greatly influenced by the Zoroastrian ideologies, Mihandust notes that since Iranian folk narratives date back to ancient times, in every one of them the two powers of "evil" and "good" are always in conflict, with combat making the narrator and the listener ponder more about the dark and light sides of life. Triumph belongs only to the followers of the "right" who resist and fight against "wrong" and "evil." In his conclusion, Mihandust comments that folk narratives are not only representatives of the internal and external characteristics of ethnic societies, but they also can be influential factors in shaping a society's future. In narratives man contemplates his behavior and character through time.[96]

The study of Iranian mythology—with the exception of studies of *Shah Namah* from folkloristic points of view—has not received its due share from the Iranian researchers. In the preface to his book-length study, Mihrdad Bahar states that considering the significant role mythology plays in providing information about the history of civilization and the social structures and customs of nations in pre-historic periods, no attempts have been made to provide a complete source study and precise analysis of Iranian mythology by the Iranian researchers. He also expresses his disappointment that mythology is still viewed as mere storytelling, with no significance and value in the space age, and suitable only for recital in old coffee-houses. Recognizing the fact that the task of thorough collection and study of sources on Iranian mythology cannot be undertaken by a single individual, Bahar points out that this responsibility should be assumed by Iranian cultural organizations. Through the cooperation of a group of researchers and experts, all the available material in Old, Middle, and Modern Iranian, as well as sources in other languages, should be compiled. The researchers should classify the sources on the basis of subject; determine their course of development and evolution through comparison; and provide analyses from historical, social, and psychological points of view. The final step would be the publication of the complete collection.[97]

Of the few essay-length studies of Iranian mythology, reference can be made to H. Davidian's essay. In his Jungian analysis of Iranian mythology, Davidian points out that studies with perspectives such as his would have considerable significance in discovering explanations for man's symbols. He believes Iranian mythology is clearer and more expressive than the mythologies of other nations. Therefore, its study may provide solutions to many ambiguities of human psychology.[98] Tabatabi's main subject of discussion is *Div* (ogre) in Iranian mythology and folk narratives and its characteristics and nature. Drawing on examples from the *Shah Namah* and Zoroastrian sources, and at the same time presenting views of different Western scholars, Tabatabai concludes that the ogre of the religious sources of ancient Iran and those which appear in the epics and folk narratives have a common source. The statements in such pre-Islamic sources as *Bundahish* and

Dinkart have been responsible for creating the concept of *Div* (ogre) in the more recent times. On the other hand, the Iranians, at the time of their migration to the Plateau, had to fight the natives, who were courageous warriors. Memories of these battles and the events that followed during the early stages the Iranians' settlement, besides providing the essence of the Iranian national epics, left images of the natives of the Plateau in the minds of the early Iranian settlers. With the passage of time and exaggerations, these images gave rise to the evil and ugly ogre. Undoubtedly the *Divs* of the Iranian epic were none other than very strong human beings, big in stature, who had other religious beliefs. So Iranians, in accordance with the *Avesta*, called them *Div*.[99]

In the category of studies on the Iranian folklore and mythology, one should also include the works that have examined the *Shah Namah* from a folkloristic or mythological point of view. A few examples include Avedis Shahsavarian's "Dāstān-i Rustam-i Zal Tibq-i Ravāyāt-i Armani" ("The Story of Rustam-i Zal According to Armenian Versions,") *Payam Nuvin* 8: 1 (1345,1966,87–90); F. Vahman "Rustam va Suhrāb va Dāstānhā-yi Shabih-i be ān dar Afsānah-hā-yi Digarān" ("Rustam and Suhrab and Similar Stories in the Folk Narratives of other Nations"), *Sukhan* 18: 1 (1347,1968,24–36); and Jalil Dustkhah, "Kaykhusraw dar Kuhhāy-yi Fārs" ("Kaykhusraw in the Mountains of Fars") in *Proceedings of the Fourth Congress of Iranian Studies* vol. 2 (September 1973): 77–90.

Narrating—mainly the professional form of it—has been the subject of few studies. Historical information and definitions of different types of narrating is provided by Bahram Bayzai.[100] Muhammad Ja'far Mahjub is the author of several essays on professional narrating. His article "Sukhanvari" is a description of a storytelling tradition which used to take place in the coffee-houses during the month of fasting (Ramazan).[101] The tradition has religious roots and, as Mahjub traces its history, was initiated during the Safavid period to spread and strengthen Shi'ism. Since, according to tradition, seventeen members of different professions lost their lives in the early stages of this religious campaign, the ceremony of *Sukhanvari* commences with the hanging of the replicas and symbols of each of the seventeen professions on skins of such animals as tigers, deer, or sheep on the walls of the coffee-house. *Sukhanvars* are *Dervishes* and belong to a certain sect of Sufis. They come from different walks of life and various backgrounds, and do not earn money for performing. In further description of *Sukhanvari*, Mahjub explains that the main core of the ceremony is the debate between the two *Sukhanvars*, mostly in verse, with one challenging the other by posing questions or problems. The one who is being challenged delivers the attire and other belongings that he carries as a *Dervish* to the one who poses the questions, and only after he has satisfied the challenger can he take them back. The debate, which originally dealt with religious questions, gradually has included other subjects. According to Mahjub, *Sukhanvari* was very popular during the early decades of the present century, but in the recent years the enthusiasm of the audience and the number of the performers have declined greatly. Later on, Mahjub published a modified version of the article in French.[102] Another work by Mahjub is his study of *Naqqāl* (the professional reciter of *Shah Namah*). Making references to classical sources regarding narrating in Iran, he states that the establishment of the "coffee-houses" during the Safavid period played a significant role in the development of oral literature in Iran. After a description of the narrating techniques by Naqqāls, Mahjub concludes that with the introduction of other forms of entertainment such as radio, television, theatre, movies, and nightclubs, the popularity of professional narrators has diminished, and their role has been reduced to that of conservers of tradition.[103]

The influence of mass media on storytelling in Iran is the subject of a study by Kazim Mo'tamidnijad. The article starts with a historical review of storytelling at different periods in Iran. With regard to the present state of professional storytelling, he expresses a view identical to the one presented by Mahjub:

> Story-telling as an ancient dramatic art and a traditional method of communication has experienced gradual decline since the rise of modern technology and the advent of new means of mass entertainment. Coffee-houses have been replaced by modern centers of attraction and even in the few remaining

> coffee-houses and teashops, television has superseded the
> story-tellers. . . . The alluring fascination of modern
> distractions . . .has overshadowed the more genuine art of story-
> telling and stripped it of the great appeal and popularity it once
> enjoyed.[104]

Mo'tamidnijad then examines the position of storytelling in relation to radio, television, cinema, and advertising commercials. In conclusion, he suggests the incorporation of storytelling into radio and television programs, with the objectives of promoting "social harmony" and literacy and raising moral standards. As can be inferred from these and other examples, when the subject of study is narrating, researchers have only been concerned with the historical development and a general description of professional storytelling. Not much attention has been paid to the audience or the narrator as an artist and a communicator.

A review of the statements made by the Iranians who have collected and/or studied folklore reveals great consistency in their view of folklore as a mirror of culture, and therefore as essential in determining the distinctive characteristics of a nation and unknown historical facts. The dominant effort is to overcome the general misconceptions about folklore and point out its significance as a cultural phenomenon which could and should be studied scientifically. In reference to the term "folklore," besides the Euro-American form of it, a variety of combinations with very similar connotations is employed. Some of the terms used include *Farhang-i Mardum* ("People's Culture"), *Farhang-i 'Ammah* (The Culture of Populace), Dā-nish-i 'Avvām (The Knowledge of Populace), *Farhang-i Tudah* (Culture of Masses), etc. The first part of each of these combinations stands for "lore" and the second part for "folk." A glance at the terms used to equate "folk" exhibits the general preconception about the "folk" or the bearers of folklore, which was also predominant in the early stages of folklore scholarship in the West. When Iranian researchers have chosen to identify the "folk," the reference is almost always to the illiterate peasant or the minimally educated urban dweller. The perfect informants and the keepers of folklore are described as uneducated, elderly peasants whose knowledge of folklore has not been contaminated or affected by education or modernization. In the present stage of scholarship, with the development of folkloristics and general rejection of the notion that folklore can be found only among certain groups of a society, of all the current terminologies used to equate "folklore," the combination "Farhang-i Mardum" (The Culture of People) seems to be the most appropriate one, for it includes all the members of a society.

Iranian researchers' perception of the "folk" as the uneducated masses has strongly influenced their preoccupations and priorities. Obsessed with the fear that folklore will disappear due to literacy, urbanization, and the dying out of older generations, Iranians engaged in the study of folklore have focused on, and repeatedly appealed for, immediate collection of folklore. This over-emphasis on collecting, and the notion that not much can be accomplished unless thorough collections have been accumulated, have been among the reasons for the slow progress in analytical studies. Even the author of a fairly recent study states, "In Iran folkloristics is still in the collecting stage and it is not time yet for discussion, comparison and the analysis of this great heritage."[105] This statement is made despite Mahjub's modified concept of folklore, in which he refutes the long-standing assumption about the inevitable disappearance of folklore. He comments that contrary to the popular belief, folklore is not disappearing, for it can be found in everybody's daily life, even among those living in large cities.[106] Another preoccupation of Iranian researchers has been the emphasis on "similarities," without much attention being paid to "differences."

Since its inception in Iran, folkloristics was faced with the great obstacle of unfavorable public opinion regarding its significance. Though the modernization and spread of education were among the factors responsible for the development of folkloristics in Iran, ironically they also hindered its progress. In the newly-modernized Iran of the early twentieth century, the intellectuals and the common people alike preferred to disassociate themselves from "old wives' tales." Fortunately, this attitude was gradually modified due to

the research of the Western scholars and to the genuine interest
and efforts of Iranian researchers themselves.

NOTES

1. *Nukhustin Kungirah-yi Nivisandigān-i Irān* (*The First Congress of Iranian Writers*) (Tehran, 1326/1937), p. 129.

2. Edward G. Browne, *Literary History of Persia: Modern Times* (1500–1924), vol. 4 (Cambridge: Cambridge University Press, 1930), p. 468.

3. Edward G. Browne, *The Press and Poetry of Modern Persia* (Los Angeles: Kalimat Press, 1983), p. 154. First edition, 1914.

4. For further information see *Nukhustin Kungirah-yi Nivisandigān-i Irān*, pp. 138–142, and Veľa Kubičkova, "Persian Literature of the 20th Century," in Jan Rypka, *History of Iranian Literature*, pp. 382–383.

5. *Nukhustin Kungarah*, p. 142.

6. For a list of the books translated and/or compiled by *Darul-Funum* teachers, see Browne's *Press and Poetry*, pp. 157–159.

7. Jan Rypka, "History of Persian Literature up to the Beginning of the 20th Century," in Jan Rypka, *History of Iranian Literature*, p. 341.

8. Veľa Kubičkova, p. 364.

9. Jan Rypka, p. 342.

10. Veľa Kubičkova, p. 379.

11. Hassan Kamshad, *Modern Persian Prose Literature* (Cambridge: The University Press, 1966), p. 40.

12. Muhammad Ali Jamalzadah, *Once Upon a Time* (*Yeki Bud Yeki Nabud*), translated by Heshmat Moayyed and Paul Sprachman (New York: Bibliotheca Persica, 1985), p. 9.

13. Hassan Kamshad, pp. 90–91.

14. Sayyad Muhammad Ali Jamalzadah, *Yiki Bud, Yiki Nabud* (*Once Upon a Time*) (Tehran: Kanun Ma'rifat, n.d. 4th edition), p. 8, cf. Haideh Dargahi, "The Shaping of the Modern Persian Short Story; Jamalzadah's 'Preface' to *Yiki Bud, Yiki Nabud*," in *The Literary Review*, 18: 1 (Fall 1974): 28.

15. Jamalzadah, *Yiki Bud, Yiki Nabud*, p. 9.

16. *Once Upon a Time*, p. 9.

17. For further information see L. P. Elwell-Sutton, "Influence of Folktale and Legend on Modern Persian Literature."

18. Sayyad Muhammad Ali Jamalzadah, "Zabān-i 'Ammiyānah" ("Folk Speech"), *Rahnamāy-i Kitāb*, 3: 5 (1339/1960): 611–615, 3: 6, 716–720. Making references to the pioneering works of people such as Talibuff, Mirza Malkum Khan, Akhunduff, Mirza Aga Khan Kirmani, Hajj Zaynu'l 'Ābidin of Maraqah the translator of *Hajji Baba of Isfahan* and few other writers, Jamalzadah explains that though these people wrote in a simple language, not much colloquialism can be found in their writings. Writers in general avoided "common" people's language, because it was considered to be degrading and vulgar.

19. *Ibid.*, 717, 718, and 719.

20. *Farhang-i Luqāti-i 'Ammiyānah* (Tehran: Intisharat-i Farhang-i Iran Zamin, no. 7, 1341/1962).

21. "Davidam u Davidam," *Payam-i Nuvin* 5: 6 (1342/1963): 10.

22. Kamshad, p. 159.

23. *Ibid.*

24. *Ibid.*

25. A review of some of Hidayat's correspondence with his friends outside the country reveals how, in order to keep his readings up to date and obtain the sources unavailable in Iran, he did not hesitate to request his friends to provide him with the books. For further information see, for example, "Nāmah-hā-yi Sadiq Hidayat" ("Hidayat's Letters") *Sukhan*, 6: 1 (1333/1954): 199–209; Parviz Natil Khanlari, "Fout-i Sadiq Hidayat" ("Sadiq Hidayat's Death") *Khabarhā-yi Danishgāh*, 5 (1330/1951) reprinted in *'Aqāid va Afkār dar bārah Sadiq Hidāyat pas az Marg* (*Views and Comments about Sadiq Hidayat after his Death*) (Tehran: Intisharat-i Bahr-i Khazar, 1346/1967), pp. 29–30. Hidayat's association with great contributors to Iranian folkloristics, namely Arthur Christensen and Henri Massé, had great influence on Hidayat's interest in folklore. On Hidayat and Christensen see for example, Mihdi Qaravi, "Mutāli 'at Irānshinasi dar Dānmārk" ("Iranian Studies in Denmark") *Rāhnamā-yi Kitāb*, 6 (1342/1963): 644–749. Henri Massé, at a lecture delivered at Hidayat's memorial ceremony, pointed out how he encouraged Hidayat to collect folklore; "Sukhanrāni Professor Henri Massé dar Majlisi Yādbud-i Chahāumin Sāl-i Marg-i Hidayat dar Pāris," ("Professor Henri Massé's Speech on the Occasion of the Fourth Anniversary of Hidayat's Death in Paris") in *Nazariyyāt-i Nivisandigān-i Buzurg-i Khāriji dar barah-yi Sadiq Hidayat, Zindagi va Asār-i u* ("*Great Foreign Writers' Views about Sadiq Hidayat, his Life and Work*, edited by H. Qaimiyan, (Tehran, 1343/1964, 3rd edition), pp. 140–150.

26. Jalal Al-Ahmad, "Hidayat-i *Buf-i Kur*" ("Hidayat of *The Blind Owl*") *'Ilm va Zindagi* 1: 1 (1330/1951), reprinted in Jalal Al-Ahmad, *Haft Maqalah* (*Seven Articles*) (Tehran: Intisharat-i Amir Kabir, 1357/1978), p. 15.

27. Amin Banani, *The Modernization of Iran: 1921–1941* (Stanford: Stanford University Press, 1961), p. 106.

28. *Ibid.*, p. 45.

29. *Ibid.*, p. 47

30. Thomas M. Ricks, "Contemporary Persian Literature," *The Literary Review*, 18: 1 (Fall 1974): 10.

31. *Nayrangistan* (Tehran: Intisharat-i Amir Kabir, 1342/1963, 3rd edition), p. 12.

32. *Ibid.*, p. 23.

33. *Ibid.*, p. 25.

34. *Ibid.*, p. 13.

35. *Ibid.*, p. 26.

36. According to Mahmud Katira'i, the main informants for *Nayrangistan* were Hidayat's mother and a house maid, "Sadiq Hidayat va Folklore-i Iran" ("Sadiq Hidayat and Iranian Folklore") in *Namah Minuvi: Majmu' ah Si u Hasht Guftar dar Adab va Farhang-i Irani bi Pas-i Panjah Sal Tahqiqat va Mutali 'at-i Mujtaba Minuvi* (*A Collection of Thirty-eight Essays on Iranian Literature and Culture Dedicated to Mujtaba Minuvi in Appreciation of his Fifty Years of Research*) edited by Iraj Afshar (Tehran, 1350/1971): 356-357; see also Mahmud Katira 'i, *Az Khisht ta Khisht* (Tehran: Intisharat-i Mu'assasah Mutali'at va Tahqiqat-i Ijtima 'i, 1348/1969), p. VI.

37. *Usanah* (Tehran: Aryan Kudah, 1310/1931). A few years earlier, however, he had written an article in French entitled "Le Magic en Perse," in *Le Voile D'Isise*, 79 (1926).

38. *Usanah* in *Majmu'ah Nivishtih-ha-yi Parakandah-yi Sadiq Hidayat* (*Collection of Sadiq Hidayat's Miscellaneous Writings*), compiled by Hassan Qaimian (Tehran: Amir Kabir, 1344/1965) second edition, p. 310, 316.

39. *Ibid.*, 296.

40. *Ibid.*, 297–300.

41. Henri Massé, *Croyances et coutumes persanes suivies de contes et chansons populaires* (Paris: G. P. Maisonneuve, 1938), p. 14.

42. *Ibid.*, p. 15.

43. "Taranah-ha-yi 'Ammiyanah ("Folksongs") in *Majmu'ah*, p. 344.

44. *Ibid.*, p. 349.

45. "Sukhanrāni Āqā-yi Mujtabā Minuvi dar Jalasih Yādbud-i Hidayat" (Mr. Mujtaba Minuvi's Speech at Hidayat's Memorial Ceremony," in *'Aqāyid va Afkār*, p. 108.

46. Qa'imiyan, "Tuzih-i Girdavarandah" ("Compiler's Comments") in *Majmu'ah Nivishtih-ha-yi Parākandah*, p. XXI.

47. M. A. and Sadiq Hidayat, "Bulbul-i Sargashtah" ("The Wondering Nightingale") *Sukhan* 3: 6–7 (1325/1946): 432–434.

48. *Nivishtah-hā-yi Parākandah*, p. XXI, and Katira'i, "Sadiq Hidayat va folklore-i Iran," 358.

49. Reprinted in *Nivishtah-hā-yi Parākandah*, pp. 120–126.

50. *Ibid.*, p. 120.

51. *Ibid.*, p. 121.

52. Both narratives are reprinted in *Nivishtah-hā-yi Parākandah*, pp. 127–130 and 131–138.

53. "Folklore yā Farhang-i Tudah: Nimunahā va Dastur-i Jam' Āvari va Tadvin-i ān" ("Folklore or the Culture of the Masses: Examples and Methods of Collection and Recording") Sukhan 2: 3 (1323/1944): 180.

54. Sadiq Humayuni, *Mardi ki bā Sāyihash Harf Mizad*, (*The Man who Talked to his Shadow*) (Tehran, 1352/1973), p. 92. In the chapter on "Hidayat va Folklore" ("Hidayat and Folklore"), pp. 85–100, he reviews Hidayat's contribution to Iranian folkloristics.

55. "Chand Nuktah dar bārah *Vis u Ramin*" ("A Few Comments about *Vis and Ramin*") in *Majmu' ah*, p. 507.

56. *Nayrangistān*, p. 9.

57. "Bayanat-i Aqā-yi Rashid Yāsimi dar bārih Folklore" ("Mr. Rashid Yasimi's Speech on Folkore") *Ta'lim va Tarbiyat* 6: 1 (1315/1936): 90.

58. For the complete text of the advertisement see Jamalzadah, *Farhang-i Lugāt-i 'Āmmiyānah*, p. 92.

59. Sadiq Hidayat, "Folklore yā Farhang-i Tudah," 182.

60. *Ibid.*

61. Soheila Shahshahani, "History of Anthropology in Iran" *Iranian Studies* 19: 1 (Winter 1986): 70.

62. "Muqaddamah" *Mardumshināshi va Farhang-i 'Āmmah-i Irān*, 1: 1 (Intisharat-i Vizarat-i Farhang va Hunar, Markaz-i Pazhuhishhā-yi Mardumshinasi va Farhang-i 'Āmmah, Summer 1353/1974): 15–16.

63. One such example is the research conducted by L. P. Elwell-Sutton and Kazim Sadat-Ishkivari, "Mountain and Plain Contrasts in Persian Folk-Literature," *Studia Fennica* 20 (1976): 331–337. With regard to the project Elwell-Sutton explains:

During the summer of 1973 I carried out two short expeditions in Iran for the purpose of collecting local folk-tales. In both cases I had the full cooperation of the National Centre for Anthropological and Folklore Research of the Iranian Ministry of Culture and Art, which has been very active during the short period since its formation in exploring this hitherto sadly neglected field and trying to build up a comprehensive collection from what must be one of the richest treasure-houses of folk-literature in the world.

64. Mahmud Khaliqi, "Muqaddamah", 17.

65. Muhsin Mihandust, *Samandar-i Chil-gis* (Tehran: Vizarat-i Farhang u Hunar, 1353/1973); Kazim Sadat Ishkivari, *Afsānah-hā-yi Ishkivir-i Bālā* (Tehran, 1352/1973); and Murtiza Hunari, *Owsungun, Afsānah-hā-yi Mardum-i Xur* (Tehran: Vizarat-i Farhang u Hunar, 3352/1973).

66. For further information see Khaliqi, 18–20.

67. Some examples include the three works by Jalal Al-Ahmad, *Awrāzan* (Tehran: Kitabkhanah Danish, 1333/1954), *Tātnishinhā-yi Buluk-i Zahrā* (Tehran, 1337/1958), and *Durr-i Yatim-i Khalij, Jazirah-i Khārk* (Tehran: Kitabkhanah Danish, 1339/1960); Sirus Tahbaz, *Yush* (Tehran: Intishārāt-i Mu'assasah Mutāli'āt va Tahqiqāt Ijtimā'i, 1342/1963); Qulam Hussain Sā'idi, *Khiāv yā Mishkin Shahr* (Tehran: Intishārāt Mu'assisah Mutāli'āt va Tahqiqāt Ijtimā'i, 1344/1965), and Ilkhchi (Tehran: Intishārāt-i Mu'assasah Mutāli'āt va Tahqiqāt Ijtimā'i, 1342/1963).

68. Muhammad Ja'far Mahjub, "Farhang-i 'Āmmah va Zindagi" ("Folklore and Life") *Hunar va Mardum* 184–185 (1357/1978): 11.

69. Hussain Kuhi Kirmani, *Pānzdah Afsānah Rustāi (Fifteen Rural Narratives)* (Tehran: Amir Kabir, 1333/1954).

70. *Afsānahā (Folk Narratives)* 2 vols., (Tehran: Amir Kabir, vol. I 1323/1944, vol. II 1325/1946). Subhi's other collections are: *Afsānahā-yi Kuhan (Old Folk Narratives)* 2 vols., (Tehran, vol. I 1328/1949, vol. II 1329/1960); *Dizh-i Hush Rubā* (Tehran: Amir Kabir, 1353/1974) 1st edition 1330/1951; *Dāstānhā-yi Divān-i Balkh* (Tehran: Amir Kabir, 1353/1974) First edition 1331/1952; *Afsānahhā-i Bu Ali Sīnā* (Tehran, 1333/1954); and *Afsānah-hā-yi Bāstāni Irān va Majār* (Tehran, 1332/1953). In addition to these collections, Subhi authored several articles about folk narratives. A German translation of nine of Subhi's folk narratives is presented by Lore Ehlers in *Persische Märchen und Schwänke* (Wien: Ferdinand Berger, Horn, 1966).

71. Though the major reason for this lack of favoritism was his engagement in popularizing and studying folklore, a subject which was

looked down upon by many intellectuals as vulgarities, his earlier religious convictions as a Baha'i might have also played an influential role.

72. Amir Quli Amini, *Folklore Iran: Dānstānhā-yi Amsāl (Iranian Folkore: The Stories of Proverbs)* (Isfahan: Chapkhanah Isfahan, 1333/1954), p. 3.

73. *Ibid.*, p. 1.

74. Amir Quli Amini, *Si Afsānah az Afsānah-hā-yi Mahalli Isfāhān (Thirty Folk Narratives from Isfahan)* (Tehran, 1343/1964): p. III.

75. *Qissah-hā-yi Mardum-i Fārs (Folk Narratives of Fars)* (Tehran, 1349/1970).

76. Abulqasim Anjavi Shirazi, *Farhang-i Mardum va Tarz-i Girdāvari va Nivishtan-i ān (Folklore and the Methodology of Collecting and Recording It)* (Tehran: Chapkhanah vizārat-i'Ittilā'at, 196) First edition 1960.

77. Sadiq Hidayat, "Folklore yā Farhang-i Tudah," 181.

78. *Masal va Tamsil (Proverbs and Stories of Proverbs)* (Tehran: Intishārāt-i Amir Kabir, 1352/1973): p. XXV.

79. *Ibid.*, pp. XXII-XXIII.

80. *Qissahā-yi Irāni (Iranian Folk Narratives)* 2nd. vol., (Tehran: Intishārāt-i Amir Kabir, 1353/1974): p. XIX.

81. See, for example, Manuchihr Lam'ah, *Farhang-i Ammiyānah 'Ashāyir-i Boyir Ahmadi va Kuhkiluyah (Folklore of Buyir Ahmadi and Kuhkiluyah Tribes)* (Tehran: Intishārāt-i Ashrafi, 1349/1970), and S. Javid, *Azarbayjān Folkorindan Nimunahlar (Examples of Azarbayjani Folklore)* (Tehran, 1344/1965).

82. Ibrahim Shakurzadah, *'Aqāyid va Rusum-i 'Ammah-yi Mardum-i Khurāsān (The Folk Belief and Customs of the People of Khurasan)* (Tehran: Intishārāt-i Bunyānd-i Farhang-i Irān, 1346/1967): p. 8.

83. Stith Thompson, *The Folktale* (New York: The Dryden Press, 1946), p. 8.

84. "Dar bārah-i Afshānah-hā-yi 'Ammiyānah" ("About Folk Narratives") *Sukhan* 6: 4 (1334/1955): 299.

85. *Ibid.*, p. 300.

86. "Afsānah-hā-yi 'Ammiyānah" ("Folk Narratives") *Sukhan* 5: 12 (1333/1954): 920–922.

87. Samad Bihrangi and Bihruz Dihqani, *Afsānah-hā-yi Azarbāyjān (Azarbayjani Folk Narratives)* (Tehran: Intishārāt-i Dunyā 1360/1981): p. 6.

88. *Dāstānhā-i 'Ammiyānah-i Fārsi"* ("Iranian Folk Narratives") *Sukhan* 10: 1 (1338/1959): 66–67. This is an introduction to a series of

articles which include the description and discussion of several well-known romances in their printed form.

89. "Mutāli 'ah dar Dāstānhā-yi 'Ammiyānah-i Fārsi" ("Study of Persian Folk Narratives") *Majallah Dānishkadah Adabiyyāt-i Tehran* 10: 1 (1341/1962): 80.

90. "Dāstānhā-yi Ablahān va Sādahluhān" ("Narratives of Numskulls and Simpletons") *Sukhan* 19: 8 (1348/1969): 757.

91. Hassan Javadi, "Tanz va Intiqād dar Dāstānhā-yi Hayvānāt," ("Satire and Criticism in Animal Stories") *Alifba* 4 (1353/1974): 1–2.

92. "Afsānah-hā-yi Mahalli Āzarbāyjan" ("Folk Narratives of Azarbayjan") in *Haft Maqālah Pirāmun-i Folklore va Adabiyyāt-i Mardum-i Āzarbāyjan, (Seven Articles about the Folklore and the Literature of Azarbayjani People)* edited by Parvin Aqajanzadah (Tehran: Intisharat-i Dunyay-i Danish, 1978): 64–86 second edition.

93. "Simāy-i Qahramān dar Dāstān-hā-yi 'Ammiyānah" ("The Characteristics of Heroes in Folk Narratives") *Sadaf*, 1: 4 (1336/1957): 275–291.

94. "Rumuz-i Qissah az Didgāh-i Ravānshināsi" ("Study of Narrative Symbols from a Psychological Point of View") *Hunar va Mardum*, 96–97 (1349/1970): 49–55 through 126 (1351/1972): 100–103.

95. Kazim Sadat Ishkivari, "Nigāhi Guzarā bi Afsānah-hā-yi Ishkivar-i Bālā" ("A Glance at Ishkivar-i Bala Folk Narratives," *Mardum Shināsi va Farhang-i 'Ammah-yi Iran* 2 (Tehran: Vizārat Farhang va Hunar, Markaz-i Mardumshinasi, 1354/1975): 58.

96. Muhsin Mihandust, "Qissah dar Qalamruv-i Adabiyyāt-i Shafāhi" ("Narrative in the Realm of Oral Literature"), *Mardumshināsi va Farhang-i 'Ammah-yi Iran* 2 (Tehran: Vizārat-i Farhang va Hunar, Markaz-i Mardumshinasi, 1354/1975): 103–113.

97. Mihrdad Bahar, *Asātir-i Irān (Iranian Mythology)* (Tehran: Intishārāt-i Bunyād-i Farhang-i Iran, 1392/1973), p. v.

98.H. Davidian, "Ahammiyat-i Barrasi Asātir-i Irāni dar Ravānshināsi Tahlili" ("The Significance of Iranian Mythology Studies on Analytical Psychology") *Sukhan* 15: 4 (1343/1964): 374–391.

99. Ahmad Tabatabai, "Div va Juhar-i Asātiri ān" ("Ogre and its Mythological Origin,") Nashriyah Dānishkadah Adabiyyāt Tabriz 16: 5 (1343/1964): 39–45.

100. Bahram Bayzai, *Namāyish dar Irān (Theatre in Iran)* (Tehran, 1345/1966).

101. "Sukhanvari" *Sukhan* 9: 6 (1337/1958): 530–535; 9: 8 (1337/1958): 779–789.

102. Muhammad Ja'far Mahjub, "Les Traditions des Bardes, les Assauts Poetiques," *Studia Iranica* 3: 1 (1973): 115–122.

103. Muhammad Ja'far Mahjub "Le conteur en Iran," *Objets et Mondes* 10: 1 (1971): 159–170.

104. The Story-Teller and Mass Media in Iran: The Role of Story Telling in Social Communications," in *Entertainment: A Cross-Cultural Examination* edited by Heinz-Dietrich Fischer and Stefan Reinhard Melnik, 58–59 (New York, 1979).

105. Muhammad Ja'far Mahjub, "Farhang-i 'Ammah va Zindagi," 10.

106. *Ibid.*, 6. A similar idea is expressed by F. Vahman in his introduction to *Farhang-i Mardum-i Kirmān: Gird Avarandah D. L. Lorimer* (*Folkore of Kirmani People: Collected by D. L. Lorimer*) (Tehran: Intishārāt-i Bunyād-i Farhang-i Iran, 1353/1974). Based on Alan Dundes' definition of folklore in *The Study of Folklore* (Englewood Cliffs, N. J.: Prentice-Hall, 1965), Vahman points out that "folk" is referred to any group of people who share a common factor. Therefore folklore is not limited to rural areas, and the folklore found among the urban dwellers is as important.

CHAPTER V

Conclusions

The contribution of travellers and Western researchers, specifically philologists, played a significant role in the inception and generation of interest in folklore in Iran. While the detailed and vivid information recorded by travellers sparked the attention and interest of Western scholars, it was the extensive research of philologists that laid the foundation for folklore studies in Iran. The development of folkloristics in Iran as a scientific field of study, however, was the direct result of a genuine interest and the scholarly efforts of the Iranian researchers themselves.

The major contribution of travellers and philologists to Iranian folkloristics is their recording examples of different genres of folklore. The materials recorded by travellers as novelties of an Eastern land to entertain and/or inform their readers are valuable data, providing information about the culture and folklore of Iran at different periods of time. Many of the customs and traditions which have either been modified or have ceased to exist due to social and cultural changes are still preserved in these source documents. The wide range of data gathered by travellers of different nationalities and backgrounds at different periods of time provide the student of Iranian culture and folklore with ample material for research. Scholars in different fields of study have constantly drawn upon travel books as historical sources of reference. Even philologists have searched in them for information regarding the dialects under their study. In folklore studies, the same function has been bestowed upon travel books. The most extensive use of travel records as source documents in a folkloristic study is provided by Henri Massé in his *Croyances et coutoumes persanes suivies des contes et chansons populaires*, in which Massé provides references and statements from different travellers. Yet the function of travel accounts need not be limited to mere historical sources of reference. The variety of information embedded in travel records can be employed by the contemporary folklorists as a data-base to complement the data gathered through fieldwork, to fill in the gaps in tracing developments, and to shed light on certain ambiguities. Nevertheless, in employing these source documents one must take into consideration the fact that they are not always void of errors and/or misinterpretations. The prejudice and presuppositions of some travellers, or their lack of sufficient knowledge about the language and culture of the country, have marred the reliability of some of the information recorded. These misinterpretations are usually easily detectable, and in cases where doubt obtains, a comparison with similar information recorded by other travellers or available in other sources provides a solution.

Though the researchers of Iranian folklore have recognized and acknowledged the significance of travellers' accounts as source documents, no further attempts have been made for their study in this perspective. In comparison, the Iranian classical sources of literature and history, which have been recognized as reservoirs of folklore have been treated differently. In the early stages of folklore scholarship Sadiq Hidayat chose a classical literary source as a subject of study from folkloristic point of view.[1] Since then several individuals have emphasized the significance of classical texts as sources for the study of folklore. In Mahmoud Khaliqi's view, the Greek sources, pre-Islamic texts in Avestan and Pahlavi languages, and the classical texts of the Islamic period, as well as the Arab and Western travellers' accounts, provide valuable sources of information on Iranian ethnology and folklore.[2] The archives of the National Center for Ethnology and Folklore Research houses data on Iranian folklore extracted from various classical literary and history texts which have been systematically classified.[3] A similar attempt in the case of travellers' accounts would provide fruitful results. In a more recent study in recognition of the importance of the classical texts, Mahmoud Omidsalar points out, "A systematic study of Persian folklore must involve not only fieldwork, but also a review of the classical Persian and Arabic texts."[4] Among the literary texts, *Shah Namah* has been the primary choice for studies from a folkloristic point of view. Few studies have focused on other literary sources. One such example is Sadiq Humayuni's "Folklore va Gulistān-i Sa'di" ("Folklore and Sa'di's *Gulistan*"). In an attempt to reveal the close relationship that exists between *Gulistan* and people's every day life, Humayuni draws on examples of proverbs that have their origin in *Gulistan*.[5]

As sources of folkloristic data, travellers' accounts with information on the different aspects of Persian life present a much greater variety than do the recordings of philologists, which include only narratives, folksongs, and some categories of folk speech. With regard to folk narratives, while philologists, due to the nature of their studies, have only focused on texts, travellers have provided, in addition to narratives, firsthand information about narrators—professional or non-professional—storytelling, and audience. Yet philologists' studies have played a more influential role in generating interest in the study of Iranian folklore. Several reasons can be given for this. One is the length of philological studies, which are much shorter than travel records. Second, unlike travel accounts, in which folk narratives or other kinds of folklore examples are interspersed throughout the work, philological studies classify them as such. Third, philological studies have a conceptual base instead of simply an observational one. While travellers' records were perceived as mere memoirs put together by individuals from different walks of life, the work presented by philologists was judged to be serious research conducted by reputable scholars. Thus, through their research, philologists provided credibility for the study of what was regarded by the majority of Iranians as "old wives' tales." Having established the significance of collecting and studying folklore, Western scholars repeatedly pointed out to Iranians the lack of sufficient research and encouraged their involvement.

A general review of folklore studies in Iran reveals a slow, but steady, progress, specifically in the area of analytical and/or contextual studies. Studies on Iranian mythology have suffered an identical fate. While the *Shah Namah* has been the subject of some studies from a mythological point of view, Iranian mythology, despite its rich resources, has not received its fair share of study by the Iranian specialists. The requirement of a knowledge of Old and Middle Iranian languages, and the lack of translations of these sources into standard Modern Persian, have been the main obstacles in the advancement of studies on Iranian mythology. On the other hand, many Iranian scholars with a knowledge of these languages have become more involved in the study of the languages themselves than in the texts and their contents. Taking these facts into consideration, the statements and suggestions made by Mihrdad Bahar still present fundamental solutions.[6]

In folklore studies, the lingering assumptions and presuppositions which were inherited from the pioneers of Iranian folkloristics have been among the major factors responsible for the slowness of progress. As stated earlier, Sadiq Hidayat's views of folklore, which were mainly based on the folkoristic trends current at his time, had great impact on the work of the researchers who followed in his footsteps.[7] This faithful subscription to the notions popularized by Sadiq Hidayat and lack of adequate information about the development of folkloristics in the West greatly affected the nature of research conducted by Iranian folklorists. For a long period of time the overemphasis on the fear of the disappearance of folklore, and the persistence of the idea that a thorough collection of different genres of folklore from all parts of the country should precede any classification and/or analytical study (both of which disregarded the dynamic nature of folklore) led researchers to concentrate mainly on collecting folklore. With regard to folk narratives, Iranian researchers' preoccupation with the making and publishing textual records did not allow the collector to pay attention to other important elements, such as the narrator and his/her style, the audience and their reactions or interaction with the narrator, and the functions of storytelling. In fact, Iranian folklorists' methodologies of collecting data are strikingly similar to the work of the Western philologists whose main concern was recording texts.

It was not until recently that Iranian researchers recognized the ongoing nature of folklore, its existence among all members of the society and not just the peasants and the illiterate, and the fact that collecting need not be an isolated effort, but can be combined with analysis. The eventual appearance of studies of an analytical nature and of statements indicating mere collection of folklore is an outdated process and emphasizing the need to train individuals to study systematically different aspects of society[8] signified modifications in the long-standing assumptions. In his study of proverbs, Kazim Sadat Ishkavari states that the prerequisite for gaining proper knowledge about a phenomenon is the study of its context.[9] Examination and discussion of the significant political and social events reflected in some folksongs is the subject of an article by Abulqasim Faqiri.[10] Iranian folklore scholarship has also suffered other shortcomings which have affected its progress noticeably. To name a few factors, reference should be made to the insufficient support of government organizations and institutions in providing adequate financial and human resources; lack of comprehensive educational possibilities in the fields of folklore and mythology studies in academia to educate interested individuals and provide potential researchers with the necessary knowledge and background about the developments and current trends of folkloristics; and the lack of up-to-date information about folklore scholarship in the West. Elimination of these inadequacies would greatly affect the directions of folklore scholarship in Iran.

In the recent years some Western researchers and Iranians educated abroad have provided new and significant material on different aspects of Iranian folklore. These studies play an influential role in expanding the scope of Iranian folkloristics, as well as providing greater exposure and recognition, which in turn could result in encouraging further research. Besides new subjects and approaches, these studies also differ in length and format. They are master's theses and doctoral dissertations and book-length studies and essays appearing in scholarly periodicals. A systematic analysis of Persian tale types was first undertaken by Adrienne Boulvin in her *Contes populaires persans du Khorassan* in 1974. Kianoosh Mo'tarif's doctoral dissertation is another attempt. Unlike Boulvin, who based her type analysis on firsthand collection of 103 narratives, Mo'tarif employs a large collection from printed sources.[11] A more comprehensive study is presented by Ulrich Marzolph. Besides providing a type-index of printed and unpublished firsthand collections of Persian narratives, Marzolph reviews in the introduction the contributions of the Western and Iranian researchers and enumerates the general characteristics of the main heroes of the narratives.[12] He concludes, "Persian tale—taking into account distinct regional peculiarities—keeps strictly within the frame of the well known and thoroughly explored Indo-European tradition."

The study of Iranian folk narratives from a sociological point of view is the subject of Elwell-Sutton's article "Family Relationships in Persian Folk-Literature." In his view Iranian folk narratives "both reflect and influence present-day popular ideas" regarding family relationships. He presents a characterization of each member of a family as depicted in folk narratives, and he concludes "To understand how the people of a given culture think, it is useful to know what they have been told as children."[13] Erika Friedl's study of women in Persian folk narratives is a subject not often explored by either Western or Iranian scholars. Her essay consists of detailed description of women's various roles as depicted in the narratives under study with references to real-life circumstances. Friedl's analysis is based on "forty-five tales from the tribal area of Boir Ahmad in Southwest Iran,...and ten tales from the same area and time period collected by an Iranian physician."[14] In her view, the reason for the survival of folk narratives is that they conform with the social and cultural criteria which are acceptable and meaningful to the members of a cultural group. She also points out that the spontaneous statements provided by informants constitute valuable data for evaluating the culture or the group under study. Both these ideas are also explored by her in an earlier work. The focus of study in Friedl's "The Folktale as Cultural Comment" is scrutinizing the narratives related by two informants in relationship to their personal background. Friedl's main thesis is that "storytellers use tales to comment on certain cultural features, especially those that are of relevance to their personality."[15] She also points out that "the constellation of narrator-tale-audience all formed by one culture can be used as a shortcut to learn something about that culture."[16] Friedl's study, besides conforming with the longstanding view about tallying of narratives with culture, also provides more evidence about the significant role the narrator's background plays in his/her choice and relating of folk narratives. Though the number of studies on non-professional narrators is very limited, professional narrators have been the subject of study by some Iranian and Western researchers. Several studies have focused on the narrating skills and style of *Naqqals* or reciters of *Shah-Namah*, who usually perform at coffee-houses. An example of studies in this category is Mary Ellen Page's doctoral dissertation. Her study of *Naqqals* is based on firsthand information and fieldwork conducted in Shiraz.[17] The study by Ilhan Basgöz, on the other hand, focuses on another group of narrators, namely the *Hikaye* tellers, or, as he refers to them, "professional wandering minstrels."[18]

Iranian folkloristics was generated and enhanced through the researches of both Western and native scholars. The contributions of Western researchers were significant in the inception and enrichment of Iranian folklore studies. Iranian folklorists, through their collections and studies, rectified public misconceptions, established the credibility of folklore as an important field of study, and encouraged further scholarship. To ensure the continuous progress of Iranian folkloristics and its advancement, harmonious scholarly cooperation between foreign and native researchers is essential.

NOTES

1. Sadiq Hidayat, "Chand Nuktah dar bārāh *Vis u Ramin*."

2. Mahmud Khaliqi "Muqaddamah," 2-12.

3. *Ibid.*, 20.

4. Mahmoud Omidsalar, "Storytellers in Classical Persian Texts," *Journal of American Folklore* 97 (1984): 205.

5. Sadiq Humayuni, "Folklore va *Gulistān-i* Sa'di" ("Folklore and Sa'di's *Gulistan*") in *Majmu'ah Maqālāt-i Chaharumin Kungarah-i Tahqiqāt-i Irāni* (*Proceedings of the Fourth Congress of Iranian Studies*) vol. 3 (September 1973): 284–294.

6. Mihrdad Bahar, p. v. An outline of his suggestions appear in Chapter IV.

7. An exaggerated example of this influence is Iraj Gulsurkhi's article "Dar bārāh Farhang-i Mardum" ("About Folklore,") in *Talash* 1: 5 (1346/1967): 44–45. Gulsurkhi's reproduction of statements by Sadiq Hidayat and representing them with statements such as "In my opinion . . . ," leaves the reader with no other choice than considering this article a case of plagiarism.

8. Ja'far Saffarzadah, "Rābitah-i Zarbul masalhā bā Zindigi Ruzmarrah-yi Mardum" ("The Relationship between Proverbs and People's Everyday Life") in *Sevvumin Kungarah-yi Tahqiqāt-i Irāni* (*Proceedings of the Third Congress of Iranian Studies*) vol. 2 (1972): 370.

9. Kazim Sadat-Ishkivari, "Zarbulmasalhāi az Ishkivar-i Bālā" ("Some Proverbs from Ishkivar-i Bala") *Hunar va Mardum* 191–192 (1357/1978): 65. Other examples of contextual study of Persian proverbs include E. Noel, "The Character of the Kurds as Illustrated by their Proverbs and Popular Sayings," in *Bulletin of the School of Oriental and African Studies* 1 (1920): 79–90, and Reuben Levy, "Persia Viewed through its Proverbs and Apologues," in *Bulletin of the School of Oriental and African Studies* 14 (1952): 540–549.

10. Abulqasim Faqiri, "Havādis dar Tarānah-hā-yi Mahalli" ("Events in Folk Songs") in *Majmu'ah Chaharumin Kungarah-yi Tahqiqāt-i Irāni* (*Proceedings of the Fourth Congress of Iranian Studies*) vol. 2 (1973): 256–266.

11. Kianush Mo'tarif, *From the Land of Roses and Nightingales: Collection and Study of Persian Folktales* 2 vols., unpublished doctoral dissertation, University of Florida, 1979.

12. Urlich Marzolph, *Typologie des Persischen Volksmärchen* (Wiesbaden: Franz Steiner Verlag, 1984).

13. L. P. Elwell-Sutton, "Family Relationships in Persian Folk-Literature," *Folklore* 87 (1976): 166.

14. Erika Friedl, "Women in Contemporary Persian Folktales," in *Women in the Muslim World*, edited by Lois Beck and Nikki Keddie, p. 630 (Cambridge, Massachusetts and London, England: Harvard University Press, 1978).

15. Erika Friedl, "The Folktale as Cultural Comment," in *Asian Folklore Studies* 34 (1975): 144.

16. *Ibid.*, p. 128.

17. Mary Ellen Page, *Naqali and Ferdowsi: Creativity in the Iranian National Tradition*, unpublished doctoral dissertation, University of Pennsylvania, 1977.

18. Ilhan Basgöz, "Turkish *Hikaye* Telling Tradition in Azerbaijan, Iran," *Journal of American Folklore* 83 (1970): 391–405.

Appendix I

Travellers' remarks regarding *Dervishes*, professional storytellers and entertainers, coffee-houses, and Iranian modes of entertainment.

I

Nicolas Sanson, *The Present State of Persia: with a Faithful Account of the Manners, Religions, and Government of the People*, translated by John Savage (London: M. Gilliflower, 1695), pp. 153–152.

They have Religious People which they call *Dervishes*, or Abdals; they lead a poor and austere Life; they preach the Alcoran in the corners of Streets, Coffee-Houses, publick Ways, and, in short where-ever they can find Auditors. They talk with a great deal of Zeal, and some of 'em have a little Eloquence. They know nothing but Fables, with which they amuse the Vulgar. They are no more esteem'd of by Men of Wit, than the *Charlatans* are in *France*.

II

John Struys, *The Voyages and Travels of John Struys Through Italy, Greece, Muscovy, Tartary, Media, Persia, East India, Japan and Other Countries in Europe, Africa and Asia, Done out of Dutch by John Morrison* (London: Abel Swalle, 1684), pp. 320–321.

But quaint is the Habit, and more strange the Customs of their Clergy. . . . These abstain from Wine, live an austere life, and never marry till they grow very old. Some go in a long coarse Robe, others half naked, and a third sort only with a Skin girded about their middle. They go about the Streets, and when they come to any large Place as the *Maydan, Basar,* or the like, sit down, and with most hideous yelling convoke an Auditory, which being assembled they make a kind of a hortatory Oration, which notwithstanding the Scope or Erg, contains little else than a commemoration of the great and worthy Acts of *Aly,* and always at Peroration vilify and curse the *Turkish* Saints *Omar, Osman* and *Abubeker,* but more eagerly against the dogmatical Decrees of the *Usbec-Tartars:* But those of that nation being of late years grown very numerous at Ispahan, assumed the boldness to oppose them, for which end the King has allowed those Worthies to go armed with Hatchets, as at present they do, and have free Toleration to knock any man down that shall offer to interrupt them. They have only one Monastery, or *coenobium,* where they all live together, which was built them at the charges of the present King: and have also a considerable Sum allowed them for their maintenance, besides what they gather from the People by mumping, or rather Mountebanking.

III

C. J. Wills, *Persia as it is; Being Sketches of Modern Persian Life and Character* (London: S. Low, Marston, Searle and Rivington, 1886), pp. 93–95.

Take any ordinary Persian, let his hair grow; take off his outer garments, leaving him but his flowing shulwar and his shirt, or perhaps not even that: clap the tall embroidered sugar-loaf hat on his head, hang a necklet of big beads round his neck, sling a panther's skin across his shoulders, let his calabash depend from his girdle, let him be unwashed and uncombed; and you have your complete dervish, without his weapons. Dirt is not, however, essential to the dervish. . . . It is in his arms that the real dervish's fancy takes most scope. Bludgeons with portentous projections; clubs bristling with spikes or knife-blades; steel axes, single-headed or double-headed, at times beautifully damascened with silver or gold; maces of steal or iron, having the head like the head of a horned bull. . . . With one or other of these curious weapons the dervish is sure to be provided. . . . He marches along at a slow and dignified pace, pretending to be lost in pious meditation. Suddenly he will rattle his calabash or extend it. "Hakk!" he will shriek, grawl, or mutter, as he may feel disposed; "Ya Hakk!" ("O God!"— literally, "O the True" [God]). . . . Or he will politely present a flower, a nut, a leaf; and if it is accepted, a present must be given him . . . .

There are story-telling dervishes: proficients, some of them, having real genius, marvellous memories, and the art of the ventriloquist and mimic at command. The dervish is permitted by custom to enter any assemblage, to seat himself at every board—a humble, uninvited, but still welcome guest.

IV

Cornelius Le Brun, *A New and More Correct Translation than has Hitherto Appeared in Public of Mr. Cornelius Le Brun's Travels into Moscovy, Persia, and Divers Parts of the East-Indies* (London, 1759), p. 275.

Here [at the *Meydah* at Isfahan] likewise are frequently seen great numbers of quack-doctors, and their merry-andrews, or buffoons, tho' they sell no medicines at all and do nothing more than amuse the crowd with idle, nonsensical stories for which they are tolerably well paid for their labour by their numerous spectators. Some of these mountebanks have their apes and monkeys, which play a thousand antic tricks, to attract the mob about them; for there is no nation under the copes of heaven so fond of trifles, and buffoonery as the Persians are; for which reason, their coffee-houses, bazars, and other places of public resort, swarm with these idle jackpuddings, and quack-doctors.

V

Sir John Malcolm, *Sketches of Persia; from the Journals of a Traveller in the East* (London: John Murray, 1827), vol. I. pp. 176–177.

The day before we left Shiraz, Derveesh Seffer, my old acquaintance, paid the Elchee a visit. This remarkable man, who has charge of the shrines (including those of Sadee and Hafiz) near Shiraz is esteemed one of the best reciters of poetry and tellers of tales in Persia; and there is no country in the world where more value is placed upon such talents; he who possesses them in an eminent degree is as certain of fortune and fame as the first actors in Europe. Derveesh Seffer, who is honoured by the royal favour, has a very melodious voice, over which he has such power as to be able to imitate every sound, from that of the softest feminine to the harshest masculine voice. The varied expression of his countenance is quite as astonishing as his voice, and his action is remarkably graceful, and always suited to his subject. His memory is not only furnished with infinite variety of stories, but with all the poetry of his country: this enables him to give interest and effect to the most meagre tale, by apt quotations from the first authors of Persia. Those told by persons like him usually blend religious feeling with entertainment and are meant to recommend charity . . . .

VI

James Morrier, *Second Journey to Persia, Armenia, and Asia Minor, to Constantinople, between the Years 1810 and 1816* (London: Longman, Kurst, Rees, Orme, and Brown, 1818), p. 44.

. . . the Dervishes and *Gousheh nishins,* (or sitters in the corner,) . . . are so frequently met with in Persia; a set of men who hold forth their doctrines in open places, sometimes almost naked, with their hair and beard floating wildly about their head, and a piece of camel or deer skin thrown over their shoulders. We were struck with the cry of a Dervish, who had taken post for a short time on the desert near to our camp, uttering his piercing exclamations of *hak* and *hou.* These cries, which are peculiarly wild when heard at a distance, the Dervishes utter to announce their arrival near a town, at the same time sounding a blast of a ram or a cow's horn, which they wear slung at their girdle.

VII

Sir John Chardin, *Sir John Chardin's Travels in Persia, with an Introduction by Brigadier-General Sir Percy Sykes* (London: The Argonaut Press, 1927), Book II, p. 203.

The *Puppet-shows* and *Juglers* ask no Money at the Door as they do in our Country, for they play openly in the public Places, and those give 'em that will. They intermingle Farce, and Juggling, with a thousand Stories and Buffooneries, which they do sometimes Mask'd, and sometimes un-mask'd, and this lasts two or three Hours. And when they have done, they go round to the Spectators and ask something. . . . For two Crowns the Juglers will come to their House. They call this sort of Diversions Mascare. . . .

VIII

Sir Arnold Wilson, *S. W. Persia, Letters and Diary of a Young Political Officer 1907–1914* (London: Oxford University Press, 1942 pp. 63–65.

I spent four more days with him, shooting every day and listening every evening to a blind story-teller, a well-known and popular figure in these remote parts. He had been in Ispahan three weeks ago and had a very good idea indeed of the truth behind the news or, at least, the news behind the newspapers. Events in Tehran and the character of the leading figures, their family history and political records, grain prices, and harvest forcasts, the probable trends of events during the next few weeks: the names of new governors of cities and provinces and a few marriages in "high life," as the French imagine we say. After a little of this he would turn to romance, sometimes classical Persian poetry, sometimes topical adaptations of well-known stanzas of Sadi and Hafiz, sometimes an old Lur or Kuhgalu song, bringing in the names of famous tribal leaders of bygone days. He had an unfailing memory and a voice like a bell. One night he recited the story of Sohrab and Rustam in its original form as told by Firdawsi: it moved me almost to tears. Speaking nearly in the dark as we sat round the small charcoal fire he relied entirely on modulations of his voice to give dramatic effect to the successive speeches of the boy Sohrab and his old father Rustam.

He held us spell-bound for nearly two hours; then tea was served and water-pipes passed round. He took a little food and began afresh. The family Chaplain came in and was received, as always, with respect. . . . The Chaplain took his seat by the Khan, salutations were exchanged with ceremony, and the orator asked the Chaplain (a Saiyid) if it was his pleasure that the company should hear some religious verse. The Chaplain readily agreed, beginning with prayer . . . after first calling for water that all might perform ceremonial ablutions. Then he began by intoning in a high voice the call to prayer for he was a *Muezzin*: all stood and followed him in his genuflexion and prostrations whilst I stood awkwardly at the door. . . . Prayers ended we took our seats again and the blind man began his psalm: a great oratorial performance, followed by a prose narrative of the sad fate of the patron saint of Persia, the martyred Huzain which reduced many of his audience to genuine tears, though it is not yet the month (*Muharram*) in which his death is called to mind. He ended on a more joyful note.

One night as a change, the Khan summoned a local *darvish* to tell us amusing stories—in a dialect which I found it hard to follow. He had a merry face, a club of immense size as his stage "property," and a wonderful capacity for mimicry and gestures. His performance was not indoors but in the courtyard where half the village had assembled. I have never heard Persians laugh loudly or unrestrainedly before. . . . A boy of 14 was with him as the butt of his jokes, or as his partner in imaginary misfortune: he too had his little jokes, on music-hall lines—of some of which the Lord Chamberlain, the L. C. C., and the Bishop of London would not have approved.

IX

Samuel Greene Wheeler Benjamin, *Persia and the Persians by S. G. W. Benjamin* (Boston: Ticknor and Company, 1887), p. 100.

What offers more attraction to a European in these tea-houses than the dancers, are the recitations from the poets. The-songs of Hafiz may be heard there, and entire cantos from the great epic of Firdousee, chanted with resonat modulations and listened to with enthusiastic rapture. Here, too, one may hear the "Arabian Nights tales" repeated without any attempts to expurgate passages offering a peculiarly oriental flavor. It is, however, these very passages which largely contribute to make of these immortal narratives a picture of oriental life and manners the most remarkable in literature.

X

Adam Olearius, *The Voyages and Travels of the Ambassadors from the Duke of Holstein, to the Great Duke of Muscovy, and the King of Persia Begun in the Year 1633 and Finish'd in 1639* (London: Thomas Daring and John Starkey, 1662), p. 298.

The *Cahwa Chane* are those places where they take Tobacco, and drink of a certain black water, which, they call *Cahwa*. . . . Their Poets and Historians are great frequenters of these places, and contribute much to the Divertisement of the Company. These are seated in a high Chair, in the midst of the Hall, whence they entertain their Auditors with Speeches, and tell them Satyrical stories, playing in the mean time with a little stick, with the same gestures, and after the same manner, as those do who shew tricks of Legerdemain among us.

XI

James Basset, *Persia, the Land of the Imams* (London: Blackie and Son, 1887), p. 269.

The social entertainment of the women consist in feasting, eating of candies, in gossip and dancing by hired dancing girls or boys. The reading of the Persian poets is sometimes one feature of an entertainment. A dervish or Mullah may be employed for this purpose; he being stationed in another apartment of the harem.

XII

Samuel Greene Wheeler Benjamin, *Persia and the Persians*, p. 173.

They [the peasants of Persia] have a decided taste for poetry, and often fly the heat of midday and find shelter under the great Chenars in the center of the village, where they listen to recitations from the Odes of Hafiz or the Shah Nameh of Firdousee.

XIII

J. B. Fraser, *An Historical and Descriptive Account of Persia from the Earliest Ages to the Present Time*, (Edinburgh: Oliver and Boyd, 1834), p. 332.

. . . when the entertainer is a pleasant, open-hearted person, mirth and good-humour abound,—wit and repartee are indulged,—stories and anecdotes are told,—and abundance of poetry is repeated.

But the relaxation to which the middle class are most attached is, to retire, after the fatigue of the day to some shady, well-watered garden near the city, and to devote their leisure to the delights of ease and social enjoyments, in such places parties of friends may frequently be seen sitting under the trees, smoking calleeoons, and listening to the odes of their most admired poets or to the tales of a kissago (storyteller), and often solacing themselves by copious libations from the wine cup.

Appendix II

A. Selection of narratives recorded by travellers.

I

Anthony Jenkinson, *Early Voyages and Travels to Russia and Persia by Anthony Jenkinson and Other Englishmen*, 2 vols. (New York: Burt Franklin, 1885), vol. 1, pp. 136–137.

Not farre from the sayd citie of *Shamakye*, there was an old Castle called *Gullistone*, now beaten down by this Sophie, which was esteemed to be one of the strongset castles in the world, and was besieged by Alexander the great, long time before he could winne it. And not farre from the said castle was a Nunnery of sumptuos building wherein was buried a kinges daughter, named *Amelecke Channa*, who slew herselfe with a knife, for that her father would have forced her (she professing chastitie) to haue married with a king of Tartary, vpon which occasion the maidens of that countrey doe resort thither once euery yere to lament her death.

II

Ibn Battuta, *Travels in Asia and Africa, 1325–1354, Translated
and Selected by H. A. R. Gibb* (London: Routledge and Kegan
Paul Ltd., 1929), pp. 95–96.

Shiraz contains many sanctuaries . . . among them is the
tomb of the Imam `Abdallah ibn Khafif, who is known there
simply as the "Shaykh" . . . the following story is told of him.
One day he went to the mountain of Sarandib [Adam's Peak] in
the Island of Ceylon accompanied by about thirty darwishes.
They were overcome by hunger on the way, in an uninhibited
locality, and lost their bearings. They asked Shaykh to allow
them to seize one of the small elephants of which are
transported thence to the king of India. The Shaykh forbade
them, but their hunger got the better of them and they
disobeyed him and, seizing a small elephant, killed and ate it.
The Shaykh however refused to eat it. That night, as they slept,
the elephants gathered from all quarters and came upon them,
smelling each one of them and killing him until they had made
an end of them all. They smelled the Shaykh too but offered no
violence to him; one of them lifted him with its trunk put him
on its back, and brought him to the inhibited district. When the
people of that part saw him, they marvelled at him and came
out to meet him, and hear his story. As it came near them, the
elephant lifted him with its trunk, and placed him on the ground
in full view of them.

III

Marco Polo, *The Travels of Marco Polo, Translated into English
from the Text of, L. F. Benedetto by Professor Aldo Ricci* (New
York, 1931), pp. 34–36.

In Persia is the city of Sava, whence the three magi set out when they came to adore Jesus Christ. In the city there are three very large and most beautiful tombs, in which the three Magi are buried. . . . Messer Marco Polo questioned many people of the city concerning these three Magi but there was no one who could tell him anything. . . . But he ultimately got to know what I will now tell you.

At three days' journey from Sava, he found a town called Cala Ataperistan, which, in our language, means the town of fire-worshipers. And it is quite rightly named, for the people there worship fire. And I will tell you why they do so. The inhabitants relate that once, in the day of old three kings of that country went to adore a Prophet who had just been born, and took with them three offerings—gold, frankincense, and myrrh—to ascertain whether that prophet were God or an earthly king or a physician. For, they said, if he takes the gold, he is an earthly king; if he takes the frankincense, he is God; if he takes the myrrh, he is a physician. When they reached the birth place of the Child, the youngest of the three kings went in alone to see it; and it seemed to him the Child was like him, seemingly of the same age and aspect; whereat he came away marvelling greatly. After him, the one of the middle age entered, and the Child appeared to him, as to the first, of his age and aspect; he too came away all amazed. Then the third and the oldest went in, and the same happened to him as to the others; he too came away all pensive. When the three kings were all together again they told one another what they had seen. They marvelled very much, and decided to go in all three together. Thus they all entered at the same time into the presence of the Child, and found it with the aspect of its real age namely but thirteen days. Then they adored the Child, and offered it the gold and the frankincense and the myrrh. The Child took all three offerings, and then gave them a closed box. Where upon the three kings went away to return to their own land. . . . After riding several days they resolved to see what the Child had given them. So they opened the box, and found a stone in it. They wondered greatly what it might be. The Child had given it to them as a token that they should abide firm as a rock in the faith that they had just accepted. For, when they had seen the Child take all three offerings, they had concluded that he was God and earthly king and physician and the Child, knowing well that this faith was born in them, had given them the stone to signify that they should remain firm and constant in their faith. The three kings took the stone and threw it into a well, for they knew not wherefore it had been given to them. As soon as the stone was thrown into the well, a flame descended from Heaven and came straight to the well into which the stone had been thrown. Seeing this great marvel, the three kings were all amazed, and repented having thrown the stone into the well, fully realizing now that it had a great and excellent meaning. They straight way took some of that fire and carried it to their country, placing it in a very fine and rich Church of theirs. And they ever keep that fire alight, and adore it as a God; and all the sacrifices and holocausts that they offer, they burn with that fire. If at any time the fire should by chance go out, they have recourse to others of the same faith, who are also fire-worshippers, and obtaining from them some of the fire that burns in their Church, they rekindle it with any other fire than that I have told you of. Often in order to find it, they have to go on a ten days' journey.

This is why the inhabitants of this country worship fire. And I assure you that they are very numerous.

All these things were told Messer Marco Polo by the people of the town. And they are all truth. I will add, too, that one of the three Magi came from Sava, another from Ava, and the third from Cashan.

NOTE: CF. Mis'ar Ibn al Muhalil Abu Dulaf, *Safar Nāmah Abu Dulaf dar Iran dar Sal-i 341 Hijri (Abu Dulaf's Travel Book on Iran in the Year 341 A.H.)*, edited by V. Minorski, translated by A. Tabatabai (Tehran: 1342/1963), pp. 40–42.

IV

Anthony Collins Basil, *Al-MuQaddasi: The Man and His Work, with Selected Passages Translated from the Arabic* (Ann Arbor: University of Michigan, 1974), p. 221.

It is said that in olden times a king of the Mashriq [Khorasan] grew angry with four hundred men of his kingdom, especially at his court, and he ordered them to be taken to a place removed from civilization, a hundred *Farsakhs* away. . . . After a considerable period of time he sent some people to enquire about them and when they arrived, they found them alive, having built huts for themselves, and they saw them fishing for their sustenance; they had also plenty of firewood there. When they returned to the king and told him about this, said he, "What name do they call "meat"? Said they, "Khwar." "And "firewood?" Said they, "Rizm." Said the king, "I have caused them to settle in that erea, so I name it Khwarizm." Moreover, he ordered four hundred Turkish maidens to be brought to them, so that to this day there remains among them resemblance to the Turks.

p. 210.

I heard one of the followers of al-Ma'dani say, "One of the kings of Khorasan ordered his minister to assemble a man from each of five districts of Khorasan, the principal districts. When they assembled the Sijistani spoke and the minister said, "This language is suitable for fighting.' Then he conversed with the Naishapuri and said, "This language is suited for litigation.' Then he spoke with the person from Marv and said, "This language is suited for government ministry.' Then he spoke with the man from Balkh and said, "This language is fit for despatches.' Then the man from Herat spoke, said he, "This language is for the cesspool."

V

H. L. Rabino, *Mazandaran and Astarabad* (London, 1928), p. 16.

From Rasht we followed the road . . . and reached the Gayshadamarda canal. This name means in *Gilak* "dead bride," and the legend is that a young bride, whilst being taken to the bridegroom's house, was drowned at this spot. . . . We crossed the Nawrud, also called Latarud, by the Murghanapurd, "chicken egg bridge." We were told that an old woman spent the best part of her life selling eggs at this crossing and that with her hard earned savings she built this bridge.

VI

Sir John Chardin, *Sir John Chardin's Travels in Persia*, p. 133.

(Local legend regarding the damp weather of Mazandaran)
   Here upon they recount the following Story; That a Courier being one day arriv'd from Mazandaran, at Ispahan, arm'd with a Bow and Sabre, a young lord that was at Court at his first Arrival there, happening to take his Bow into his Hand, to make a Trial of it, as it is usual among them to do, found it so slack, that he said smiling to him, *What is this Mounsieur Courier, you have a Bow a Child can Bend? That may be my Lord*, reply'd he, *but if you are so very strong draw out my sabre.*

p. 146.

   They say, among other things of him [Abbas the Great], that having one Day all his Noblemen round about him at a Feast, he commanded, that the Bottles of Tobacco, which were to be served up to them, should have the Cups belonging to them full of Horse-dung dry'd and pounded, instead of Tobacco. . . . The King asked the Grandees from time to time, *How do you like that Tobacco? It was a Present from my Vizir of Hamaden, who, to reconcile me to taking it sent me the most excellent Tobacco in the World. Each of them answered him, Sire, it is most wonderful Tobacco; there is none that is more exquisitely good.* At length the King, addressing himself to the General of Courtches, who are the ancient Militia of *Persia,* . . . said to him *My Lord I pray you tell me freely, and sincerely, what do you think of this Tobacco? Sire,* reply'd he, *I swear by your sacred Head, it smells like a thousand flowers.* The Kind turned, and looking on them all with Indignation, *Cursed be that Drug, he said, that cannot be discerned from the Dung of Horses.*

VII

John Baptist Tavernier, *The Six Travels of John Baptista Tavernier, Baron of Aubonne, through Turkey and Persia to the Indies, during the Space of Forty Years* (London: Moses Pitt, 1684), p. 167.

The Gaurs would not be thought to give Honour to Fire under the title of Adoration. For they do not account themselves Idolaters, saying that they acknowledge but only one God, Creator of Heaven and Earth, whom they only adore. As for the fire, they preserve it and reverence it, in remembrance of the great Miracle, by which their Prophet was delivered from the Flames. One day being at Kerman, I desir'd to see that Fire, but they answer'd me, they could not permit me. For say they, one day the Kan of Kerman being desirous to see the Fire, not daring to do otherwise, they shew'd it him. He it seems expected to see some extraordinary Brightness; but when he saw no more than what he might have seen in a Kitchen or a Chamber-fire, fell a swearing and spitting upon't as if he had been mad.

Whereupon the Sacred Fire being thus profan'd, flew away in the form of a white Pigeon. The Priests considering then their misfortune, which had happen'd through their own indiscretion, fell to their Prayers with the People, and gave Alms; uponwhich, at the same time, and in the same form the Sacred Fire returned to its place, which makes them so shy to shew it again.

VIII

Thomas Herbert, *Travels in Persia: (1627–1629)* (London, 1928), p. 183.

. . . Albors: a mountain of great fame . . . by reason of that pyre of idol-fire, which (if tradition may be credited) has continued unextinguished for full fifty generations. Furthermore, upon this high mountain it is (say the inhabitants) that Pischyton, eldest son to Gustasp (who in Jakob's day ruled Persia), is, endowed with power of not dying, with thirty other immortal Chyrons who by Zertoost's doom are to continue there till Doomsday. So as, if any could find the place, they may . . . be likewise made immortal.

IX

Jonas Hanway, *An Historical Account of the British Trade over the Caspian Sea, with a Journal of Travels and the Revolutions in Persia*, 2 vols. (London, 1762), pp. 174–175.

The SHAH [Nader Shah] having appointed a certain general as governor of a province, imposed an exorbitant tax on it, to be levied in six months. At the expiration of the time the governor was sent for to the camp, and ordered to produce the account. He did so, but it amounted only to half the sum demanded. The SHAH called him a rascal; and telling him he had stolen the other half of the money, ordered the executioners to bastonade him to death. This man's estate was also confiscated, but all his effects fell very short of the demand. The servants of the deceased were then ordered to come into the SHAH's presence; he enquired of them if there was anything left belonging to their master? They answered ONLY A DOG. He then commanded the dog to be brought before him; and observed that he appeared to be much honester than his master had been; however, that he should be led through the camp from tent to tent, and beaten with sticks, and wherever he expired, the master of such tent should pay the sum deficient. Accordingly the dog was carried to the tents of the ministers successively, who hearing the case, immediately gave sums of money, according to their abilities, to procure the removal of the dog; by which means the whole sum the SHAH demanded was raised in a few hours time.

X

Adam Olearius, *The Voyages and Travels of the Ambassador from the Duke of Holstein*, p. 314.

There are also those, who never cut their Mustachoes, which by that means cover over their Mouth; and this they do in rememberance of their Prophet *Haly*, who wore them in that manner . . . they say *Haly* wore his Mustachoes so, for the following reason: That when *Mahomet* took that voyage to Paradise . . . *Haly* follow'd him. At first they made some difficulty at the gate to let him in, till such time as he told the Porter, that he was *Schir Chodda*, that is, God's Lion. Being got in, he saw that the Angels made *Mahomet* drink of a certain excellent Wine, whereof he was so happy as to have one Goblet presented to him, which he took off, but some drops of the Divine drawght sticking on his Mustachoes, he would never afterwards suffer them to be cut.

p. 255.

There is one [bath] behind the Garden belonging to the King's Palace, which they call *Hamam   Charabe*. It is now half destroy'd, and there is a story told of it, which I conceive pleasant enough to deserve insertion into this Relation. They say, that there lived, heretofore at *Caswin* a very famous Physician, named *Lokman*, a black Arabian, who had acquir'd so great reputation, not only by the Books he had written, but also by many other excellent productions of his understanding, that the Inhabitants have still a very great veneration for his memory. . . . This *Lokman* having attain'd a great age, and being upon his Death bed, sent for his Son, and told him, that he would leave him an inestimable Treasure, and having commanded to be brought him three Glasses, full of certain medicinal waters, he said they had the vertue to raise up a Dead man to life, if they were apply'd before the Body began to corrupt. That, casting upon the Deceas'd the water which was in the first Glasse, the Soul would return into the Body; that, upon the pouring of the second, the Body would stand upright, and that upon the third, the Person would be absolutely alive, and should do all things as before; That however he had very seldom made use of this Experiment, out of a fear of committing a sin, by undertaking to intermeddle with that which is reserv'd to God alone; and that out of the same Consideration, he exhorted him to be very carefull how he made use of it, as being a secret rather to be admir'd, than put often to experience. With these exhortations *Lokman* dying, his Son was very mindfull of the advice he had given him, and pretending the same tendernesse of Conscience as his Father had express'd before him, he receiv'd the Glasses, till he might have occasion to make tryal of them upon himself. Accordingly being at the Point of Death, he commanded a man that had waited on him, to make use of those Glasses, as his Father had taught him. The man having caus'd his Master's body to be brought into the Bath we spoke of before, poured upon it the two first Glasses which wrought the effect, which *Lokman* had promised they should, insomuch that the Master sitting up, and impatient to return to Life, cries out *bris, bris*, that is to say, *pour, pour,* at which words the Fellow was so frightened, that he let the third Glasse fall down to the ground; so that the unfortunate *Lokmansade* was forc'd to lye down again, and take the Journey which all other mortales do. The *Persians* confidently affirm, that, near this ruinous Bath, that Voice of *bris, bris*, is still many times heard. They relate several other stories of this *Lokman*, but I shall forbear any accompt of them, thinking it enough to have produced one, to shew the vanity of all the rest.

XI

James Basset, Persia, *The Land of the Imams*, p. 227.

It is related of one of the Shahs that on visiting the shrine [of Imam Reza] he saw there a blind man. The king inquired how long a time he had been here seeking the recovery of his sight. The man replied "Ten years." Then said the king, "You must be a very bad man; I therefore give you until morning an opportunity for prayer. If by that time the saint has not granted your request, I will take your head off." It is said that Reza was moved with pity for the blind man and restored his sight that very night, and in the morning the Shah gave to him a valuable present.

XII

Samuel Greene Wheeler Benjamin, *Persia and the Persians*, pp. 215–216.

Another story of the evening is one which is widely current in Persia. It may have some mystical relation to the so-called solar myths about which professors Max Muller, Wolf, and others have expended such floods of hypothetical ink. An archer came one on a time from Turkey to Persia with a great renown for strength. He challenged all with the champions of Persia to shoot an arrow farther than he. The Shah was greatly shaken in his mind lest the credit of the Empire should be imperilled on the question of archery. But there came a man from the south, who bade the Shah cease his apprehensions, for he declared himself able to outshoot the world. The day for the contest arrived. The Turkish archer was indeed a wonder, for he shot a shaft to a prodigious distance. But the Persian champion, being a scientific wag, put mercury on his arrow and aimed towards the sun. As the whizzing shaft neared the glowing luminary, the mercury being volatile gave increased momentum to the arrow, which ceased not to speed forward until it reached the banks of Gihoon. Another version of this story states that this contest really took place in order to settle the question of the boundry between Persia and Turan, and that the contestants stood on the summit of Demavend.

Another ingenious and highly characteristic story was told on this occasion, well illustrating the subtile imagination of the cultivated Persian. It is an allegory intended to typify the different effects produced on the mind and nerves by wine, opium, and hashish. Three men, each under the influence of one of these intoxicants, arrived after nightfall at the gate of a city. He who was under the effect of alcohol was furious when he found the gate closed, and vociferated, "Let us burst in the gate at once! I will do it with my sword!" The opium-eater said, "Nay, we will tarry here until sunrise; then the gate will be opened, and we can enter without discomfort." But the hashish eater murmured, with feeble voice, "Neither way is good; because we can steal through the keyhole, as we can make ourselves small."

XIII

Sir Percy Sykes, *Ten Thousand Miles in Persia, or Eight Years in IRAN* (New York: Charles Scribner's Sons, 1902), p. 156.

In the adjacent hills is a shrine in honour of the *Banu-i Fars*, the mother, or more likely the daugher, of Yezdijird. The legend runs that when fleeing from the Arabs, she begged some refreshment of a peasant. He immediately fetched and milked his cow, but the malicious beast kicked over the bowl when filled and the royal fugitive departed thirsty. Until a few years ago, cows were sacrificed at the expence of the Zoroastrians, the killing and eating being done by Mohamedans. The act was evidently retributive, and the sacrifice was only stopped after a reference to Bombay.

Sir Percy Sykes, *Ten Thousand Miles in Persia, or Eight Years in IRAN* (New York: Charles Scribner's Sons, 1902), pp. 413-414.

Ancient Neh, . . . is undoubtedly what is known as Kala Sha'h Duzd . . . legend has it that Sha'h Duzd or King Thief forced Zal to pay tribute, until Rustam grew up, when the overlord was challenged to single combat. All their weapons having been exhausted, they wrestled until, by mutual consent, a halt was made for refreshment. Rustam of subtlety indulged sparingly, but his less careful opponent drank his fill and was easily worsted, thereby sealing his own doom.

XIV

Sir Arnold Wilson, *South West Persia*, p. 37–38.

Lurs and Bakhtiari . . . tell many stories of them [bears]. . . . They account for its intelligence by saying that the first bear was a tribesman who hid himself under a pile of wool in order to avoid entertaining Hazrat Ali, the Patron saint of Persians. His wife excused herself from giving hospitality on the ground that she was a lone woman and as much by custom exempt. But the saint knew better, and called the man out from under the wool, saying "From now on you and your seed need not fear that you will entertain good men. You shall keep your covering: become a bear."

XV

E. Treacher Collins, *In the Kingdom of the Shah* (London: T. Fisher Unwin, 1896), pp. 54–55.

They [vineyards] seem to have existed from very ancient times, and a story, which is well worth quoting, attributes to the famous king Jemsheed the discovery of wine. He was immoderately fond of grapes, and desired to preserve some, which were placed in a large vessel and lodged in a vault for further use. When the vessel was opened the grapes had fermented; their juice was so acid that the king believed it must be poison. He had some bottles filled with it, and "Poison" written on them. These were placed in his room. It happened that one of his favorite ladies was affected with nervous headache. The pain distracted her so much that she took a bottle of the fermented juice and swallowed its contents. The wine (for such it had become) overpowered the lady, who fell into a sound sleep, and awoke much refreshed. Delighted with the remedy, she repeated the doses so often that the king's "poison" was all drunk. He soon discovered this and forced the lady to confess what she had done. A quantity of wine was made and Jamsheed and all his court drank the beverage, which from the manner of its discovery, is to this day known in Persia by the name Zeher-e khoosh, or "the delightful poison".

XVI

George N. Curzon, *Persia and the Persian Question* (London: Longmans, Green and Co., 1892), 2 vols., vol. 1, p. 397.

. . . on one occasion, according to a well-known story, Fath Ali Shah found an honest critic in his Poet Laureate. "What do you think of my verses?" said the king. "May I be your sacrifice, I think they are great rubbish," was the frank rejoinder. "Take the donkey to the stable," shouted the indignant Shah; and the order was obeyed. A little while later the King sent for the poet again, and read out to him some more of his own compositions. The poet without a word, began to walk away. "Where are you going?" cried the Shah. "Back to the stables," answered the fearless Laureate. It is to the credit of the King that he was so pleased with the repartee that he released the poet, and ordered his mouth to be stuffed with sugar-candy as a mark of his extreme approbation.

XVII

Edward Stack, *Six Months in Persia* (London: Sampson Low, Marston, Searle, and Rivington, 1882), 2 vols., vol. I pp. 166–167.

In the evening I went out with some of the gilded youth of Kaha, to see an old fort on the top of the hill some 500 feet high. . . . The fort, they said, belonged to a Kafir monarch, and was taken by the Commander of the Faithful (*Amir ul Muminin*), but they evidently had no clear notion as to who the latter sacred personage might be. In the cliff below the fort there is a small cave, which is credited with endlessness . . . , and is further remarkable for harboring a dragon (azhdaha) who guards the buried treasure of the deceased Kafir, and comes down every Friday night to drink of the stream in the valley (usually dry), and to kill and devour any man he may happen to meet; this done he returns to his cave.

XVIII

Charles Edward Stewart. *Through Persia in Disguise, with Reminiscences of the Indian Mutiny . . . by Colonel Charles E. Stewart, ed. from his Diaries by Basil Stewart* (London: G. Routledge and Sons Ltd., 1911), pp. 318–320.

THE COBBLER ASTROLOGER

A certain cobbler, who lived at Ispahan and was no longer young, married a young and ambitious wife. She was not at all satisfied with her position as a cobbler's wife, but wished to be a fine lady and gave out that her husband was a noted astrologer, and could foretell events. The news of this astrologer reached the ears of the Shah's daugher, who, having lost her jewels, one day when the cobbler had brought her some shoes which he had repaired, told him the story of her loss, and asked him to tell her where the jewels were. While the poor man was meditating very unhappily on the difficulty of his position, he saw a rent in the Princess's skirt, and said, "Look at the rent," to call her attention to it. The Princess said at once "You are quite right; when I went to the bath, I did place my jewels in the rent in the wall of the bathroom," and she went there and found her jewels. She gave a large reward to the cobbler, and it was noised abroad what a wonderful astrologer the old man was. Amongst others, the Shah heard the story.

Shortly afterwards a robbery took place in the palace, the thieves having carried off a large part of the Shah's treasures.

The cobbler was sent for, and the Shah told him that he must tell him the names of the robbers, and enable him to capture them, and obtain the return of his jewels, that if he did not do so within forty days, he would be executed. The poor cobbler went home in utter despair, and told his young wife this story, saying "See what you have done for me by saying I am an astrologer." The cobbler, to keep count of the number of days he had to live, put forty date-fruits into a jar, and determined to eat one every evening. That night, before going to bed, he took the jar, ate one date, and said, "That is one, and there are thirty-nine left." The robbers had heard of the Shah's threat, and one of them was outside watching. When he heard the cobbler say, "There is one, and there are thirty-nine remaining," he thought that the cobbler was an astrologer, and had discovered there were forty thieves engaged in the robbery; so he went and told the story to his comrades, and said, "The astrologer knows all about it, come one of you and listen with me to-morrow." So the next night two robbers were listening, when the cobbler, before going to bed, ate the second date, and said, "There are two, and there are thirty-eight left," the robbers were convinced that he knew all about them. The following night there were three of the robbers watching, and when they heard the cobbler say, "There are three, and thirty-seven are left," they became more than ever convinced that the cobbler was an astrologer, and before the forty days were finished, they felt sure that the cobbler knew all about it, and would inform the Shah, so they thought it best to confess their crime to the cobbler, and tell the whole story, and where the treasure was concealed.

The cobbler informed the Shah, who seized the treasure, and rewarded the cobbler magnificently.

XIX

J. P. Ferrier, *Caravan Journeys and Wanderings in Persia, Afganistan, Turkistan and Beloochistan: with Historical Notices of the Countries Lying between Russia and India Translated by Capt. William Jesse, edited by H. D. Seymour* (Karachi: Oxford University Press, 1976), pp. 102–103.

This halt [Zaffouroonee] was at a wretched village protected by a mud wall . . . a ruined carvansarai-shah, the largest in Persia, is in front of it. Tradition says that in former days there were 1700 rooms within its walls, also baths, a mosque, and handsome gardens. I suspect that tradition is, in this case, somewhat of a romancer—not an uncommon thing though the ruins that surround it certainly occupy a considerable space. The Cufic characters and arabesques upon various parts of the building denote its Arabic origin, but the Persians, in their love for the marvellous, give it the following.

A Persian, they say, finding an immense treasure on this spot, made a vow to employ it in good works, and the first was the construction of the caravanserai. The foundations were just finished, when a merchant with three *Kharvars*—nearly a ton— of saffron, came that way. He had left Khorassan with his purchase, and travelled to Bagdad, in the hope of disposing of it on advantageous terms; but trade was bad; he saw in perspective a certain loss, and when he arrived in the city of the Caliphs he thought it preferable to return to his own country with his merchandise, and wait for better times. Halting at Zaffouroonee, the rich man saw and addressed him thus.: "Friend, what makes thee look so sad?" "Sad" replied the merchant, "I have enough to make me sad," and related the history of the bootless errand he had been on. "Oh, is that the cause of your grief? Here, men," said he to his masons, "shoot the saffron on the ground and mix it with the mortar." This was done and he paid the astonished merchant three *Kharvars* of precious stones for his three *Kharvars* of saffron. This is a good specimen of a Persian tale, and, absurd as it is, it finds believers amongst them, even the educated. To seem to doubt its truth might bring one into trouble. "See" said a pilgrim, turning to his companions, and taking up a brick, "they have quite the colour and smell of saffron." There was no arguing with them after this, especially as the bricks were as red as cochineal.

X X

Sir John Malcolm, *Sketches of Persia*, vol. I., p. 171.

The Shaikh-ool Islam . . . illustrated his arguments with anecdotes of religious and learned men, of which I shall give those that struck me as the happiest. "The celebrated Abu Yusuph," he said, "who was chief judge of Baghdad in the reign of the Caliph Hadee, was a very remarkable instance of that humility which distinguishes true wisdom. . . . It is related of this judge," said the Shaikh-ool-Islam, "that on one occasion after a very patient investigation of facts he declared that his knowledge was not competent to decide upon the case before him," "Pray, do you expect," said a pert courtier, who heard this declaration, "that the Caliph is to pay your ignorance?" "I do not" was the mild reply; "the Caliph pays me, and well, for what I do know; if he were to attempt to pay me for what I do not know, the treasures of this empire would not suffice."

vol. II, p. 103.

A Persian of our party, called Meerza Ibrahim, who had been at Demavand, increased our curiosity by a detail of the wonders we should see when we visited that place. "Amongst others," said he, "is the cave that was once the habitation of the Deev-e-Seffeed, who was slain by Roostem; and if fortunate," he added, "you may catch a glimpse of the Deev's daughter, whose dwelling is on the point of an inaccessible rock, at the edge of which she now and then appears; and is reported, not withstanding her age, which cannot be less than two thousand four hundred years, to be active with her distaff, and looking as well as ever."

"Higher up the mountain," continued our informant "amid rocks and snow, which forbid all mortal approaches dwells Zohak, the most wicked of kings, surrounded by a court of magicians and sorcerers; this at least is the belief of the worshippers of fire."

XXI

Edward Scott Waring, *A Tour To Sheeraz by the Route of Kazroon and Feerozabad* (London: W. Blumer and Co., 1807), pp. 126–127.

They have a story of an inhabitant of Tung-stear (to the southward of Bushire), finding a watch which someone had dropped. He held it in his hand till he heard it beating, which he thought to be extraordinary, as it neither walked nor moved. He put it to his ear, and heard it more distinctly. After considering some time he cried out, "A qoormsaq too kojaee darbia" (Wretch, where are you? Come out!) and threw it in a passion on the ground. The watch still went; he then very deliberately took up a large stone, and broke it into pieces. The noise ceased, and congratulating himself upon it, he cries out "Akir kooshteed," (Have I killed you!?)

XXII

Lady Mary Leonora (Waulfe) Sheil, *Glimpses of Life and Manners in Persia* (New York: Arna Press, 1973), first edition 1856, pp. 93–94.

By way of illustrating its [Turkish language] harshness and fitness for command, the Persians say that when Adam was doomed to quit Paradise, the Angel Gabriel conveyed the commands from heaven to the first sinner in Persian, but without effect, for Adam refused to obey. Gabriel then tried Arabic, Sanskrit, and all other languages now known, without result, till, in despair and ire, he roared in Turkish "Kiopekoghlee, chick boorden" (be off, you dog!) on which Adam scampered off without further delay.

XXIII

Sir Henry Layard, *Early Adventure*, vol. II, pp. 224–227.

Saleh who was a skillful story-teller, and very ingenious in inventing explanations to satisfy inquiries with regard to my motive for visiting ancient ruins and wandering in foreign lands, held forth to a curious and attentive audience until a late hour in the night. . . . He then related how he had accompanied some English travellers to the city of Shapur, which he described as being between Shiraz and Bushire. There they discovered figures sculptured on the rocks, amongst which Shapur himself was to be seen, with the king of India prostrate under the belly of his horse. Beneath was some writing which they interpreted. It stated that the king of India had surrounded Shapur for many months in his capital, but all his efforts to capture it having failed, he was thinking to raise the siege, when the Persian monarch, hearing that such was his intention, collected all the provisions contained in the city together, and after setting apart sufficient for the nourishment of its inhabitants for three days, threw the remainder from the walls into the river. The strategem succeeded. The king of India, believing that there could be no scarcity where there was so much waste, made preparations to retire with his army. It happened that the daughter of Shapur, having seen the king from the battlements of her father's castle, had fallen in love with him. She therefore wrote on a piece of paper, "O king, why do you abandon the siege of this city? Know that Shapur has destroyed his provisions to deceive you, and that in three days it must surrender," and placed it in a casket which she threw into the river. The king of India perceived the casket as it was floating down the stream, and ordered it to be brought to him. Having read the message of the daughter of Shapur, he invested the city more closely. In three days, as she had predicted, it surrendered.

Shapur escaped, but his daughter remained and was taken to wife by the king of India. On their wedding night she was restless and could not sleep. On being asked the reason by her husband, she replied that there was a cotton-seed in the mattress which incommoded her. "Where, then did you sleep," he inquired, "when in your home, that so small a thing should have disturbed your rest?" "On my father's breast," she answered. "How then, O lady," exclaimed the king, "could you have betrayed him whose love for you was so great for one whom you had only seen from the castle wall?" Having further upbraided her for her perfidy, he caused her to be bound to a mule, which, being set free, galloped off to the mountains, and she was never heard of more. Shapur, having collected together his followers, returned to make war against the king of India, whom he ultimately overthrew and captured. But, in consideration of the punishment which his prisoner had inflicted upon his unnatural daughter, he spared his life, and gave him his liberty after compelling him to pass under the belly of his horse. The sculptures which the Feringhi had discovered represented, Saleh concluded, this incident in the history of the great Persian monarch.

pp. 258–260. The following is an example of versions of the same narrative being reported by different travellers:

The Lurs have numerous stories about bears, who they believe are endowed with intelligence far superior to that of other animals, and to have almost human habits and feelings. . . . The origin of the bear, they said, was the following. Hazret Ali, the son-in-law of the Prophet, travelling in disguise and weary, approached a tent to rest. Its owner who was a sordid wretch, seeing a stranger coming and wishing to shirk the duties of hospitality, hid himself under a heap of wool--for it was the time of sheepshearing--and desired his wife to tell the traveller that her husband had gone to the mountains, and that, being a woman and alone, she could not receive him as her guest. She did as she was bidden, but the Vali of God knew that the man had concealed himself. Addressing him, "Rise, O bear!" he exclaimed, "and dwell henceforth in the woods!" The wool adhered to the inhospitable Lur; he lost his speech, fled to the mountains and became the first bear.

pp. 264–265.

When passing the next night in an Arab tent, I met a man from Shustar, who related several anecdotes to me, amongst which was the following version of the story of Midas and his asses' ears. King Shapur had horns, of which he was greatly ashamed. Fearing that his subjects might learn the fact, and that his dignity would be thus compromised, he ordered every barber who shaved his head to be put to death immediately afterwards, so that the secret might not transpire. At length, one who was about to experience this fate succeeded in persuading the king to spare his life, and to employ no one else, so that the secret, which he took a solemn oath not to reveal, might remain with him alone. For three years he kept his oath; but, at last the secret becoming too heavy a load for him to bear, to release himself from it he went to the mouth of a well and called out, "O well I know that king Shapur has horns."

Shortly afterwards a shepherd passing by the well cut a reed growing at its edge to make himself a pipe to pipe to his sheep. The first time he played upon it, instead of music there only came from it the words, "Shapur has horns! Shapur has horns!" The king soon learnt that his secret had been betrayed and sent for the barber, who confessed that although he had divulged it to no one, according to his oath, he had been compelled in consequence of the intolerable burden of keeping it, to deliver himself of it at the mouth of a well. Shapur accepted his excuse and graciously pardoned him.

pp. 268–269. Several versions of the following narrative are recorded in Sayyad Abulqasim Anjavi Shirazi's collection *Mardum va Shāhnāmah (People and Shah Namah)* (Tehran: Intishārāt Amir Kabir, 1354/1975), pp. 107–125.

One of the Baktiari, who was seated with us round the fire in the evening, related the following tale. The Musjedi-Suleiman was the "Pa Takt" of that great and wise king. There all the monarchs of the earth came to his salam or audience, except Rustem, who, jealous of the renown of the prophet-king, resolved to try his strength in single combat with him. Accordingly, he mounted his renowned charger, Raksh, and took the road to Soloman's capital. As he drew near to it, he met a beautiful youth riding a milk-white steed. This was Hazrat Ali, Amir-el Mumenin, the Commander of the Faithful. But he was disguised, and was not recognized by Rustem, who, addressing him, asked the way to the city. "I am the cup-bearer of King Soloman," replied Ali, "and come from the foot of his throne!" "And I" exclaimed the hero, "am Rustem, and defy your master, whom I will this day deprive of his kingdom." "First," answered the son-in-law of Mahomet, "contend with me, and if I am vanquished do as you propose."

Thereupon Rustem seized the youth by his girdle, counting upon an easy victory over such a stripling. But he laboured in vain until evening to throw him, the blood flowing from his eyes, nostrils, and mouth in consequence of the violence of his efforts. As night approached he ceased to wrestle with Ali, who lifting him from the ground hurled him so high into the air that he reached the fourth heaven, when he fell heavily to the earth again. "If such are the servants of Soloman," exclaimed Rustem, recovering from the effects of his fall, "What must the strength of Solomon himself be?" and returning to his own kingdom, ever afterwards paid tribute to the great king.

B. Narratives recorded by philologists as dialect specimens.

I

D. L. R. Lorimer, *The Phonology of the Bakhtiari, Badakhshani, and Madaglashti Dialects of Modern Persian* (London: Royal Asiatic Society Prize Publication Fund, vol. VI, 1922), pp. 171–172.

A certain man had two sons. The younger said to his father: "father, give me that which is due to me." Thereupon the father divided his property up between his sons. Some days later the younger son gathered his belongings together and journeyed off to a distant country. There he wasted his substance in riotous living. When he had dissipated the whole of it a severe famine fell on that country and he got into great straits. He went to one of the men of that country and entered into partnership with him, and the man sent him out into the desert to feed his swine, and he was glad to eat the same food that the swine ate, and no one gave him anything.

Then he thought within himself, and said to himself: "How many servants are there in my father's house who receive pay and have more than enough of bread, while I am dying of hunger. Now I will arise and go to my father and say: "O father, I have sinned against God and against you and I am not worthy to be called your son, now support me in any fashion as one of your servants.'"

Then he arose and went to his father. Now when he was a long way off his father saw him, and pity came into his heart and he ran and caught him in his arms and kissed him.

II

V. Ivanov, "Two Dialects Spoken in the Central Persian Desert," *Journal of the Royal Asiatic Society* (1926): 418–419.

There was a man, he had a donkey. His donkey, however, was old and thin, and his back was ulcerated. The man wanted to sell his ass. He took it to bazars, but no customer wanted to buy it. The man became sad. Later in the day he returned to his house. He wife asked him, saying: hast thou sold the ass or not? He replied: no, I have not sold it. (The woman) said: dost thou know what we shall do? This woman said: there is a nice cat. Thou take it to bazars. Say: this donkey is valued at three farthings. Take the ass to bazars, say: I sell it for three farthings, and the cat goes with it. This donkey costs three farthings, the cat costs six tumans. Whosoever takes the ass must also take the cat, I do not sell (them) separately. When morning dawned the man saddled his ass. The cat he also tied on one side. He went

to bazars and shouted: I sell this donkey at three farthings.
People began to crowd.

III

V. Ivanov, "Notes on Khorasani Kurdish," *Journal of Asiatic
Society Bengal* (1927):218–219.

There were 'Ali the fool and 'Ali the wise, both were
brothers. 'Ali (the wise) once said to "Ali the fool: "go to the
village, bring me some bread from the house." 'Ali the fool
started, went to the village. He took an ovenful of bread, then
went to his tree, got a stick, and went back. Suddenly, he looked
behind him and noticed his own shadow. Saw what appeared to
him to be another man. He said to it: "art thou hungry?" (And
he himself?) said: "eh!" He took two loaves and threw them to
it. Then he went half a farsakh, looked behind him and again
saw his shadow. He said: "poor man, he is still hungry! Will give
him a loaf." He took (another loaf) and threw it to it. (So) he
wasted his bread. Having reached his brother, 'Ali the wise,
asked: "hast though brought the bread?" He replied: "there was
a man on the road who was hungry, so I have given it to him to
eat." 'Ali the wise said: "what a (foolish) thing thou hast done!"
(He) said (further): "remain here, and I will go to the village to
bring the bread." 'Ali, the fool, said: "go!"
　　'Ali, the fool, began to drive the herd. He brought it to a
spring. There was a mulberry tree. 'Ali climbed the tree and
shook off the berries, and on whatever sheep the berries fell he
took and ate them. He kissed the head of (every such sheep).
But those on whom no berries fell he killed. Then he moved the
herd from that place. They went to a river-bed, and he allowed
the sheep to drink. Whatever he tried to do to get the herd from
that stream-bed, they would not go. He said: "o you scoundrels!
You want to soak your shoes in the water." He took out his knife

from his pocket and cut the hoofs from the legs of the sheep. Those animals died.

'Ali, the wise, arrived from the village and asked: "'Ali, where are the sheep? What hast thou done with them?" He replied: "they did not obey me, so I killed them." 'Ali, the wise, said: "o, may fire fall into the tent of thy father! Come, let us go to the village!" So they came to the village. They had a good cow. ('Ali, the wise) said: "dear brother, take this cow and sell it." 'Ali, the fool, replied: "all right, no harm in it."

He took the cow and went. He walked about two farsakhs from the village and came across a lizard. He said to the lizard: "wilt thou not buy a cow?" There was a lizard on the top of the rock, it moved its head. 'Ali the fool said: "tomorrow at noon I will come, then thou wilt give me ten tumans." Again the lizard moved its head. 'Ali walked back to his village. 'Ali, the wise, asked the brother: "what hast thou done with the cow?" He said: "I have sold it." The brother asked: "how much was given to thee? To whom has thou sold it?" 'Ali, the fool, said: "I have given it to a lizard." 'Ali, the wise, said: "may thy house be ruined! With this thou hast done the same as with the sheep. Hurry up, thou ruined one, let us go!"

So both started on their way. They came to the place of the lizard. They saw a lizard on the rock. 'Ali, the wise, said: "thou ruined one, thou hast no sense. In what grave can this lizard have money? Come on. This year thou wilt make me die of hunger." 'Ali, the fool, said to the lizard: "bring, give me money!" The lizard crawled into its hole. He then took a spade and digged out the hole of the lizard, hit it with a stick and killed it. Then he returned to the village.

IV

V. Ivanov, "The Dialect of Gozarkhon in Alamut," *Acta Orientalia* (1929):367.

Fox made a habit of devouring every year the Lion's cubs. A year he went to catch the Lion's cubs and to devour (them). (But) the Lion appeared himself to catch the Fox. Then the Fox said pretendingly: I did not devour thy cubs. (But) I (can) go now (and) bring thy enemy. Let me go. The Lion said: wilt thou go at once to bring my enemy? The Fox said: yes. I will go at once (and) bring thy enemy. The Fox went. As he went, he saw on the road that the Bear was just coming from that side. He came before the Bear. Said: salam 'alaykum. (The Bear) replied: *'alaykum salam.* (The Fox) said: Mr. Bear, I have something to tell you. (The Bear) said: well, what is it, tell (me). (The Fox) said: the Lion wants to give you the governorship of Mazandaran. (The Bear) said: where is the Lion? (Perhaps) he will give the governorship of Mazandaran to thee? (The Fox) said: Mr. Bear, when we go to the Lion, whatever he asks from thee, say "yes." They went to the Lion. The Fox said pretendingly: now I have brought thy enemy. The Lion asked: Mr. Bear, didst thou devour my cubs every year? The Bear replied: yes. Three times he asked: didst thou devour my cubs?- and the Bear replied: yes. On the fourth time the Lion jumped and caught him. He caught his skin on the head, and tore it. Then the Fox, standing farther aside, said (to the Bear): Mr. Bear, I congratulate you on the robe of honour which Mr. Lion has granted you for the governorship of Mazandaran. Take it now.

V

V. Ivanov, "Persian as Spoken in Birjand," *Journal of the Asiatic Society of Bengal* 24 (1928):266-267.

Once upon a time there was a king who had three sons: two were completely blind, and the third had no eyes. The one who was blind came before his father, and said: father, give me rifle, I want to go out hunting. (The king) said: go into the clothing room, there are three rifles: two of them are broken, and the third has no stock. The son took the last one, went out to the fields. He saw three crows lying down, two of them were dead, the third had no breath. He took up the one which had no breath, brought it before his father, and said: father, give me a cauldron, I want to cook this crow. The king said: in the workshop there are three cauldrons, two of them broken, and the third is without a bottom. The son came, filled the cualdron with water, and then placed it over the fire, putting the crow into it. Then he put on more fuel. He put so much fuel that the bones of the crow melted, the flesh remaining raw as it was. Then he began to eat it. He ate so much that the folds of his coat burst, though his stomach did not feel anything. Then he came before his father, and said: father, I am thirsty, think of (giving me) water. The king said: go into such and such a garden, there are three streams, two of them are dry, the third has not a drop. The son went to the stream that had not a drop, and began to swallow water. He drank so much that he could not lift his head.

VI

Ann. K. S. Lambton, *Three Persian Dialects* (London: The Royal Asiatic Society, 1938), p. 11.

A peasant came to the city. He was going along in the bazaar. He reached the shop of a confectioner. Confectionary of different kinds was set out in the shop. This confectioner was sitting and looking. The peasant thought that the confectioner was blind. He went (forward) quietly. The peasant held his two fingers before his (the confectioner's) eyes. The confectioner said to him, "Why did you do this?" The peasant said, "I thought you were blind." "I am not blind; I see." The peasant said, "If you see why do you not eat?"

p. 29.

The door of a man's house was stolen. He went and pulled out the door of the mosque and put it on his shoulder. He was taking it to his house, someone said to him, "Why have you pulled down the door of the house of God?" He said, "The door of my house has been stolen; I do not know the thief; God knows the thief, let him go and take the door of his house from my thief."

p. 61.

A man had a guest, and he brought supper for his guest. He laid it before him. He went out to bring water. When he came (back), he saw the guest had eaten all there was. He said "Sir, eat." He said, "What shall I eat? There is not anything for me to eat." The master of the house said, "How, is there nothing? (There is) the spoon and tray and plate and table and chair; my house is ruined because I have brought you, O son of a burnt father, to my house as a guest."

VII

Georg Morgenstierne, "Stray Notes on Persian Dialects," *Norsk Tidsskrift for Sprogvidenskap* 19 (1960):99–100.

Two thieves arrived together at a spring. One of them was called Wise, the other Fool. They agreed to go thieving. One of them went, took out his ass, loaded a sack on it, and went into the bazzar. He stole bottles in the glass-blower's shop, and loaded them on his ass. But the ass brayed. They caught him, that is the watchmen arrested him. Night fell, and they kept him in custody. His comrade, the wise thief, had gone and had dug a trench. He had entered the king's treasury to steal. At last, with enormous efforts, he had penetrated under the king's palace, very slowly. He made a hole with his pick-axe. He saw: "Here is the king's house, and the king is asleep in his bed". He put his head out, and saw that there was no treasure there, but the king was asleep. At that moment he saw that a monkey, with a sword in its hand, was the king's sentinel. A white sheet covered the king's face. An ant tumbled down from the ceiling, and fell on the king's breast. The monkey uttered a cry. It drew the sword to cut the ant into two pieces. The wise thief raised a cry: "Why (are you doing so)? Watch your hand, the king is being killed." The king awoke from his sleep and said: "What is it?" He answered: "I am a thief, I have come to break into your treasury. But your good fortune was supreme, and I put my head out (of the hole at the right moment). The monkey your sentinel, wanted to kill the ant, in order that it should cause you no harm. But you would have been (cut) into two pieces by the sword. The king quickly rose and seized the thief. He kissed both his cheeks. He said: "You were my Good Fortune. I have bestowed my kingdom upon you. My life was only to last until now, but you have rendered me to life." He placed him on the throne in his own place. Next day the sun rose and the night-watch brought the thief from the glass-blower into the king's audience hall. The wise thief saw him. He said: "This is the foolish thief." At once he made him lay down, and took some sticks. (The Wise Thief) said: Strike him down, let him die under the stick. Because he was a fool, and did not listen to me." It was finished.

VIII

Oskar Mann, *Kurdisch-Persische Forschungen: Die Mundarten von Khunsâr, Mahallāt, Natānz, Nāyin, Sāmnân, Sîvānd und sô-kohrfld* Bond 1, Abteilung 3 (Berlin und Leipzig, 1926), p. 161.

Eines Tages ging Mulla Nasruddin in ein Seminar. Er sah, das einem Studenten ein Kran ins Wasser gefallen ist. Der Student tat den Stock ins Wasser, das der Kran an ihm haft und herauskomme. Mulla Nasruddin begann zu lachen. Er sagte: "Ihr Studenten seid Esel, und da sagen die Leute, das die Mulla's Esel

seien. He, Eselsmann, mach die Spitze des Stockes mit deinem
Speichel feucht! Dann tu den Stock ins Wasser, das der Kran an
ihm hafte und herauskomme!"

IX

Gilbert Lazard, "Textes en Tāleši de Māsule" *Studia Iranica*
(1979):51–53.

Il y avait un frère et une soeur. Le nom du frère était
Mahmud. Ils étaient bergers et demeuraient dans la montagne
avec leur troupeau. Ce garçon avait une fiancée. Chaque soir il
allait jouer avec sa fiancée. La maison de sa fiancé était très
loin. Un soir il va jouer avec sa fiancée. (litt. au jeu de fiancée).
Il laissait sa soeur toute seule à la maison. Sa soeur était
couchée.

Tout à coup elle voit quatre hommes armés de fusils
arriver près de leur troupeau. La jeune fille se lève et dit:
"Qu'allez-vous faire?" Les voleurs disent: "Ne parle pas ou (litt.
car) nous te tuerons; nous devons emmener ce troupeau". La
jeune fille voit qu'elle (litt. elle-même) est seule; quant à son
frère, il est parti jouer avec sa fiancée. Elle [se] dit: "Que puis-je
faire pour que mon frère sache que des voleurs sont venus et
vont emmener notre troupeau?"

Tout à coup elle a une idée: "Il serait bon que j'alerte
mon frère avec la flûte". Elle va trouver les voleurs et dit: "Tant
que je ne joue pas de la flûte pour notre troupeau, [les bêtes] ne
se lèvent pas. Je vais passer devant vous, jouer de la flûte et le
troupeau me suivra. Allons!" Les voleurs acceptent; ils disent:
"Joue de la flûte. La jeune fille prend la flûte et joue (litt. chante)
sur (litt. dans) la flûte:

> "Mahmud, viens, Mahmud, viens.
> Le troupeau est parti, le troupeau est parti.
> Le troupeau avec le chien est parti.

> Cent trente agneaux sont partis.
> La laine de quarante moutons est partie.
> Le chien avec la chaîne est parti.
> Le boeuf avec le bât est parti.
> Le peigne avec la laine cardée est parti.
> La tent avec l'occupant(e) est partie".

Son frère Mahmud était assis avec sa fiancée dans la maison. Tout à coup il entendit la flûte résonner. Il écouta et vit qu'elle disait:

> "Mahmud, viens . . ."

Il comprit que des voleurs allaient emmener son troupeau et que sa soeur l'appelait avec la flûte.

Aussitôt il prend son bâton, accourt (litt. vient à la course) et rejoint les voleurs. Il se bat avec eux. Il casse la tête à deux ou trois. Les voleurs voient qu'il est très brave. Ils laissent là le troupeau et s'enfuient. Mahmud [les] poursuit très loin jusqu'à ce qu'il les culbute par-dessus la montagne. [Puis] il [re]vient chez lui.

X

Arthur Christensen, *Contributions à la dialectologie iranienne.* (Cobenhavn: Det kgl. Danske videnskabernes selskab. Historisk-filologiske Meddelelser, 1930), p. 297.

Un Européen, qui habitait la Perse, livra dix moutons à son domestique avec l'ordre d'aller les présenter à l'ami de l'Européen. Le domestique prit un mouton pour lui-même et mena les neuf autres à l'ami de son maître avec une lettre dans laquelle [le maître] avait écrit: "Je t'envoie dix moutons; prends-les comme un dépôt". L'[autre] Européen lut la lettre et remarqua qu'on y avait écrit "dix moutons". Il compta les moutons et constata qu'il n'y en avait que neuf. Il dit au domestique: "Il devrait y avoir dix moutons; pourquoi n'y en a-t-il que neuf?" Le domestique dit: "Que dirai-je, Monsieur? en voilà tout ce qu'il y a". L'homme dit: "Mais enfin, on a écrit dans la lettre "dix moutons", et voilà qu'il n'y en a que neuf. "Que dirai-je, Monsieur?" reprit le domestique, "ce n'est pas ma faute qu'il a écrit "dix"." L' Européen pensa, que ce domestique ne savait peut-être pas combien est dix et combien neuf. Il appela dix de ses domestiques à lui et dit au domestique de son ami. "Compte ceux-ci et vois combien il y en a". Le domestique dit: "Voilà dix personnes". Puis le maître dit à ses propres domestiques: "Que chacun saisisse un mouton!" Chacun des domestiques saisit un mouton, mais un d'eux resta les mains vides. Le maître dit au domestique [de son ami]: "Vois-tu que ces neuf hommes tiennent chacun un mouton, mais que celui-là seul n'en a pas?" Le domestique répondit: "Que dirai-je, Monsieur? Ce n'est pas ma faute: ces neuf personnes ont été adroites, et ont pris chacun un mouton, mais celui-là seul a été paresseux et n'a pas pu ensaisir un."

p. 299.

Un homme alla dans un café et commanda du café. Quand on lui apporta le café, et qu'il avança la main pour prendre la cuillère et la mettre dedans, il vit la queue d'une souris. Il tira, et une souris morte apparut de dedans la tasse. Il dit au cafetier: "Pourquoi as-tu jeté une souris morte dans la tasse?" Le cafetier répondit: "Tu n'as donné que deux chahis; veux-tu qu' [à ce prix] un chameau sorte de dedans?"

Bibliography

Abolhamd, Abdolhamid. *Bibliographie française de civilisation iranienne, par Abdolhamid Abolhamd et Nasser Pakdaman*, 3 vols. Tehran: Tehran University Publications, 1972-1974.

Abu Dulaf, Mis'ar Ibn al-Muhalil. Safarnāmah-yi *Abu Dulaf dar Irān dar Sāl-i 341 Hijri* (*Travel Accounts of Abu Dulaf in Iran in 341 A. H.*), edited by V. Minorsky, translated by A. Tabatabai. Tehran: n.p., 1342/1963.

Afshar, Iraj. *Fihrist-i Maqālālt-i Fārsi (Index Iranicus)*, 2 vols. Tehran: Tehran University Publications, 1961.

————. *Fihrist Nāmah-yi Kitābshināsihā-yi Irān* (*A Bibliography of Bibliographies on Iranian Studies.*) Tehran: Faculty of Letters, University of Tehran, 1963.

————. *Rāhnāma-yi Tahqiqāt-i Irāni* (*A Guide to Iranian Studies.*) Tehran: Markaz-i Barrasi va Mu'arrafi Farhang-i Iran, 1970.

Ahmad, Nafis. *Muslim Contribution to Geography*. Lahor: Sh. Muhammad Ashraf, 1972.

Al-Ahmad, Jalal. *Awrāzān*. Tehran: Kitabkhanah Danish, 1333/1954.

————. *Durr-i Yatim-i Khalij, Jazirah-yi Khark*. Tehran: Kitabkhanah Danish, 1339/1960.

————. "Hidayat-i *Buf-i Kur*" ("Hidayat of the *Blind Owl*.") In *'Ilm va Zindagi* 1: 1 (1330/1951), reprinted in Jalal Al-Ahmad, *Haft*

Maqālah (*Seven Articles.*) Tehran: Intishārāt-i Amir Kabir, 1357/1978, pp. 3–25.

———. *Tātnishinha-yi Buluk-i Zahra.* Tehran: Danish, 1337/1958.

Ali, S. M. tr. *Arab Geography; Being the Translation of Section II of M. Reinaud's Introduction Générale à la Géographie des Orientaux* (Géographie d'Abulf eda, tome i). Aligarh: Institute of Islamic Studies, Muslim University, 1960.

Amini, Amir Quli. *Folklore-i Irān: Dāstānhā-yi Amsāl (Iranian Folklore: The Stories of Proverbs.*) Isfahan: Chāpkhanah Isfahān, 1333/1954.

———. *Si Afsānah az Afsānah-ha-yi Mahalli Isfahan (Thirty Folk Narratives from Isfahan.*) Tehran: n. p., 1343/1964.

Anjavi Shirazi, Abulqasim. *Farhang-i Mardum va Tarz-i Girdāvari va Nivishtan-i ān (Folklore, and the Methodology of Collecting and Recording it.*) Tehran: Chāpkhānah Vizārat-i 'Ittilā'āt, 1968. First Edition, 1960.

———. *Mardum va Shahnamah (People and Shah Namah,*) 2 vols. Tehran: Intishārāt-i Amir Kabir, 1354/1975.

———. *Masal va Tamsil (Proverbs and the Stories of Proverbs.*) Tehran: Intishārāt Amir Kabir, 1352/1973.

———. *Qissah-ha-yi Irani (Iranian Folk Narratives),* 3 vols. Tehran: Intisharat-i Amir Kabir, vol. I: 1352/1973, vol. II: 1353/1974, vol. III 2535/1976.

Arberry, Arthur J. *British Contribution to Persian Studies.* Edinburgh: Longmans, Green and Co., 1942.

Arnold, Arthur. *Through Persia by Caravan,* 2 vols. London: Tinsley Brothers, 1877.

Arnold, Sir T. W. "Arab Travellers and Merchants, A. D. 1000–1500." In *Travel and Travellers of Middle Ages* edited by Arthur Percival Newton, pp. 88–103. New York: Alfred A. Knopf, 1926.

Asmussen, J. P. "Remarks on Some Iranian Folk-tales Treating of Magic Objects, Especially AT 564." *Acta Orientalia* 28: 3–4 (1965): 220–243.

Babazadah, Shahla. *Fihrist-i Tusifi-yi Safarnamah-ha-yi Ālmāni-yi Mujud dar Kitabkhanah-yi Milli-yi Iran (Annotated Bibliography of*

German Travel Books in the National Library of Iran.) Tehran: Kitabkhanah Milli Iran, 3978.

Bahar, Mihrdad. *Asātir-i Irān (Iranian Mythology.*) Tehran: Intishārāt-i Bunyād-i Farhang-i Irān, 135 /1973.

Bailey, H. W. "A Half-Century of Irano-Indian Studies." *Journal of the Royal Asiatic Society* (1972): 99–110.

Banani, Amin. *The Modernization of Iran: 1921–1941.* Stanford: Stanford University Press, 1961.

Barbaro, Josafa. *Travels into Tana and Persia, by Josafa Barbaro and Ambrogio Contarini.* London: Hakluyt Society 1873

Barthold, V. V. *La Découverte de l'Asie; Histoire de l'orientalisme en Europe et en Russie traduit du Russe et annoté par B. Nikitine.* Paris: Payot, 1947.

Basgöz, Ilhan. "Turkish *Hikaye* Telling Tradition in Azerbaijan, Iran." *Journal of American Folklore* 83 (1970): 391–405.

Basil, Anthony Collins. *Al-Muqaddasi: The Man and His Work, with Selected Passages Translated from Arabic.* Ann Arbor: Dept. of Geography, University of Michigan, 1974.

Basset, Rev. James. "Grammatical Notes on the Simnflnî Dialect of the Persian Language." *Journal of the Royal Asiatic Society.* (1884): 120–139.

————. *Persia, the Land of the Imams: A Narrative of Travel and Residence 1871–1885.* London: Blackie and Son, 1887.

Bayzai, Bahram. *Namāyish dar Irān (Theatre in Iran.*) Tehran: Chāp-i Kāviān, 1344/1965.

Bell, Gertrude L. *Safar Nameh; Persian Pictures, A Book of Travel.* New York: Boni and Liveright, 1928.

Benjamin, Samuel Greene Wheeler. *Persia and the Persians by S. G. W. Benjamin.* Boston: Ticknor and Co., 1887.

Benjamin of Tudela, *The Itinerary of Rabbi Benjamin of Tudela.* Translated and edited by A. Asher, 2 vols. New York: "Hakesheth" Publishing Co., 1840.

Bérézine, E. *Recherches sur les dialectes persans.* Casan: Imprimerie de l'Université, 1853.

Bihrangi, Samad and Bihruz Dihqani, *Afsānah-hā-yi Āzarbayjān* (*Azarbayjani Folk Narratives.*) Tehran: Intishārāt-i Dunyā, 1360/1981.

Boulvin, Adrienne. *Contes populaires persans du Khorasan*, 2 vols. Paris: Travaux de l'institut d'études Iranienne de l'université de la sorbonne nouvelle, 1975.

————. "Uslub-i 'Ilmi-yi Tanzim-i Mavvād-i Qissah-hā-yi 'āmmiyānah" ("Systematic Methodology of Folk Narrative Classification.") *Sukhan* 21 (1971): 1159-1170.

Braaksma, M. H. *Travel and Literature; An Attempt at a Literary Appreciation of English Travel Books About Persia from the Middle Ages to the Present Day.* Groningen: J. B. Walters, 1938.

Bricteux, Auguste. *Contes persans.* Liege: n. p., 1910.

Browne, Edward Granville. *Literary History of Persia: Modern Times (1500–1924).* Vol. 4. Cambridge: Cambridge University Press, 1930.

————. "The Persian Manuscripts of the Late Sir Albert Houtum-Schindler, K. C. I. E." *Journal of the Royal Asiatic Society* (1917): 657–694.

————. *The Press and Poetry of Modern Persia.* Los Angeles: Kalimat Press, 1983. First Edition, 1914.

————. *A Year Amongst the Persians,* Cambridge: Cambridge University Press, 1927.

Brun, Cornelius Le. *A New and More Correct Translation than has hitherto Appeared in Public, of Mr. Cornelius Le Brun's Travels into Moscovy, Persia, and Diverse Parts of the East-Indies.* London: J. Warcus, 1759.

Cejpek, Jiři. "Iranian Folk-Literature." In Jan Rypka, *History of Persian and Tajik Literature,* edited by Karl Jahn, pp. 609–709. Netherlands: D. Reidel, Dordrecht, 1968.

Chardin, Sir John. *Sir John Chardin's Travels in Persia, with an Introduction by Brigadier-General Sir Percy Sykes.* London: The Argonaut Press, 1927.

————. *The Travels of Sir John Chardin into Persia and the East Indies. The First Volume Containing the Author's Voyage from Paris to*

Isphahan to which is added, the Coronation of his Present King of Persia, Solyman the Third. London: Moses Pitt, 1686.

Chodzko, Alexander Borejko. *Grammaire de la langue persane.* Paris: Imprimerie Nationale, 1852.

————. *Specimens of the Popular Poetry of Persia, as Found in the Adventures and Improvisations of Kurroglou, the Bandit Ministrel of the People Inhabiting the Shores of the Caspian Sea, Orally Collected and Translated, with Philological and Historical Notes.* London: Harrison Co., 1842.

————. *Théatre persan: Choix de Téaziés.* Paris: E. Leroux, 1878.

Christensen, Arthur. *Contes persans en langue populaire.* Kobenhavn: Det Kgl. Danske Videnskabernes Selskab. Historisk-filologiske Meddelelser, I, bd., 8, 1918.

————. *Contributions á la dialectologie iranienne: dialecte Guiläki de Recht, dialectes de Färizänd, de Yaran et de Natanz, avec un supplément contenant quelque textes dans le Persan vulgaire de Téhéran.* Kobenhavn: Det Kgl. Danske Videnskabernes Selskab. Historisk-fililogiske Meddelelser, 1930.

————. "Les Dialectes d'Awromän et de Päwä, textes recueillis par Åge Meyer Benedictsen." *Det Kgl. Danske Videnskabernes Selskab. Historisk-filologiske Meddeleser* 6: 2 (1921): 3–128.

————. "Le dialect de Sämnän, essai d'une grammaire Sämnäni.‾e avec un vocabulaire et quelques textes suivi d'une notice sur les patois de Sängsar et de Läsgird." *Det Kgl. Danske Vidensk. Selskab. Skrifter, Historisk og Filosofisk*, Afd II, no. 4 (1915): 227–300

————. "Juhi in the Persian Literature." In *A Volume of Oriental Studies Presented to Edward G. Browne on his 60th Birthday* edited by T. W. Arnold and Reynold A. Nicholson, pp. 129–136. Cambridge: The University Press, 1922.

————. *Persische Märchen.* Düsseldorf-Köln: Eugen Diederichs Verlag, 1958.

————. "La princesse sur la feuille de myrte et le princesse sur le pois." *Acta Orientalia* 14 (1936): 241-257.

————. "Qissah-ha-yi Iräni" ("Iranian Narratives.") translated by K. Jahandari. *Sukhan* 7: 2 (1335/1956): 17–25, and 148–263.

————. "Les sots dans la tradition populaire des Persans." *Acta Orientalia* 1 (1923): 43–75.

Clavijo, Ruy Gonzalez. *Embassy to Tamerlane, 1403–1406, translated by Guy Le Strange, edited by. E. Denison Ross.* London: George Routledge and Son, Ltd., 1928.

Clouston, William Alexander. *Some Persian Tales From Various Sources.* Glasgow: Bryce, 1892.

Cocchiara, Giuseppe. *The History of Folklore in Europe*, translated by John N. McDaniel. Philadelphia: Institute for the Study of Human Issues, 1981.

Condie, Stephen A. *Fairy Tales of a Parrot Adapted from the Persian.* London: Ernest Nister, 1892.

Curzon, George. *Persia and The Persian Question*, 2 vols. London: Longmans, Green and Co., 1892.

Daftari, Farhad. "Bibliography of the Publications of the Late W. Ivanow." *Islamic Culture* 45 (1971): 55–67.

Dargahi, Haidah. "The Shaping of the Modern Persian Short Story; Jamalzadah's "Preface' to *Yiki Bud, Yiki Nabud.*" *The Literary Review* 18: 1 (Fall 1974): 18–37.

Davidian, H. "Ahammiyat-i Barrasi Asātir-i Irāni dar Ravānshināsi Tahlili" ("The Significance of Iranian Mythology Studies in Analytical Psychology.") *Sukhan* 15: 4 (1343/1964): 374–391.

Dieulafoy, Jane. *Le Perse, La Chaldée et la Susiane.* Paris: Librarie Hachette et Cie, 1887

Dresden, M.J. "Survey of the History of Iranian Studies." *Handbuch der Orientalistik*, vol. 4, part 2, no. 1 (1968): 168–189.

Dundes, Alan. *The Study of Folklore.* Englewood Cliffs, N. J., Prentice-Hall, 1965.

Dustkhah, Jalil. "Kaykhusraw dar Kuhhā-yi Fārs" (Kaykhusraw in the Mountains of Fars.") *Proceedings of the Fourth Congress of Iranian Studies* vol. 2 (September 1973): 77-90.

Edwards, Edward. *A Catalogue of the Persian Printed Books in the British Museum.* London: British Museum, 1922.

Ehlers, Lore. *Persische Märchen und Schwänke.* Wien: Ferdinand Berger, Horn, 1966.

Elwell-Sutton, Laurence Paul. *Bibliographical Guide to Iran*. New Jersey: Barnes & Noble Books, 1983.

————. "Collecting Folktales in Iran." *Folklore* 93: 1 (1982): 98–104.

————. "Family Relationships in Persian Folk-Literature." *Folklore* 87 (1976): 160–166.

————. *A Guide to Iranian Area Study*. Ann Arbor: J. W. Edwards, 1952.

————. "The Influence of Folk-Tale and Legend on Modern Persian Literature." *Iran and Islam*. Edinburgh: Edinburgh University Press, 1971. pp. 247–254.

————. "Magic and the Supernatural in Persian Folk-Literature," *Ve Congres International d'Arabisants et d'islamisants*. Actes. 5 (1970): 189–196.

————. *Mashdi Galeen Khanom; the Wonderful Sea-Horse and other Persian Tales*. London: Geoffrey Bles, 1950.

————. "Mountain and Plain—Contrasts in Persian Folk-Literature." *Studia Fennica* 20 (1976): 331–337.

————. "The Role of Darvish in the Persian Folk-Tale." *Proceeding of the 26th International Congress of Orientalists* 2 (1968): 200–203.

————. "Scaldheads and Thinbeards in Persian Folk-Tale Literature." *Laographia dettion tes Ellenikes Laographikes Hetaireias* 22 (1965): 105–108.

————. "The Unfortunate Heroine in Persian Folk-Literature." In *Yādnāmah Irāni Minorski* edited by M. Minovi, Iraj Afshar, pp. 37–50. Tehran: Tehran University Publications, 1969.

Enayat, Hamid. "The Politics of Iranology." *Iranian Studies* 6 (Winter 1973): 2–20.

The Encyclopaedia of Islam, New Edition, edited by E. Von Donzel, B. Lewis and C. H. Pellat. Leiden: E. J. Brill, 1960–1985.

Faqiri, Abulqasim. "Havādis dar Tarānah-hā-yi Mahalli" ("Events in Folksongs.") *Majmu'ah Chāhārumin Kungarah-i Tahqiqāt-i Irāni* (*Proceedings of the Fourth Congress of Iranian Studies*), vol. 2 (1973): 256–266.

————. *Qissah-ha-yi Mardum-i Fārs* (*Folk Narratives of Fars*). Tehran: Markaz-i Nashr-i Sipihr, 1349/1970.

Ferrier, J. P. *Caravan Journeys and Wanderings in Persia, Afghanistan, Turkistan, and Beloochistan: with Historical Notices of the Countries Lying Between Russia and India,* translated by Capt. William Jesse, edited by H. D. Seymour. Karachi: Oxford University Press, 1976.

Fihrist-i Maqālāt-i Mardumshināsi Mu'assasah-i Mutali'ā t va Tahqiqāt Ijtimā'i (An Index of Anthropological Articles: Social Sciences Research Institute Publications.) Tehran: Tehran University Publications, 1977.

Fihrist-i Mundarajāt-yi Majalliha-yi 'ilmi va 'Ulum-i Ijtimā'i Iran (Content Pages, Iranian Science and Social Sciences Journals), 5 vols. Tehran: Markaz-i Asnād va Madārik-i 'Ilmi Iran, 1969-1973.

Forbes, Duncan. *A Grammar of the Persian Language.* London: Wm. H. Allen and Co., 1861.

Fouchecour, Charles Henri D. *Éléments pour un manuel de persan.* Paris: Publications Orientalistes de France, 1976. First Edition, 1952.

Fraser, James Baillie. *An Historical and Descriptive Account of Persia from the Earliest Ages to the Present Time.* Edinburgh: Oliver & Boyd, 1834.

————. *A Winter's Journey From Constantinople to Tehran with Travels Through Various Parts of Persia.* 2 vols., London: Richard Bentley, 1838.

Friedl Erika. "The Folktale as Cultural Comment." *Asian Folklore Studies* 34 (1975): 127–144.

————. "Women in Contemporary Persian Folktales." In *Women in the Muslim World,* edited by Lois Beck and Nikki Keddie, pp. 629–650. Cambridge, Massachusetts and London, England: Harvard University Press, 1978.

Fyzee, A. A. A. "Wladimir Ivanow (1886–1970)." *Journal of the Asiatic Society of Bombay* 45–46 (1970-1971): 92–97.

Gabriel, Alfons. *Die Erforschung Persiens; die Entwicklung der abendländischen Kenntnis der Geographie Persiens.* Wien: A. Holzhausens Nfg. 1952.

Gibbon, C. M. "Some Persian Folk-lore Stories Concerning the Ruins of Persepolis." *Journal of the Asiatic Society Bengal* 5: 8 (1909): 279–297.

Gladwin, Francis. *Persian Moonshee.* London: Wilson and Co., 1801.

Gray, Charles. *A Narrative of Italian Travels in Persia in the Fifteenth and Sixteenth Centuries.* London: Hakluyt Society, 1873.

Gulsurkhi, Iraj. "Dar bārah Farhang-i Mardum" ("About Folklore"). *Talash* 1: 5 (1346/1967): 44–45.

Gulzara: Princess of Persia, or the Virgin Queen: Collected from the Original Persian., n.p., 1816.

Hafiz Abru. *Jughrafiyā-yi Hafiz Abru,* edited by Mayel Heravi. Tehran: Intishārāt-i Bunyādi-i Farhang-i Irān, 1970.

Hanaway, William L., Jr. "Formal Elements in the Persian Popular Romances." *Review of National Literatures* 2: 1 (1971): 139–160.

————. "Popular Literature in Iran." In *Iran: Continuity and Variety,* edited by Peter J. Chelkowski, pp. 59–75. Fourth Annual New York University Near Eastern Round Table. New York: Center for Near Eastern Studies, 1971.

Hanway, Jonas. *An Historical Account of British Trade over the Caspian Sea, with a Journal of Travels from London through Russia into Persia and Back through Russia, Germany and Holland,* 2 vols. London: T. Osborne, 1754.

Harvard University Library. *Catalogue of Arabic, Persian and Ottoman Turkish Books.* Cambridge: Harvard University Press, 1968.

Hedayat Hosain, M. "Douglas Craven Phillott (1860–1930)." *Journal of the Asiatic Society Bengal* 27 (1931): cl, ⁻–cl, ⁻iii.

Herbert, Thomas. *Travels in Persia (1627–1629).* London: G. Routledge and Sons, Ltd., 1928.

Hidayat, Sadiq. "Āqā Mushah." *Majallah Musiqi* 1: 8 (1318/1939). Reprinted in *Majmu'ah Nivishtih-hā-yi Parakandah Sadiq Hidayat,* compiled by Hassan Qaimian, pp. 122–124. Tehran: Intishārāt Amir Kabir, 1344/1965. Second Edition.

————. "Chand Nuktah dar bārah *Vis u Ramin* ("A Few Comments about *Vis and Ramin*) in *Majmu'ah Nivishtah-hā-yi Parakandah Sadiq Hidayat,* pp. 486–523.

————. "Folklore yā Farhang-i Tudah: Nimunahā va Dastur Jam'āvari va Tadvin-i ān" ("Folklore, or the Culture of Masses: Examples and Methods of Collecting it.") *Sukhan* 2: 3 (1323/1944): 179–184; 2:

4 (1324/1945): 265–275; 2: 5 (1324/1945): 337–342; 2: 6 (1324/1945): 420–424.

———. "Lachak Kuchulu-yi Qirmiz." *Majallah Musiqi* 2: 2 (1319/1940). Reprinted in *Majmu 'ah Nivishtih-ha-yi Parakandah Sadiq Hidayat*, pp. 127–130.

———. "Matalha-yi Farsi" ("Persian Folk Narratives.") *Majallah Musiqi* 1: 8 (1318/1939). Reprinted in Majmu 'ah Nivishtih-ha-yi Parakandah Sadiq Hidayat, pp. 120–121.

———. *Nayrangistan.* Tehran: Intisharat-i Amir Kabir. 1342/1963. Third Edition.

———. "Sang-i Sabur." *Majallah Musiqi* 3: 7–8 (1320/1941). Reprinted in *Majmu' ah Nivishtih-ha-yi Parakandah Sadiq Hidayat*, pp. 131–138.

———. "Shangul u Mangul." *Majallah Musiqi* 1: 8 (1318/1939). Reprinted in *Nivishtih-ha-yi Parakandah Sadiq Hidayat*, pp. 124–126.

———. "Taranah-ha-i 'Ammiyanah" "Folksongs." *Majallah Musiqi* 1: 7–8 (1318/1939). Reprinted in *Majmu'ah Nivishtih-ha-yi Parakanda Sadig Hidayat*, pp. 344–364.

———. *Usanah.* Tehran: Aryan Kudah, 1310/1931. Reprinted in *Majmu'ah Nivishtih-ha-yi Parakandah-i Sadiq* Hidayat, pp. 296–327.

Hillelson, S. "The Source of a Story in the Mathnawi and a Persian Parallel to Grimm's Fairy Tales." *Journal of the Royal Asiatic Society* (1937): 474–477.

Humayun, Q. *Asnad-i Musavvar-i Urupaiyan az Iran; az Avayil-i Qurun-i Vasta ta Avakhir-i Qarn-i Hijdahum (European Illustrated Documents of Iran from the Beginning of the Middle Ages to the Eighteenth Century.)* Tehran: Tehran Universty Publications, 1348/1969.

Humayuni, Sadiq. "Folklore va *Gulistan-i* Sa'di" ("Folklore and Sa'di's Gulistan.") *Mojmu'ah Maqalat-i Chaharumin Kungarah-yi Tahqiqat-i Irani (Proceedings of the Fourth Congress of Iranian Studies)* vol. 3 (1973): 284–294.

———. *Mardi ki ba Sayahash Harf Mizad. (The Man Who Talked to his Shadow.)* Tehran: 'Atai, 1352/1973.

Hunari, Murtiza. *Owsungun, Afsānah-hā-yi Mardum-i Xur.* Tehran: Vizarat-i Farhang u Hunar, 1352/1973.

Ibn al-Balkhi. *Fārsnamah; Qadimtarin Tarikh va Jughrafiya-yi Fārs ba Muqaddamah va Havāshi bih Kushish-i 'Ali Naqi Bihruzi (Farsnamah; The Oldest History and Geography of Fars, with an Introduction and Notes by 'Ali Nagi Bihruzi.)* Shiraz: Ittihādiyahi Matbu'āti-yi Fars, 1343/1964.

Ibn Battuta. *Travels in Asia and Africa, 1325–1354,* Translated and Selected by H. A. R. Gibb. London: Routledge and Kegan Paul Ltd., 1929.

Ibn Fazlan. *Safar Nāmah-yi Ibn Fazlan (The Itinerary of Ibn Fazlan),* translated by A. Tabatabai. Tehran: Intishārāt-i Bunyād-i Farhang-i Irān, 1345/1966.

Ibn Hauqal. *The Oriental Geography of Ebn Hauqal an Arabian Traveller of the Tenth Century,* translated by Sir William Ouseley. London: n. p., 1800.

————. *Surat al-Arz,* translated by Ja'far Sho'ar. Tehran: Intisārāt-i Bonyād-i Farhang-i Irān, 1345/1966.

Ibn Khurdadbeh, Abu'l-Kasim Obaidallah ibn Abdallah. *Kitab al-Masalik wa'l-Mamalik,* edited by M. J. De Goeje, Bibliotheca Geographorum Aribocorum VI. Leiden: E. J. Brill, 1889.

Ibnu'l Balkhi. *The Farsnama of Ibnu'l Balkhi,* edited by G. Le Strange and R. A. Nicholson. London: Luzac and Company, 1962.

Istakhri, Abu Ishaq Ibrahim. *Masālik va Mamālik; Tarjumah-yi Fārsi-yi al-Masālik va'l-Mamālfk az Qarn-i V/VI Hijri, Ta'lif-i Abu Ishaq Ibrāhim Istakhri (Masalik va Mamalik, by Abu Ishaq Ibrahim Istakhri; Persian Translation of Maslik va'l Mamalik from V/VI Century A. H.),* edited by Iraj Afshar. Tehran: B. T. N. K., 1347/1968.

Ivanov, Vladimir. "The Dialect of Gozarkhon in Alamut." *Acta Orientalia* (1929): 352–368.

————. "The Gabri Dialect Spoken by the Zoroastrians of Persia." *Rivista degli Studi Orientali* 17 (1937): 1–39.

————. "Jargon of Persian Mendicate Darvishes." *Journal of the Asiatic Society of Bengal.* New Series, 23 (1927): 243–245.

————. "Notes on Khorasani Kurdish." *Journal of Asiatic Society of Bengal* 23 (1927): 167–236.

————. "Persian as Spoken in Birjand." *Journal of the Asiatic Society of Bengal* 24 (1928): 235–351.

————. "Pidar-Sukhta." *Journal of the Royal Asiatic Society* (1927): 96–97.

————. "Some Persian Darvish Songs." *Journal of the Asiatic Society of Bengal, New Series*, 23 (1927): 237–242.

————. "Two Dialects Spoken in the Central Persian Desert." *Journal of the Royal Asiatic Society* (1926): 405–431.

Jackson, A. V. William. "Our Interest in Persia and the Study of her History, Language, and Literature." *International Congress of Arts and Sciences* 3 (1906): 357–366.

Jaktaji, Mohammad Ali. *Fihrist-i Tusifi-yi Safarnāmah-hā-yi Farānsavi-yi Mujud dar Kitābkhānah-yi Milli-i Irān (Annotated Bibliography of French Travel Books in the National Library of Iran.)* Tehran: Kitābkhānah-i Milli, 1976.

————. *Fihrist-i Tusifi-yi Safarnāmah-hā-yi Inglisi Mujud dar Kitābkhānah-yi Milli Irān (Annotated Bibliography of English Travel Books in the National Library of Iran.)* Tehran: Kitābkhānah Milli, 1976.

Jamalzadah, Siyyad Muhammad Ali. "Davidam u Davidam." *Payam-i Nuvin* 5: 6 (1342/1963): 10–28.

————. *Farhang-i Luqāt-i 'Āmmiyānah*. Tehran: Intishārāt-i Farhang-i Iran Zamin, no. 7, 1341/1962.

————. *Once Upon A Time (Yiki Bud Yiki Nabud.)* Translated by Heshmat Moayyed and Paul Sprachman. New York: Biblioteca Persica, 1985.

————. *Yiki Bud, Yiki Nabud (Once Upon a Time.)* Tehran: Kānun Ma'rifat, n. d. (Fourth edition).

————. "Zabān-i Āmmiyānah" ("Folk Speech"). *Rahnamay-i Kitab* 3: 5 (1339/1960): 611–615, 3: 6 (1339/1960): 716–720.

Javadi, Hassan. "Tanz va Intiqad dar Dāstānhā-yi Hayvānāt" ("Satire and Criticism in Animal Stories.") *Alifba*, 4 (1353/1974): 1–22.

Javid, S. *Āzarbāyjan Folklorindan Nimunahlar (Examples of Azarbayjani Folklore.)* Tehran: (Chāpp-i Ittihād), 1344/1965.

Jenkinson, Anthony. *Early Voyages and Travels to Russia and Persia by Anthony Jenkinson and other Englishmen*, 2 vols. New York: Burt Franklin, 1885.

Jones, Sir William. *A Grammar of the Persian Language.* London: W. Blumer and Co., 1804 (6th edition).

Jordanus de Severac Friar. *Mirabilia Descripta; The Wonders of the East by Friar Jordanus*, translated by Sir Henry Yule. London: Hakluyt Society, 1863.

Kaempfer, Englebert. *Dar Darbār-i Shāhanshah-i Irān (At the Court of the King of Kings of Iran)*, translated by K. Jahandari. Tehran: Anjuman-i Āsār-i Milli, 1350/1971.

Kamshad, Hassan. *Modern Persian Prose Literature.* Cambridge: The University Press, 1966.

Katirai, Mahmud. Az Khisht tā Khisht. Tehran: Intishārāt-i *Mu'assisah-yi Mutali'at va Tahqiqāt-i Ijtima'i*, 1348/1969).

————. "Sadiq Hidayat va Folklor-i Irān" ("Sadiq Hidayat and Iranian Folklore.") In *Nāmah Minuvi: Majmu'ah Si u Hasht Guftār dar Adab va Farhang-i Irāni bi Pās-i Panjāh Sāl Tahqiqāt va Mutāli'āt-i Mujtabā Minuvi (A Collection of Thirty Eight Essays Dedicated to Mujtaba Minuvi in Appreciation of his Fifty Years of Research)*, edited by Iraj Afshar, pp. 355–368. Tehran: n. p., 1350/1971.

Kazemi, Asqhar. *Fihrist-i Kitābhā-yi Almāni dar bārah-yi Irān (A Bibliography of German Books on Iran.)* Tehran: Tehran University Publications, 1970.

Khaliqi, Mahmud. "Muqaddamah" *Mardumshināshi va Farhang-yi Āmmah-yi Irān*, 1: 1 (Intishārāt-i Vizārat-i Farhang va Hunar, Markaz-i Pazhuhishhā-yi Mardumshināsi va Farhang-i 'Āmmah, Summer 1353/1974): 2–21.

Komissarov, D. S. "Qissah-ha-yi Fārsi." In *Haft Maqālah az Irān-shināsān-i Shuravi (Seven Articles by Russian Iranologists)*, translated by A. Azmudah, pp. 71–79. Tehran: Mark-az-i Nashr-i Sipihr, 1972.

Komroff, Manuel. *Contemporaries of Marco Polo, Consisting of the Travel Records to the Eastern Parts of the World of William Rubruck. 1253–1255, the Journey of John Pian de Carpini 1245–1247; the Journal of Friar Odoric 1318–1330 and the Oriental*

Travels of Rabbi Benjamin of Tudela 1160–1173. New York: Liveright Publishing Corp., 1973.

Kotov, Fedor Afanasiyev. "Of a Journey to the Kingdom of Persia." In *Russian Travellers to India and Persia: 1624–1798 Kotov, Yefremov, Danibegov,* translated and edited by P. M. Kemp. Delhi: S. L. Kaeley, M. A., 1959.

Kramer, J. H. "Djugrafiya." In *The Encylopaedia of Islam: A Dictionary of the Geography, Ethnography and Biography of Muhammadan Peoples,* Supplement, edited by M. Th. Houtsma, A. J. Wensink, H. A. R. Gibb, W. Heffening, Levi Provincal, pp. 61–73. Leiden: E. J. Brill, 1938.

Kubičkova, Veľa. "Persian Literature of the 20th Century." In Jan Rypka, *History of Iranian Literature* edited by Karl Jahn, pp. 353–418. Netherlands: D. Reidel, Dordrecht, 1968.

Kuhi Kirmani, Hussain. *Pānzdah Afsānah Rustāi (Fifteen Rural Narratives.)* Tehran: Amir Kabir, 1333/1954.

Kurti, Alfred. *Persian Folktales.* London: G. Bell and Sons Ltd., 1971.

Lam'ah, Manuchihr. *Farhang-i 'Āmmiyānah-i 'Ashāyir-i Boyir Ahmadi va Kuhkiluyah (Folklore of Buyir Ahmadi and Kuhkiluyah Tribes.)* Tehran: Intishārāt-i Ashrafi, 1349/1970

Lambton, Ann K. S. *Three Persian Dialects.* London: Royal Asiatic Society, 1938.

Layard, Sir Henry. *Early Adventures in Persia, Susiana, and Babylonia* 2 vols. London: John Murray, 1887.

Lazard, Gilbert. "Persian and Tajik." In *Current Trends in Linguistics* edited by Thomas A. Sebeok, pp. 64–96. The Hague: Mouton, 1970.

———. "Textes en Tāleši de Masule." *Studia Iranica* 8 (1979): 33–66.

Levy, Reuben. "Persia Viewed Through its Proverbs and Apologues." *Bulletin of the School of Oriental and African Studies* 14 (1952): 540–549.

———. *The Three Dervishes, and Other Persian Tales and Legends, for the Most Part Translated from hitherto Unpublished Bodleian Manuscripts.* London, New York: H. Milford, Oxford University Press, 1923.

Lorimer, D. L. R. "Is There a Gabri Dialect of Modern Persian?" *Journal of the Royal Asiatic Society* (1928): 287–319.

————. "Notes on the Gabri Dialect of Modern Persian." *Journal of the Royal Asiatic Society* 12 (1916): 423–489.

————. *Persian Tales, Written down for the First Time in the Original Kermani and Bakhtiari and Translated by D. L. R. Lorimer and E. S. Lorimer.* London: Macmillan and Co. 1919.

————. *The Phonology of the Bakhtiari, Badakhshani, and Madaglashti Dialects of Modern Persian.* London: Royal Asiatic Society Prize Publication Fund, vol. VI, 1922.

M. A. and Sadiq Hidayat. "Bulbul Sargashtah." *Sukhan* 3: 6–7 (1325/1946): 432–434.

Machalski, Franciszek. "Notes on the Folklore of Iran." *Folia Orientalia* 12 (1970): 141–154.

Mackenzie, C. F. *Persian Wonder Tales Adapted from the Persian.* Glasgow: Blackie and Son Limited, 1928.

Mahjub, Muhammad Ja'far. "Le conteur en Iran." *Objets et Mondes* 10: 1 (1971: 159–170).

————. "Dāstānhā-yi 'Āmmiyānah-yi Fārsi" ("Iranian Folk Narratives") *Sukhan* 10: 1 (1338/1959): 64–68.

————. "Farhang-i 'Āmmah va Zindagi" ("Folklore and Life.") *Hunar va Mardum* 184–185 (1357/1978): 2–11.

————. "Mutāli'ah dar Dāstānhā-yi 'Āmmiyānah Fārsi" ("Study of Persian Folk Narratives.") *Majallah-yi Dānishkadih-yi Adabiyyāt-i Tehrān* 10: 1 (1341/1962) 68–112, 10: 2 (1342/1963) 211–237.

————. "Sukhanvari." *Sukhan* 9: 6 (1337/1958): 530–535; 9: 7, 631–637; 9: 8, 779–789.

————. "Les Traditions des Bardes, les Assauts Poetiques." *Studia Iranica* 3: 1 (1973): 115–122.

Malcolm, John Sir. *Sketches of Persia; from the Journals of a Traveller in the East,* 2 vols. London: John Murray, 1827.

Mann, Oskar. *Kurdisch-Persische Forschungen: Die Mundarten von Khunsâr Mahallāt, Natānz, Nâyin, Sāmnân, Sīvānd und Sô-Kohrüd.* Bond 1, Abteilung 3. Berlin und Leipzig, 1926.

Marzolph, Urlich. *Typologie des Persischen Volksmärchens*. Wiesbaden:
    Franz Steiner Verlag, 1984.

Massé, Henri. "Contes en persan populaire" *Journal Asiatique*, Tome
    206 (1925): 71–157.

————. *Croyances et coutumes persanes suivies des contes et
    chansons populaires*, 2 vols. Paris: G. P. Maisonneuve, 1938.

————. "Sukhanrāni Professor Henri Massé dar Majlis-i Yādbud-i
    Chahārumin Sal-i Marg-i Hidayat dar Pāris" ("Professor Henri
    Massé's Speech on the Occasion of the Fourth Anniversary of
    Hidayat's Death in Paris." In *Nazariyyāt-i Nivisandidān-i Buzurg-i
    Khāriji dar bārah-yi Sadiq Hidayat, Zindagi va Āsār-i U* ("*Great
    Foreign Writers' Views about Sadiq Hidayat, his Life and Work*,
    edited by H. Qaimian, pp. 140-150. Third edition. Tehran: n. p.,
    1343/1964.

Mehdavi, Ann Sinclair. *Persian Folk and Fairy Tales*. New York: Alfred A.
    Knopf, 1965.

Mihandust, Muhsin. "Qissah dar Qalamruvi Adabiyyāt-i Shafāhi"
    ("Narrative in the Realm of Oral Literature.") *Mardumshināsi va
    Farhang-i 'Āmmah-yi Iran*. 2 (Tehran: Vizārat-i Farhang va Hunar,
    Markaz-i Mardum-Shinasi, 1354/1975): 103–113.

————. *Samandar-i Chil-gis*. Tehran: Vizārat-i Farhang u Hunar,
    1352/1973.

Minorski, Vladimir. "The Gflrān." *Bulletin of the School of Oriental and
    African Studies*, 11, pt. 1 (1943): 75–103

Minuvi, Mujtaba. "Sukhanrāni Āqā-yi Mujtaba Minuvi dar Jalasih Yādbud-i
    Hidayat" ("Mr. Mujtaba Minuvi's Speech at Hidayat's Memorial
    Ceremony.") In *'Aqāyid va Afkār dar bārah-yi Sadiq Hidayat pas
    az Marg* (*Views and Comments about Sadiq Hidayat after his
    Death*.) Tehran: Intishārāt-i Bahr-i Khazar, 1346/1967, pp. 105–
    108.

Morgan, J. de. *Misson scientifique en Perse*, tome V (Etudes
    linguistique). Paris: Impremérie Nationale, 1904.

Morgenstierne, Georg. "Iranian Research in the North." *Le Nord* 2–3
    (1941): 135–146.

————. "Persian Texts from Afganistan." *Acta Orientalia* 6 (1928): 309–
    328.

————. "Stray Notes on Persian Dialects." *Norsk Tidsskrift for Sprogvidensksp* 19 (1960): 73-140.

Morrier, James. *A Journey Through Persia Armenia and Asia Minor, to Constantinople, in the Year 1806 and 1809.* Philadelphia: M. Carey and Wells and Lilly, 1816.

————. *Second Journey to Persia, Armenia, and Asia Minor, to Constantinople, between the Years 1810 and 1816.* London: Longman, Kurst, Rees, Orme, and Brown, 1818.

Motamed-Nejad, Kazem. "Story-Teller and Mass Media in Iran: The Role of Story Telling in Social Communications." In *Entertainment: A Cross-Cultural Examination* edited by Heinz-Dietrich Fischer and Stefan Reinhard Melnik, pp. 43-62. New York: Hastings House, 1979.

Mo'tarif, Kianush. *From the Land of Roses and Nightingales: Collection and Study of Persian Folktales* 2 vols. Unpublished Doctoral Dissertation, University of Florida, 1979.

"Nāmah-hā-yi Sadiq Hidayat" ("Hidayat's Letters.") *Sukhan* 6: 1 (1333/1954): 199–209.

Nasir Khosraw. *Safar Nameh-yi Hakim Nāsir Khosraw Qhobādiani Marvazi,* edited by M. Dabir Siyaqhi. Tehran: Tehran University Press, 1954/1975.

Natil Khanlari, Parviz. "Fout-i Sadiq Hidayat," ("Sadiq Hidayat's Death.") *Khabarha-yi Danishgah* 5 (1330/1951). Reprinted in *'Aqāyid va Afkār dar bārah-yi Sadiq Hidayat pas az Marg (Views and Comments about Sadiq Hidayat after his Death.)* Tehran: Intisharat-i Bahr-i Khazar, 1346/1967. pp. 27–34.

Nawabi, Y. M. *A Bibliography of Iran; A Catalogue of Books and Articles on Iranian Subjects Mainly in European Languages.* Tehran: Iranian Cultural Foundation, 1969–1984.

New York (City) Public Library. *List of Works in the New York Public Library Relating to Persia.* New York: n. p., 1915.

Nicholson, R. A. "Some Notes on Arabian and Persian Folklore." *Folklore* 41: 4 (1930): 345–358.

Nikitin, Basile. *Les Kurdes: Étude sociologique et historique.* Paris: Éditions d'Aujourd '-hui, 1975.

————. "La poésie lyrique kurde." l'Ethnographie 45 (1947–59): 39–53.

————. "Quelque fables kurdes d'animaux." *Folkore* XL: 2 (1929): 228–244.

————. "Un sujet de fable, variantes kurde et persane." *Revue d'Ethnographie et des Traditions Populaires*, Année 3, n⁰ 10 (1922): 129–140.

————. "Superstitions des Chaldéens du plateau d'Ourmiah." *Revue d'Ethnographie et des Traditions Populaires*, Année 4, n⁰ (1923): 149–181.

————. "La vie domestique kurde." *Revue d'Ethnographie et des Traditions Populaires*, Anée 3, n⁰ 11 (1922): 334–344.

Nikitin, Fedor Kotov Athanasius. "The Travels of Athanasius Nikitin of Twer." In Richard Henry Major, *India in the Fifteenth Century*. London: Hakluyt Society, 1857.

Noel, E. "The Character of the Kurds as Illustrated by their Proverbs and Popular Sayings." *Bulletin of the School of Oriental and African Studies* 1 (1920): 79–90.

Nukhustin Kungirah-yi Nivisandigān-i Irān (*The First Congress of Iranian Writers.*) Tehran: n. p., 1326/1937.

Olearius, Adam. *The Voyages and Travels of the Ambassadors from the Duke of Holstein, to the Great Duke of Muscovy, and the King of Persia, Begun in the Year 1633 and Finish'd in 1639.* London: Thomas Daring and John Starkey, 1662.

Olcott, Frances Jenkins. *Tales of the Persian Jenii Retold by Frances Jenkins Olcott.* Boston: Houghton Mifflin Company, 1917.

Omidsalar, Mahmoud. "Storytellers in Classical Persian Texts." *Journal of American Folklore* 97 (1984): 205–212.

Oranski, I. M. "Old Iranian Philology and Iranian Linguistics." In *Fifty Years of Soviet Oriental Studies (1917–1967)*, USSR Academy of Sciences Institute of the Peoples of Asia. Moscow: Nauka Publishing House, 1967.

I. Osmanov, A. Bertels, and P. Aliev, compilers, *Persidskie Skazki* (*Persian Tales.*) Moscow, 1958.

Ouseley, Sir William. *Travels in Various Countries of the East, more Particularly Persia*, 3 vols. London: Rodwell and Martin, 1819–1823.

Page, Mary Ellen. *Naqali and Ferdowsi: Creativity in the Iranian National Tradition.* Unpublished Doctoral Dissertation, University of Pennsylvania, 1977.

Parham, Sirus. "Simāyi Qahramān dar Dāstānhā-yi 'Ammiyānah" ("Characteristics of Heroes in Folk Narratives.") *Sadaf* 1: 4 (1336/1957): 275–291.

Pearson, James Douglas. *A Bibliography of Pre-Islamic Persia.* London: Mansel, 1975.

————. *Index Islamicus.* Cambridge, England: W. Heffer 1958.

Pegolotti, Friar Francesco Balducci. "Notices of the Land Route to Cathay and of Asiatic Trade in the First Half of the Fourteenth Century by Francis Balducci Pegolotti. In Henry Yule, *Cathay and the Way Thither.* pp. 279–308. London: Hakluyt Society, 1886.

Pethahiah, ben Jacob. *Travels of Rabbi Petachia, of Ratisbon, who in the Latter end of the Twelfth Century Visited Poland, Russia, Little Tartary, the Crimea, Armenia, Assyria, Syria, the Holy Land, and Greece*, translated by A. Benisch. London: Longman and Co., 1861.

Phillott, Douglas Craven. "Bibliomancy, Divination, Superstitions, amongst the Persians." *Journal of the Royal Asiatic Society* 2: 8 (1906): 339–342.

————. *Higher Persian Grammar.* Calcutta: Calcutta University, 1919.

————. "Note on the Huma or Lammergeyer." *Journal of the Royal Asiatic Society* 2: 10 (December 1906): 532–533.

————. "A Note on Sign-, Gesture-, Code-, and Street-language, etc., amongst the Persians." *Journal of the Royal Asiatic Society* 3: 9 (November 1907): 619–622.

————. "A Persian Nonsense Rhyme." *Journal of the Royal Asiatic Society* 2: 7 (1906) 332–333.

————. "Some Current Persian Tales, Collected in the South of Persia from Professional Story-Tellers." *Memoirs of the Asiatic Society of Bengal* 1: 18 (1905–1907): 375–412.

————. "Some Lullabies and Topical Songs Collected in Persia." *Journal of the Royal Asiatic Society* 2: 3 (March 1906): 32–35.

————. "Some Persian Riddles Collected from Dervishes in the South of Persia." *Journal of the Royal Asiatic Society* 2: 4 (April 1906): 88–93.

————. "Some Street Cries Collected in Persia. *Journal of the Royal Asiatic Society* 2: 7 (July 1906): 283–285.

————. "Two Persian Equivalents for Peter Piper." *Journal of the Royal Asiatic Society* 2: 10 (December 1906): 529.

Polo, Marco. *The Travels of Marco Polo, Translated into English from the Text of L. F. Benedetto by Professor Aldo Ricci, with an Introduction and Index by Sir E. Denison Ross*. New York: The Viking Press, 1931.

Power, Eileen. "The Opening of the Land Routes to Cathay." In *Travel and Travellers of the Middle Ages* edited by Arthur Percival Newton, pp. 124–158. New York: Alfred A. Knopf, 1926.

Qaimian, Hassan. "Tuzih-i Girdāvarandah" ("Compiler's Comments.") In *Majmu'ah Niwishtih-ha-yi Parakandah Sadiq Hidayat*, compiled by Hassan Qaimian, pp. I–LXV. Tehran: Intishārāt Amir Kabir, 1344/1965. Second Edition.

Qaravi, Mihdi. "Mutali'āt Iranshināsi dar Dānmārk," ("Iranian Studies in Denmark.") *Rahnamay-i Kitab* 6 (1342/1963): 644–749.

Rabino, H. L. *Mazandaran and Astarabad*. London: Gibb Memorial Series, New Series, VII, 1928.

Ricks, Thomas M. "Contemporary Persian Literature." *The Literary Review* 18: 1 (Fall 1974): 4–17.

Rosen, Georg. *Elementa Persica: Persische Erzählungen mit Kurzer Grammatik und Glossar*. Leipzig: Verlag von Veit & Comp., 1915.

Ross, Edward Denison. *The Persians*. Oxford: The Clarendon Press, 1931.

Ruysbroek, Willem van. *The Journey of William of Rubruck to the Eastern Parts of the World, 1253-55, as Narrated by Himself with Two Accounts of the Earlier Journey of John of Pian de Carpine, Translated from the Latin and Edited, with an Introductory Notice by William Woodville Rockhill*. London: Hackluyt Society, 1900.

Rypka, Jan. "History of Persian Literature up to the Beginning of the 20th Century." In Jan Rypka, *History of Iranian Literature* edited by Karl Jahn, pp. 69–351. Netherlands: D. Reidel, Dordrecht, 1968.

Saba, Muhsin. *Bibliographie Française de l'Iran; bibliographie methodique et raisonnée des ouvrages française parus depuis 1560 jusqu'á nos jours.* Tehran: n. p., 1951.

————. *English Bibliography of Iran.* Tehran: Center for Studies and Research on the Iranian Civilization, 196?.

Sackville-West, Victoria. *Passenger to Tehran.* London: Leonard and Virginia Woolf, 1926.

————. *Twelve Days; An Account of a Journey Across the Bakhtiari Mountains in South Western Persia.* London: Leonard and Virginia Woolf at the Hogarth Press, 1928.

Sadat Ishkivari, Kazim. *Afsānah-hā-i Ishkivir-i Bālā* Tehran: Vizārat-i Farhang u Hunar, 1352/1973.

————. "Nigāhi Guzarā bi Afsānahā-yi Ishkivar-i Bālā" ("A Glance at Ishkivar-i Bala Folk Narratives.") *Mardum Shināsi va Farhang-i 'Āmmah-yi Irān,* 2 (Tehran: Vizarāt-i Farhang va Hunar, Markaz-i Mardumshināsi, 1354/1975): 58–63.

————. "Zarbulmasalhāi az Ishkivar-i Bālā" ("Some Proverbs from Ishkivar-i Bala.") *Hunar va Mardum* 191–192 (1357/1978): 64–68.

Sadiq, H. "Afsānah-hā-yi Mahalli Āzarbāyjān" ("Folk Narratives of Azarbayjan.") In *Haft Maqālah Pirāmun-i Folklore va Adabiyyāt-i Mardum-i Āzarbāyjan (Seven Articles About the Folklore and Literature of Azarbayjani People)* edited by Parvin Aqajanzadah, pp. 64–86. Tehran: Intishārāt-i Dunyāy-i Dānish, 2537/1978. Second Edition.

Saffarzadah, Ja'far. "Rābitah-yi Zarbulmasalhā ba Zindigi Ruzmarrah-yi Mardum" ("The Relationship between Proverbs and People's Everyday Life.") In *Sevvumin Kungarah-yi Tahqiqāt-i Irāni (Proceedings of the Third Congress of Iranian Studies)* vol. 2 (1972): 366–373.

Sa'idi, Qulamhussain. *Ilkhchi.* Tehran: Intishārāt-i Mu'assisah Mutāli'āt va Tahqiqāt-i Ijtimā'i, 1342/1963.

————. *Khiav ya Mishkin Shahr.* Tehran: Intishārāt Mu'assisah Mutāli'āt va Tahqiqāt-i Ijtimā'i, 1344/1965.

Salemann, Carl und Valentin Shukovski. *Persische Grammatic.* Leipzig: Otto Harrassowitz, 1947. First Edition 1889.

Sanson, Nicolas. *The Present State of Persia: with a Faithful Account of the Manners, Religions, and Government of that People, Translated by John Savage.* London: Gilliflower, 1695.

Sattari, Jalal. "Rumuz-i Qissah az didgāh-i Ravānshināsi" ("Study of Narrative Symbols from Psychological Point of View.") *Hunar va Mardum* 96–97 (1349/1970): 49–55 through 126 (1351/1972): 100–103.

Shafa, Shuja'al-din. *Jahān-i Irānshināsi (The World of Iranology.)* Tehran: Kitabkhanah Pahlavi, 1969.

Shahshahani, Soheila. "History of Anthropology in Iran." *Iranian Studies* 19: 1 (Winter 1986): 65-86.

Shahsavarian, Avedis. "Dāstān-i Rustam-i Zāl Tibq-i Ravāyāt-i Armani" ("The Story of *Rustam-i Zal* according to Armenian Versions.") *Payam Nuvin* 8: 1 (1345/1966): 87–90.

Shakurzadah, Ibrahim. *'Aqāyid va Rusum-i 'Āmmah-yi Mardum-i Khurāsān (The Folk Belief and Customs of the People of Khurasan.)* Tehran: Intishārāt-i Bunyād-i Farhang-i Irān, 1346/1967.

Sheil, Lady Mary Leonora (Waulf). *Glimpses of Life and Manners in Persia.* New York: Arno Press, 1973. First Edition 1856.

Soane, E. B. "A Southern Kurdish Folksong in Kermanshahi Dialect." *Journal of the Royal Asiatic Society* (1909): 35–51.

Stack, Edward. *Six Months in Persia* 2 vols. London: Sampson Low, Marston, Searle, and Rivington, 1882.

Stewart, Charles Edward. *Through Persia in Disguise, with Reminiscences of the Indian Mutiny. by Colonel Charles E. Stewart, edited from his Diaries by Basil Stewart.* London: G. Routledge and Sons Ltd., 1911.

Struys, John. *The Voyages and Travels of John Struys Through Italy, Greece, Muscovy, Tartary, Media, Persia, East India, Japan and other Countries in Europe, Africa and Asia, Done out of Dutch by John Morrison.* London: Able/Swalle, 1684.

Subhi Muhtadi, Fazlullah. *Afsanaha (Folk Narratives)* 2 vols. Tehran: Amir Kabir, vol. I 1323/19-44, vol. II 1325/1946.

————. *Afsānahā-yi Bāstani Iran va Majār.* Tehran: n. p. 1332/1953.

————. Afsānahā-yi Bu Ali Sinā. Tehran: n. p. 1333/1954.

————. *Afsanahā-yi Kuhan* 2 vols. Tehran: n. p., vol. I 1328/1949, vol. 2 1329/1960.

————. *Dāstānhā-yi Divān-i Balkh.* Tehran: Amir Kabir, 1353/1974. First Edition 1331/1952.

————. *Dizh-i Hush Rubā.* Tehran: Amir Kabir, 1353/1974. First Edition 1330/1951.

Suratgar, Olive. *I Sing in the Wilderness; An Intimate Account of Persia and the Persians.* London: E. Stanford, 1951.

Sweeny, Sean. "Girdāvari Āsār-i Adabi va 'Āmmiyānah-yi Iran" ("Collecting Iranian Folk-literature.") *Rahnamay-i Kitab* 4 (1339/1960): 458–460.

Sykes, Ella Constance. "Persian Family Life." *Journal of the Central Asian Society* I (1914): 3–11.

————. "Persian Folklore" *Folklore* 12 (1901): 261–280.

————. *Story-Book of the Shah, or Legends of Old Persia.* London: John Macqueen, 1901.

————. "A Talk About Persia and its Women." *National Geographic Magazine* 21 (1910): 847–866.

————. *Through Persia on a Side-Saddle.* Philadelphia: J. B. Lippincott Company, 1898.

Sykes, Sir Percy. *Ten Thousand Miles in Persia, or Eight Years in IRAN.* New York: Charles Scribner's Sons, 1902.

Tabatabai, Ahmad. "Div va Juhar-i Asātiri ān" ("Ogre and its Mythological Origin.") *Nashriyah Dānishkadah Adabiyyāt Tabriz* 16: 5 (1343/1964): 39–45.

Tahbaz, Sirus. *Yush.* Tehran: Intisharāt-i Mu'assisah Mutāli'at va Tahqiqāt Ijtima'i, 1342/1963.

Tavernier, John Baptist. *The Six Travels of John Baptista Tavernier, Through Turkey and Persia to the Indies, during the space of Forty Years.* London: Moses Pitt, 1684.

Thompson, Stith. *The Folktale.* New York: The Dryden Press, 1948.

Treacher Collins, E. *In the Kingdom of the Shah.* London: T. Fisher Unwin, 1896.

Ullens de Schooten, Marie-Thérèse. *Lords of the Mountains, Southern Persia and the Kashkai Tribes.* London: Chatto and Windus, 1956.

United States Library of Congress, Reference Department, *Iran; A Selected and Annotated Bibliography Compiled by Hafiz Farman.* Washington: Library of Congress, 1951.

University of Chicago, *Catalogue of the Middle Eastern Collection, First Supplement.* Boston, Massachusetts: G. H. Hall and Co., 1977.

Vahman, Feridun. "Dastānhā-yi Ablahān va Sādahluhān" ("Narratives of Numbskulls and Simpletons." *Sukhan* 19: 8 (1348/1969): 755–765, and 19: 9 (1348/1969) 897–911.

———. *Farhang-i Mardum-i Kirmān: Gird Āvarandah D.L. Lorimer (Folklore of Kirmani People: Collected by D. L. Lorimer.)* Tehran: Intishārāt-i Bunyad-i Farhang-i Irān, 1353/1974.

———. "Jam 'Avari-i Afsānah-hā-yi Irāni" ("Collecting Iranian Folk Narratives.") *Sukhan* 18 (1347/1968): 171-177.

———. "Rustam va Suhrāb va Dastānhā-yi Shabih-yi be ān dar Afsānah-ha-yi Digarān" ("Rustam and Suhrab and Similar Stories in the Folk Narratives of Other Nations.") *Sukhan* 18: 1 (1347/1968): 24–36.

Vambéry, Armenius. *The Life and Adventures of Armenius Vambery Written by Himself.* New York: F. A. Stokes Company, 1914.

Varthema, Ludvico di. *The Itinerary of Ludvico di Varthema of Bologna from 1502 to 1508, as Translated from the Original Italian Edition of 1510 by John Winter Jones, F. S. A. in 1863 for the Hakluyt Society with a Discourse on Varthema and his Travels in Southern Asia by Sir Carnac Temple, BT.* London: The Argonut Press, 1928.

Waring, Edward Scott. *A Tour to Sheeraz by the Route of Kazroon and Feerozabad.* London: W. Blumer and Co., 1807.

Weber, Henry. *Tales of the East* 3 vols. Edinburgh: James Ballantyne and Company, 1812.

Weryho, Jan M. "Si.̄stāni-Persian Folklore." *Indo-Iranian Folklore* 4 (1962): 276–307.

Wills, Charles James. *In the Land of the Lion and Sun or Modern Persia: Being Experiences of Life in Persia during a Residence of Fifteen Years in Various Parts of that Country from 1886 to 1881.* London: Macmillan and Co., 1883.

————. *Persia As It Is: Being Sketches of Modern Persian Life and Character.* London: S. Low, Marston, Searle and Rivingston, 1886.

Wilmot-Buxton, Ethel Mary. *Stories of Persian Heroes Retold from the Shah Namah of Firdausi.* New York: Thomas Y. Crowell Company, 1908.

Wilson, Sir Arnold Talbot. *A Bibliography of Persia.* Oxford: Clarendon Press, 1930.

————. "Early Spanish and Portugese Travellers in Persia." *The Asiatic Review* 22 (October 1926): 641–656.

————. *Persian Gulf; An Historical Sketch from the Earliest Time to the Beginning of the 20th Century.* Oxford: The Clarendon Press, 1928.

————. "Some Early Travellers in Persia and Persian Gulf." *Journal of the Central Asia Society* 12 (1925): 68–82.

————. *South West Persia: Letters and Diary of a Young Officer 1907–1914.* London: Oxford University Press, 1942.

Windfuhr, Gernot L. *Persian Grammar: History and State of Its Study.* The Hague: Mouton Publishers, 1979.

Yasimi, Rashid. "Bayānāt-i Aqā-yi Rashid Yasimi dar bāb-i Folklore" ("Mr. Rashid Yasimi's Speech on Folklore." *Ta'lim va Tarbiyat* 6: 1 (1315/1936): 86–93.

Yule, Sir Henry. *Cathay and the Way Thither* 2 vols. London: Hakluyt Society, 1866.

Zamani, Muhammad. *Kitābshināsi-yi Farhang-i 'āmmah va Mardomshināsi-yi Irān (A Bibliography of Folklore and Anthropology of Iran.)* Tehran: n. p., 1971.

Zarrinkub, 'Abdulhussain. "Afsānah-hā-yi 'āmmiyānah" ("Folk Narratives.") *Sukhan* 5: 12 (1333/1954): 918–926.

————. "Dar bārah-yi Afsānah-hā-yi 'āmmiyānah" ("About Folk Narratives"). *Sukhan* 6: 4 (1334/1955): 294–300.

Zuwiyya-Yamank, Labib. *Harvard College Library Catalogue of Persian Books*. Cambridge: Harvard College Library, 1964.

For Product Safety Concerns and Information please contact our EU
representative GPSR@taylorandfrancis.com
Taylor & Francis Verlag GmbH, Kaufingerstraße 24, 80331 München, Germany